# COVERING THE BASES

The Most Unforgettable Moments
in Baseball in the Words of
the Writers and Broadcasters
*Who Were There*

Benedict Cosgrove

With a Foreword by Ron Rapoport

CHRONICLE BOOKS
SAN FRANCISCO

Printed in the United States of America

Cosgrove, Benedict.
    Covering the bases : the most unforgettable moments in baseball in the words of the writers and broadcasters who were there / Benedict Cosgrove; with a foreword by Ron Rapoport.
       p. cm.
    Includes index.
    ISBN 0-8118-1150-6 (pb)
     1. Baseball—United States—History.   I. Title.
GV863.A1C64 1997
796.357'0973—dc20              96-14861
                                    CIP

Book design by Martine Trélaün
Illustrations by Karen Smidth

Distributed in Canada by Raincoast Books
8680 Cambie Street
Vancouver, BC V6P 6M9

10 9 8 7 6 5 4 3 2 1

Chronicle Books
85 Second Street
San Francisco, CA 94105

Web Site: www.chronbooks.com

## FOR MY PARENTS—

With love and gratitude.

**I'd like to offer** my humble thanks to the following good people, all of whom had a hand—often invisible—in the completion of this book:

Jeffrey Schulte, for the original idea behind the whole thing, and for patience and encouragement as the idea mutated into its present shape; Lindsay Anderson, for faith in the project from the very beginning; Dorothy Clarke and Cliff Westfall for putting up with me in D.C.; Don Bowden and Stanley Rubenstein at AP/Wide World in New York; Bill Burdick at the National Baseball Library and Archive in Cooperstown; the harried and unfailingly helpful staff at the Library of Congress; Jill Jacobson and Martine Trélaün for envisioning and then so wonderfully executing the book's design.

Several other folks helped me muddle through in one way or another, whether they knew it at the time or not: Greg Cantrell (for one long night of yammering about baseball); Jasmine Dellal; Joe Donnelly; Howard Harrison; Sunny Jim Mason; Denyse Jones; Steve Summers; Bettie Serveert; The Replacements; and a host of others who I'll probably remember the moment this thing's gone to press.

That this book got finished at all—and that it might, in the end, bring some pleasure to the reader—can be attributed to the collective support of the aforementioned; that it might contain errors of fact, as well as of judgment, is my responsibility alone.

Finally, and most deeply, thanks to Francesca. For everything.

———◦—◦—◦———

# Contents

# Foreword

---

## BY RON RAPOPORT

**The difference between** literature and journalism is the difference between John Updike and me.

Updike's glorious "Hub Fans Bid Kid Adieu" is often cited as an exemplar of sports reporting, an opinion that will get no argument from me. The last game of Ted Williams's career will long be remembered for two things: the home run he hit in his last at-bat and Updike's account of it, which has since been anthologized about as often as "Sonnets from the Portuguese."

Yet if you take your favorite sportswriter out for a mug of the sponsor's product some evening, you might be surprised, once you were both sufficiently relaxed, to find him playing devil's advocate in regard to Updike's masterpiece.

For one thing, Updike's article ran, by my inexact estimate, about 7,500 or 8,000 words. For another, it appeared in *The New Yorker* nearly a month after the event it celebrated. And when we consider Updike's references to Euclidean geometry, to Jason, Achilles, and Nestor (the Tinker, Evers, and Chance of the Greek League, perhaps) and a joke about Thomas Aquinas, well, perhaps we can agree that there is not a daily publication in America that could have accommodated it. It amuses me to imagine some harried editor sitting in a newspaper office late at night shouting, "The game's been over for four hours! Where the hell is Updike?"

The requirements of daily sports journalism are so strict they cannot give genius the breathing room it generally requires. The best story in the world, the fledgling writer soon learns, means nothing if it is filed after the presses have begun to roll. Thus does the stress created by the quest for the perfect sentence soon begin to pale in comparison to the tyranny of the ever-ticking clock.

"Hell, no, I can't do what Updike does," our by-now completely relaxed sportswriter may be muttering into his glass. "But he can't do what I do, either."

In the present collection, Ben Cosgrove makes no claim for sustained literary brilliance, although I must note that a lineup containing Jim Murray, Red Smith, Thomas Boswell, Shirley Povich, Dave Anderson, Jerry Izenberg, Ira Berkow, Bob Stevens, and John Hall can play for my team any day. Rather, Cosgrove has let the event be his guide, to choose those moments in baseball lore that intrigue him the most and then to follow the journalistic record wherever it may lead.

The results of this effort are fascinating on a very elemental level. A man—no women in this collection, alas—who goes to a ballpark on a given day does not know what he will find. It may be a game that will be forgotten before the next one is played or one that will echo through the ages.

Here is the essential problem. When he is called upon to report a perfect game—or a three-run homer in the bottom of the ninth—the reporter does not sit back, slap his neighbor on the back, join in the celebration and wait for the replay. Adrenaline pumping as much as that of the hero of the moment, he goes to work. If he is honest, there may be a little part of him that recoils and says, "This is too big for me." And all the while, the clock is ticking.

Seeing how reporters have reacted to this sort of pressure over the years is highly instructive. Some fall back on the obvious: the who-what-when-where-why that is always available to the uninspired. Some revel in a method of expression once highly prized by baseball writers, a sort of jargon that might be termed calling things what they ain't. ("It must chagrin the Giants aplenty to see how they kiboshed themselves" is one of my favorites from these pages.)

Even those who are lucky enough to be paid a timely visit by their muse must be sure it is not the devil in disguise. With so little time to think things through, there is always the possibility that what seemed brilliant in the heat of the moment it was written will be embarrassing when it is read in the cold light of the following day.

That is why it is such a pleasure to come across such nuggets of inspiration as this from Curley Grieve's account of Don Larsen's perfect game:

> Twenty-seven up—twenty-seven down.
> Gilliam, Reese, Snider.
> Robinson, Hodges, Amoros.
> Furillo, Campanella, Maglie.
> That was the order, inning after inning, until the ninth when left-handed Dale Mitchell came on to bat for Sal Maglie, who had pitched magnificently himself. The tension that had mounted with each rise and fall of Larsen's arm seemed on the verge of explosion

when Umpire Babe Pinelli's right hand shot up in the shadows of the still horseshoe arena to signalize a third strike, which made the twenty-seventh consecutive out.

Signalize? All right, so the only one who was perfect that day was Larsen. But Grieve was on deadline, remember, and who can blame him if, after the exhilaration of creating those first four spare and evocative sentences (What a Dodger batting order that was!), one clumsy word got the best of him?

In recent years, an added difficulty has arisen. The World Series and most other important games are played at night, making deadlines that once were merely difficult nearly impossible. I can scarcely look at my own contribution to these pages—an account of Kirk Gibson's mythic home run in the 1988 World Series—without remembering the one true emotion all of us in the press box that night at Dodger Stadium felt: terror.

Our entire evening's work was suddenly useless, the clock was mocking us and here we were racing through screaming fans for the elevator, then piling frantically into a small interview room off the Dodger locker room. We were all but prostrate with gratitude when we discovered Gibson there waiting for us.

In five quick minutes, he took us through all the events leading up to the home run—where he had been, what he had thought, what he had said and been told, how he had felt—without requiring the prompting of a single question. We raced upstairs, rewrote without the luxury of thought, and met our deadlines. Then we took a deep breath and silently saluted Gibson. As far as we were concerned, he had performed *two* heroic acts that night.

Baseball goes back a long way, of course, and there are reports in this book that are outmoded in the extreme. Thus, it will quickly be noticed, that the convention of a sportswriter leaving the press box after a game and confronting the athletes who played in it is a relatively recent one.

In the accounts of Fred Merkle's famous failure to run to second base, for instance, the only quote we encounter is from the president of the National League, and it turns out to be a misleading one; he eventually did order the game replayed. What Merkle thought of his blunder—not to mention what his manager, his teammates, the opposing team, the fans, and the umpires thought—went unreported until days after the fact.

The consequences of this mode of reporting reached their zenith following the home run Babe Ruth either did or did not call in the 1932 World Series. As Cosgrove points out, the debate surrounding that event has hardly subsided since the ball was hit. Yet in the hectic moments afterwards, nobody thought to walk up to Ruth and simply ask him.

There is another oddity in the reporting of that game, too. Though John Drebinger of the *New York Times* mentioned in his lead sentence that Ruth hit two home runs off of the Cubs' Charlie Root, he did not get around to describing the big one until the 34th paragraph!

"(Root's) feelings well can be imagined," Drebinger wrote by way of summation. Again, it did not seem to occur to him to ask the unfortunate pitcher to speak for himself.

A more aggressive generation of reporters—spurred on by the addition of radio and television—has eliminated this approach, but there are times when I am not sure that this is entirely beneficial. Reporters are so often bent on getting player reaction, even if it is of the "see-the-ball, hit-the-ball" variety, that sometimes they deprive their readers of learning what happened in favor of how the participants *felt* about what happened.

It is true, of course, that fans can now see or hear what happened for themselves, and it's heartening to see how the broadcasters represented here captured the raw emotion and excitement of the events as they were unfolding. But those who are unable to tune in are too often cheated of the step-by-step elements of the drama. So are future generations of readers.

Grantland Rice's account of Walter Johnson coming out of the bullpen to redeem himself in the 1924 World Series is overwrought at times ("The wall-eyed goddess known as Fate . . . led Walter Johnson to the pot of shining gold that waits at the rainbow's end"). But Rice's descriptions of the catcher dropping a routine pop foul and of Johnson's ultimate triumph make us glad he didn't interrupt it to let us know how finally winning the Series made Johnson feel.

So, no, there is precious little of the literature of baseball in this book. Those seeking that commodity will find the bookstores shelves groaning under its weight, and much of it is brilliant, indeed. But the baseball journalists represented here had a different function to perform, and for the most part they acquitted themselves admirably.

And, unlike Updike, none of them saved the score of the game for the last paragraph, either.

# Introduction

———•◆•———

**Having begun, and then** abandoned, and then begun once again the writing of this introduction more times than I care to admit, I think I'll just start off as I originally intended, and back into it with that time-honored preemptive maneuver: the disclaimer.

So . . . this book is *not* intended solely as a list of the century's 25 greatest baseball moments, for the simple reason that no two fans would ever agree on which 25 events to include. Any attempt to corral such a slippery series of moments into a "best of" roster is, it seems to me, an act poised somewhere between lunacy and unbridled arrogance.

But (and here's a disclaimer to the disclaimer) there's no question that people, as a rule, enjoy making lists. Music, book, and film critics, for instance— not *all* of whom are arrogant lunatics—routinely present their readers and listeners with best-of lists, and, admittedly, most of us routinely pay them heed. In that tradition, then, I hereby present a collection of daily newspaper sportswriters and radio announcers covering 25 of my own favorite great baseball moments.

At this point, of course, the reader's probably asking, Who is this guy, and why do a bunch of his favorite baseball moments warrant a book? And, more importantly, why are DiMaggio and Mays and Mantle and all those other players who, when you get right down to it, have helped define the game over the years—why are those guys relegated to bit parts in this collection?

Pretty good questions.

First, in answering who I am, I'd reply, simply, that I'm a baseball fan. That's not how I introduce myself, of course ("Hi. Ben Cosgrove, ball fan."), but I'm not overstating it when I say that baseball has been one of the few constants over the course of my life. I know I'm not unique in this. Most of my friends who are ball fans are the same way.

Through the years, I've followed the game in the papers and on the radio with an occasionally unconscious dedication evident in few other realms of my life. There have been periods, certainly, when other matters took precedence over baseball; but it became clear, thankfully—after some time—that a person's life can encompass a multitude of pursuits, and that those pursuits can, rather than curtailing the enjoyment of one or the other, illumine and accentuate the pleasures of each. It was a great day, therefore, when I knew, in my bones, that sex, rock and roll, literature, and baseball are far from mutually exclusive.

At the same time, despite the difficulties of remaining a fan in the 1990s (wasn't that strike in '94 just so much *fun?*), I've gotten past the point of wondering whether such devotion to a bunch of millionaires in pajamas is pathetic, or vaguely ennobling.

It's probably neither. Perhaps it's both.

In the end, it doesn't really matter much either way. I just love the game.

Now, the question of why my list of favorite moments might warrant a book leads comfortably into the thicket of question three: namely, where are the rest of the immortals? Where's DiMaggio? Where, fer chrissakes, is Willie Mays?

Okay . . . Even though I never saw DiMaggio or Mantle play, and Mays was playing at something less than his prime by the time I knew who he was, their absence certainly calls for an explanation. And here it is: this book is not merely an index of definitive moments in the careers of players who, for whatever reason, have some significance for me, or who would be high on anyone's list of the game's greats.

In other words, it's not the notoriety of the moment, or the player, or the team per se that guarantees or denies an event its own chapter in this book. After all, if that were the case, Mays's catch off of Vic Wetrz's clout in the 1954 Series would be chronicled here, rather than, say, Fred Merkle's infamous base running error in 1908. At heart, though, this book is a collection of reporting on the events *as they happened*, and while sportswriters certainly mentioned Mays's grab in their newspaper stories, The Catch did not, in and of itself, make the next day's headlines.

I'll repeat that the events covered in this book were, admittedly, subjectively chosen; that is, they are included here because of the resonance they maintain in the heart and mind of one avowed fan. But they've also gained a place in this anthology because 1) they unquestionably were memorable baseball events, and 2) they garnered memorable coverage on the radio and in the next day's newspapers. The aim, then, is to present the immediacy and magnitude of the events, in the words of those who were there, whether those words were hoarsely shouted into a microphone or hastily pounded out upon a typewriter—or a laptop—as the drama unfolded.

Here, the famous dictum that poetry "takes its origin from emotion recollected in tranquillity" is stood on its head; much of the rough poetry of the best baseball coverage, after all, takes its origin from emotion recorded, and celebrated, in pandemonium.

The great Paul Gallico put it this way:

> There are two factors that combine to make the unforgettable sports story: the event itself, or the character or characters involved and the witness thereto, the sportswriter, who reacts to what he sees and, filled with the excitement and the still reverberating echoes of the class of teams or individuals, sets his typewriter to churning. He is burning to let his readers share his experience, to make them see it, hear and feel it as he has, in short, to tell them the story of a marvelous happening.
>
> The sportswriter's task is unlike any other, for when he takes his seat in the press box or ringside, he never knows what he is going to see. He can prepare neither his adjectives nor his state of mind. Something unforeseen and unpredictable is about to take place and he must attune himself to be the eyes and ears and the interpreter of the event for those who could not be there.

That unique, mysterious aspect of sportswriting—of the "unforseen and unpredictable" unfolding, or exploding, before the writer's eyes—rings true throughout this book. Even events that might appear inevitable by the time they actually occur, like Ripken breaking Gehrig's record, or Seaver winning his 300th game, or Aaron passing Ruth, have within them seeds of drama that other preordained events rarely, if ever, contain. A political press conference, for example, might offer the folks covering it a certain number of surprises; but aside from the tension of determining whether the pol at the podium is lying through his teeth, or is merely being evasive, or is simply confused, everyone in the room knows pretty much what to expect.

So that, again, is this book's goal: to take the reader back to some of the game's most stirring, controversial, mind-blowing moments, and provide a sense of what it might have been like to witness the unforseen, and the unpredictable. And it's also with that immediacy in mind that the reader is presented not only with the words of some of the century's leading sportswriters, but some of the voices that have through the years brought the game over the airwaves to millions of listeners.

That said, I hope that no radio passage in this book is seen as merely a counterpoint to the written accounts of a given game; at heart, the words of

Scully and Hodges and Gowdy and the rest are included here as indications of the power of a skilled announcer to transport the listener to the park. Personally, I don't mind watching television highlights of a game, but if I can't be at the stadium, I'd rather listen to the game on the radio than watch it on the little screen. The appeal of radio, of course, is that it leaves something to the imagination, and I would urge the reader to approach the partial radio transcripts herein as mildly truncated instances of the announcer's observation and the reader's imagination melding on the spot.

For instance, when Bill White and Jack Buck call Kirk Gibson's 1988 World Series home run off of Dennis Eckersley, it's fascinating to follow the thread of their conversation as they keep the listener (reader) completely on top of the game. When Gibson's homer leaves his bat, even gleaned from the printed page, Buck's astonishment is thrilling.

———◆———

Still, the main emphasis of the book is the sportswriting found in the daily papers. Far from a concerted, scholarly history of American sportswriting, this book can nonetheless be read as a sort of piecemeal, de facto retrospective of some of this century's great—and perhaps not-so-great (see below)—baseball coverage, from the turn of the century through the 1990s. At the same time, while I'm not going to belabor the obvious ("Man, they sure use a lot more quotes from players in their articles nowadays, don't they?"), it must be said that some of the writing in this book, and especially the older writing, might strike modern readers as . . . well, as pretty ridiculous.

Nobody in their right mind will claim that Grantland Rice's piece, for instance, on the 1924 World Series is, by today's standards, terribly well written. As Ron Rapoport notes in his Foreword to this volume, Rice's language is bombastic; the very sequence of events is, at best, mysterious; and the entire article is riddled with redundancies. In its own way, though, the piece is also tremendous, classic sportswriting, happily bludgeoning the reader into acknowledging that, yes, yes, the seventh game in 1924 was mighty exciting; and maybe, for an instant, while being pulled along by Rice's almost torturously grandiose prose, we might feel that we were actually there as Walter Johnson finally gained his crown.

Which explains, in part, why Rice is a legend. Some other writers in this collection, however, are not legends. They're not even vaguely famous. Some of them, in fact, aren't even all that great. Case in point: Lou Smith's piece in the *Cincinnati Enquirer* on Vander Meer's second no-hitter, despite some moments of real immediacy and passion, is more enjoyable than memorable. And that's okay.

At times, of course, the good, the bad, and the ugly sportswriters are indistinguishable. Just count how many times in this book the image of a Hollywood scriptwriter is invoked to illustrate the implausibility of what a writer just witnessed on the field, and you'll get an idea of how large a role clichés, for instance, sometimes play in the writings of even the most revered sportswriters. (Personally, I didn't have the heart to count the scriptwriter references, but there were plenty. The great Shirley Povich, for example, writing about Bobby Thomson's legendary home run, put it this way: "Hollywood's most imaginative writers on an opium jag could not have scripted a more improbable windup of the season . . ." Now, that's pretty damn good, but when you've seen several dozen writers say pretty much the same thing about a dozen other events, you start to feel that the reader with a healthy sense of humor will probably weather such repetitions and similarities a lot better than some academic with a fetish for originality.)

The point is that Lou Smith might not be as skilled a writer as Red Smith—hell, he might not be as skilled a writer as *Lonnie* Smith—but there's little doubt the man was a sportswriter to the core.

Smith and the other lesser-known, second-tier writers in this collection are here for two reasons: first, they were lucky enough to see, in their capacity as reporters, unforgettable events. Second, and just as importantly, I wanted to get across a feeling of what it's like for folks to pick up the day's paper the morning after a memorable baseball event, and read the local sportswriters grappling with the momentous.

Now, I'm not singling out Lou Smith because I dislike or dismiss his reporting. If that were the case, he wouldn't be in this collection, and the point would be moot. On the contrary, Smith's piece is one of my favorites in the book, for reasons that are as ineffable as those that make Grantland Rice's ornate freight train of a narrative somehow stay on the tracks, carrying us along with it.

The point is, some of the writers herein are great. Some aren't. But here's another phenomenon unique to sportswriting: when it's terrific, it's fun to read; when it's not so terrific, it can still, on occasion, be fun to read. A few of those occasions can be found in this book. Literary snobs are thus duly warned, and hereby discouraged from proceeding further.

While we're on the subject of the quality of the writers found in these pages, readers will note that some of the most eloquent writers the game has known will not be found here. Roger Angell is not here, nor are David Halberstam, Lawrence Ritter, Donald Hall, Tom Verducci, and any number of other folks whose words have added to our appreciation of the national pastime without smothering it in treacle.

(Timely interjection: Like most people I know, I have a great aversion to writers who suddenly find their nascent poetic sensibilities stirred by the sight of a baseball diamond. After all, contrary to what some folks might say, baseball is not life. Baseball is an often beautiful, infrequently exciting, mysterious game without a clock. Life, on the other hand, is an infrequently beautiful, often exciting, mysterious game with the biggest clock of them all. There's a huge difference.

And yet, some writings do occasionally capture whatever it is that draws us to the game. The late, great A. Bartlett Giamatti, for instance, wrote that baseball

> breaks your heart. It is designed to break your heart. The game begins in the spring, when everything else begins again, and it blossoms in the summer, filling the afternoons and evenings, and then as soon as the chill rains come, it stops and leaves you to face the fall alone. You count on it, you rely on it to buffer the passage of time, to keep the memory of sunshine and high skies alive, and then just when the days are all twilight, when you need it most, it stops.

So, some folks can get away with that sort of thing. Most of us, however, can't, and really shouldn't try.

At any rate, Angell, Ritter, and the rest are absent from these pages due to a simple twist of fate (or to wise career decisions, depending on your perspective): namely, those folks made their reputations as writers on baseball mainly through magazines and books.

The folks in this collection, on the other hand, had to get their stuff out *in the moment*, with editors breathing down their necks or berating them over the phone, while the crowds were still going apeshit and the next morning's (or that very evening's) edition of the paper waited on their copy. Granted, the writers who work for the sports weeklies and for magazines have to deal with deadlines and heavy-breathing editors and all that stuff. Of course they do. But this book is, in large part, about the daily sports pages, and about the writers who appear in them day after day after day.

There are, of course, a bunch of tremendous newspaper sportswriters—Jimmy Cannon, Edwin Pope, Bob Broeg, Jerome Holtzman, Claire Smith, Scott Ostler, Joan Ryan, and on and on—who have not made it into this collection, simply because they either weren't present at a chosen event, or, if they were, their copy from that event just didn't work for this book.

The astute (or, at the very least, not-brain-dead) reader will also note that not one woman sportswriter is to be found in this collection. Pretty ridiculous, eh? Perhaps. But I'll point out that only in relatively recent years have women made it into the front rank of the nation's sportswriters; and, while I saw a handful of pieces by women during my research that covered the events featured in this anthology, the few that I found were not the best, or even the most interesting examples for their particular moments.

Thus, I felt that to include a piece *merely* because it was written by a woman amounted to a greater disservice than to risk censure by presenting an all-male compilation. If readers know of pieces written by women that they feel deserved a place in this book, I apologize. Anyway, it remains clear that while sportswriting is not the white male preserve it once was, it's not exactly the Rainbow Coalition, either. Here's to hoping the walls continue to fall.

In the meantime, go out and buy Ron Rapoport's collection of women sportwriters, *A Kind of Grace*.

That said . . . Grantland Rice is here, and Gallico, and Red Smith, and a raft of celebrated and forgotten folks who, by happy chance, were witnesses to and able to give voice to strange and wonderful doings on the diamond.

Those doings have a certain symmetry, a symmetry that lends baseball one of its trademark characteristics: namely, an unmatched continuity. In this book alone, Hank Aaron and Eddie Mathews appear together in two separate chapters, in two prominent but entirely different capacities; Carlton Fisk hits one of the game's most famous home runs and, a decade later, catches Tom Seaver's 300th victory; Pete Rose plays in Stan Musial's last game, as a rookie, and 22 years later, a few seasons after breaking Musial's National League record for hits, he passes Cobb as the all-time hits leader—57 years to the day after Cobb played his last game. Hollywood's most imaginative writers on an opium jag, indeed.

Lastly, putting this book together allowed me the opportunity to happily wade through an enormous amount of baseball history. "It took me," in the words of Greil Marcus, "to microfilm machines unspooling the unambiguous public speech of my own childhood—and it is queer to crank through old newspapers for the confirming date of some fragment of a private obsession one hopes to turn into public speech . . . "

Marcus was writing not about baseball, but about politics and punk rock and nihilism; still, somehow, the sentiment fits.

My hope, in the end, is that the average fan will enjoy sharing in that not-so-private obsession, and the accompanying public speech, by finding in this book the same thrill I often experienced in compiling it: the thrill produced by the words of a sportswriter or radio announcer who was *there* at the precise moment when one player, or one team, stood indelibly apart from the rest.

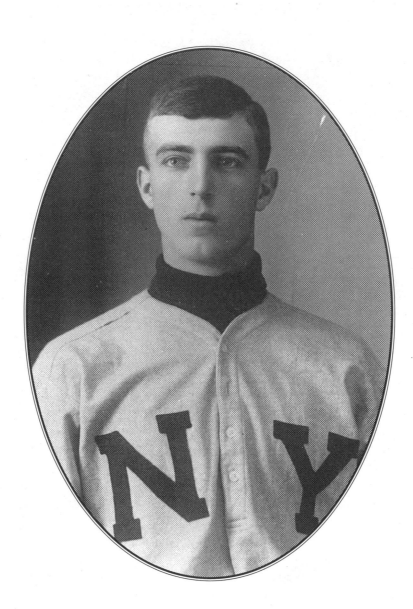

Fred Merkle, New York Giants

# The Play at Second Base

## FRED MERKLE'S IGNOMINIOUS BONER

September 23, 1908

**Few faithful ball fans** would admit to never hearing of "Merkle's Boner." Fewer still, however, would be able to tell you exactly what Fred Merkle did (or didn't do), on that long-ago September afternoon, to earn so ignominious a place in diamond history.

Nonetheless, it's probably fair to say that those folks in the know, and those who know nothing of the particulars of the brouhaha described below, are similar in at least one respect: none of us would want to be associated with such an unfortunate phrase.

Give it a try. Frost's Boner. Mason's Boner. Ziegler's Boner. Fill-in-the-blank-with-your-name-here's Boner. Sorry, but I don't think many folks would be happy going to their graves with that sort of baggage. Fred Merkle, though, had to do just that. (Another fine ballplayer who will forever be remembered for a momentary lapse on the playing field might at least gain some solace in knowing that no one has taken to calling his epic flub in '86 "Buckner's Boner.")

Merkle was a solid young first baseman with John McGraw's New York Giants, a capable teammate of the great Christy Mathewson, and a generally well-liked guy who happened to make the grandest base-running error of all time in a crucial game against the Cubs during the 1908 pennant race.

Or did he?

It's generally accepted that Merkle, on first base in the bottom of the ninth inning, failed to touch second base on a seemingly game-winning RBI single by his teammate, Al Bridwell. As another Giant, Moose McCormick, scored from third on Bridwell's shot, Merkle bolted to the dugout as fans (or "potato bugs," as Charles Dryden calls them in his piece below) stormed the field. Apparently, this sort of retreat in the face of the Goths pouring from the stands wasn't that uncommon at the time.

At any rate, the Cubs claimed Merkle never touched second (which he would have had to do to complete the play and make the run official); the umpire agreed, the game was declared a tie, and the Giants eventually lost the pennant to the Cubs in a one-game playoff at the end of the year—immediately after which a bunch of the Cubs were violently attacked at the Polo Grounds by incensed Giants fans. Ah, the game's glory days.

Both McGraw and Mathewson, however, were quoted in the newspapers the day after the game was declared a tie, arguing that Merkle had, in fact, touched second base. Mathewson (generally regarded as the most respectable and best-loved player of his day) had this to say:

> I had started from the field when I heard Evers [of the famed Tinker/Evers/Chance combination] yell to Hoffman, 'Throw the ball to second.' I remembered the trick they had tried to play at Pittsburgh [when the Cubs' Johnny Evers had tried to get the ump to call a Pirate runner out for not touching second base], and I got Merkle by the arm and told him to go to second. In the meantime the ball had been thrown in, high over Evers's head, and fell near where the shortstop ordinarily stands. Merkle touched the bag, and I was near him when he did it.
>
> One of the Chicago players then turned to [umpire] Emslie for a decision. 'I saw no such play,' Emslie replied, and walked off. When he said that, I hollered to the other players to 'Come on,' and we went to the clubhouse.

On the same day, McGraw (whom George Bernard Shaw called "the real and most authentic Most Remarkable Man in America") was quoted in the papers as saying, "As a matter of fact, Merkle tells me he did reach and touch second base. No Chicago player was on second base with the ball, anyway. It's simply a case of squeal. Chicago has been trying to get away with this all season."

Later, McGraw and other Giants vigorously defended Merkle, even after the Giants lost the pennant to the Cubs. Outfielder Fred Snodgrass, who a few years later would be saddled with blame for blowing the 1912 Series against the Red Sox, pointed out that the Giants lost five games after the September 23rd uproar in the Polo Grounds, and that they then lost the playoff game itself. Hard to blame Merkle for that.

For his part, McGraw continued to assert that the Giants had fairly won the game, and that to blame Merkle, or to call him stupid for "losing" the pennant, seriously missed the point of the crazy finale: namely, that they wuz robbed.

*New York Times*

Censurable stupidity on the part of player Merkle in yesterday's game at the Polo Grounds between the Giants and Chicago placed the New York team's chances of winning the pennant in jeopardy. His unusual conduct in the final inning of a great game perhaps deprived New York of a victory that would have been unquestionable had he not committed a breach in baseball play that resulted in Umpire O'Day declaring the game a tie.

With the score tied in the ninth inning at 1 to 1 and the New York's having a runner, McCormick, on third base waiting for an opportunity to score and Merkle on first base looking for a similar chance, Bridwell hit into centre field. It was a fair hit ball and would have been sufficient to win the game had Merkle gone on his way down the base path while McCormick was scoring the winning run. But instead of Merkle going to second base to make sure that McCormick had reached home with the run necessary to a victory, Merkle ran toward the clubhouse, evidently thinking that his share in the game was ended when Bridwell hit the ball into safe territory.

Manager Chance of the Chicago club quickly grasped the situation and directed that the ball be thrown to second base, which would force out Merkle, who had not reached that corner.

Manager Chance, who plays first base for the Chicago club, ran to second base and the ball was thrown there, but immediately pitcher McGinnity interfered in the play and a scramble of players ensued, in which, it is said, McGinnity obtained the ball and threw it into the crowd before Chance could complete a force play on Merkle, who was far away from the base line. Merkle said that he had touched second base, and the Chicago players were equally positive that he had not done so.

Manager Chance then appealed to Umpire O'Day, who was head umpire of the game, for a decision in the matter. The crowd, thinking that the Giants had won the game, swarmed upon the playing field in such a confusion that none of the "fans" seemed able to grasp the situation, but finally their attitude toward Umpire O'Day became so offensive that the police ran into the crowd and protected the umpire, while arguments were being hurled pro and con on the point in question by Manager Chance and McGraw and the umpire.

Umpire O'Day finally decided that the run did not count, and that inasmuch as the spectators had gained such large numbers on the field that the game could not be resumed, O'Day declared the game a tie. Although both umpires O'Day and Emslie, it is claimed, say they did not see the play at second base, Umpire O'Day's action in declaring that McCormick's run did not count was based upon the presumption or fact that a force play was made on Merkle at second base.

The singular ending of the game aroused intense interest throughout the city, and everywhere it was the chief topic of discussion. Early in the evening a report was widely circulated that President Pulliam had decided the game was a tie and must be played again. When this rumor reached Mr. Pulliam he authorized the following statement: "I made no decision in the matter at all and I will not do so until the matter is presented to me in proper form. The statement on the 'ticker' that I had declared the game a tie is entirely unauthorized."

Well, anyway, it was a classy baseball game from the time in the first inning when Roger Bresnahan makes an entrance, accompanied by a dresser, who does him and undoes him in his natty mattress and knee pads, till the end of the ninth, when Bridwell singles safely to centre, bringing in what looks like the winning run.

And, from a spectacular point of view, that mix-up at the finish was just the appropriate sensation to a bang-up, all-a-quiver game. They all know they have seen a mighty snappy game of ball; that New York has brought over one more run than the enemy, whether the run counts or not; that McGinnity in holding on to the ball after the ninth-inning run, has done so with the idea that it belongs to the home team, and that good Master O'Day has said, as he exits: "I didn't see the play on second—the run doesn't count."

Up to the climactic ninth it was the toss of a coin who would win. For here is our best-loved Mathewson pitching as only champions pitch, striking out the power and the glory of the Cubs, numbering among his slain Schulte in the first, Pfeister in the third, Steinfeldt in the fourth, Pfeister in the fifth, Hayden and Schulte in the sixth, Hayden in the eighth, and Evers and Schulte in the ninth—these last in one-two order. Proper pitching, and for this and other things we embrace him.

But then, Pfeister is pitching good ball, too. Not so good as the Matty article, for this isn't to be expected, or desired, even. Pfeister doesn't strike anybody out, and Pfeister gives an occasional base on balls, and once he hits a batter, but aside from these irregularities Pfeister must be accounted in the king row of Wednesday matinée pitchers. The gentleman who feels the weight of the delivery, and thereafter takes his base, is the plodsome McCormick. It is in the second inning, and Pfeister whirls up a curve that doesn't break right. In fact, it breaks directly in McCormick's tummy, and Pfeister is forced to figure out the joke's on him. After the heroic Dr. Creamer has emptied half a hydrant on the prostrate McCormick the latter walks wanly to first, but he has to wait to walk home till the ninth inning.

Meantime, the game has progressed swiftly, remarkable for excellent plays by a number of us on either side, and remarkable also for the in-and-out work of Evers at second for Chicago.

It is in the fifth that the Cubs, or one of them, find the solitary run that represents the day's work. Hofman has been thrown out at first by Bridwell, and then the admirable Tinker takes his bat in his hand and faces Matty with determination writ large on his expressive features. Mr. Tinker drives the ball away out to right centre for what would be a two-bagger if you or I had made it, gentle reader—and this is no disparagement of the Tinker, for he is well seeming in our sight. As the ball approaches Master Donlin this good man attempts to field it with his foot. It's a home run all right, when you get down to scoring, but if this Donlin boy was our boy we'd have sent him to bed without his supper, and ye mind that, Mike.

We found the stick all right in the sixth, and tied the score. Herzog—and, by the way, he led the batting list yesterday in the absence of Tenney; that is, the playing absence, for Fred was among those present in the stand—Herzog, then, belts boldly to Steinfeldt, and it's a hit all right, but the throw that Steinfeldt makes to first is particularly distressing, and Herzy goes on to second. Bresnahan yields up a sacrifice bunt. Donlin hits over second base, Herzog scores, and 18,000 people go out of their minds.

It is at this stage of the game that reputable prophets speak confidently of ten innings, mayhap eleven, or so many thereof as may be pulled off before day becomes night. But darkness never stops this Wednesday game at the Polo Grounds. It goes the limit without interference by the dimming skies. We fancy ourselves mightily in the ninth, after Devlin has made a clean single to centre. To be sure, Seymour has just gone out at first on a throw by Evers, but we have a chance. Devlin is on first and the start is splendid. But here is McCormick, with a drive over to Evers, who throws out Devlin at second, and we're not very far advanced—and two are down and out. Merkle, who failed us the day before in an emergency is at bat, and we pray of him that he mend his ways. If he will only single we will ignore any errors he may make in the rest of his natural life.

On this condition, Merkle singles. McCormick advances to third, and everybody in the inclosure slaps everybody else and nobody minds. Perfect ladies are screaming like a batch of Coney barkers on the Mardi Gras occasion, and the elderly banker behind us is beating our hat to a pulp with his gold-handled cane. And nobody minds. Aided by these indications of the popular sentiment, Master Bridwell hits safely to centre, McCormick trots home, the reporter boys prepare to make an asterisk under the box score of the game with the line—"Two out when winning run was scored"—the merry villagers flock on the field to worship the hollow where the Mathewson feet have pressed, and all of a sudden there is a doings around second base. McGinnity, walking off the field with the ball, as is the custom of some member of the winning team, is held up by Tinker and Evers, who insist that the run does not count, as Merkle has not touched second. And then begins the argument which will keep us in talk for the rest of the season, and then some. Certainly the Cubs have furnished us sport.

## Another View

# CHARLES DRYDEN
*Chicago Tribune*

Minor league brains lost the Giants today's game after they had it cleanly and fairly won by a score of 2 to 1. In the ninth round Merkle did a bone-head base running stunt identical with the recent exhibition which Mr. Gill, also a minor leaguer, gave at Pittsburgh three weeks ago. But this time, "Hank" O'Day had his eagle eye peeled and the winning run which the Giants compiled in the ninth inning was tossed into the discard.

It must chagrin the Giants aplenty to think how they kiboshed themselves. In a swell combat worth going miles to see, Mathewson had the better of Pfeister, and the game looked as safe as the Bank of England when Bridwell tore off what should have been a hit in the ninth.

Tinker's home run in the fifth was all the Cubs had in the way of visible assets. Steinfeldt's bum heave and a couple of singles knotted the count in the sixth after a most gallant defense. Then came the bone-head finish, which left the bugs puzzled and wondering. And they won't know what happened until they see the public prints—i.e., newspapers—in the morning.

The facts in the case gleaned from active participants and survivors are these: Hofman fielded Bridwell's knock and threw to Evers for a force play on the absent Merkle. But McGinnity, who was not in the game, cut in ahead and grabbed the ball before it reached the eager Trojan. Three Cubs landed on the Iron Man from as many directions at the same time and jolted the ball from his cruel grasp. It rolled among the spectators, who had swarmed upon the diamond like an army of starving potato bugs.

At this thrilling juncture "Kid" Kroh, the demon southpaw, swarmed upon the human potato bugs and knocked six of them galley-west. The triumphant Kroh passed the ball to Steinfeldt after cleaning up the gang that had it. Tinker wedged in, and the ball was conveyed to Evers for the force out of Merkle, while Capt. Donlin was still some distance off towing that brilliant young gent by the neck.

Some say Merkle eventually touched second base, but not until he had been forced out by Hofman, to McGinnity, to six potato bugs, to "Kid" Kroh, to some more Cubs, and the shrieking, triumphant Mr. Evers, the well-known Troy shoe dealer. There have been some complicated plays in baseball, but we do not recall one just like this in a career of years of monkeying with the national pastime.

Still later Hank (O'Day) submitted gracefully to an interview by war scribes. He said Merkle was forced at second base and the game ended in a tie, at 1 to 1. None of the Giants remained to make public statements. Part of the crowd lifted a player in white to their shoulders and bore him to the clubhouse. The Giant thus honored was not Mr. Merkle. He left long before the trouble started, and his departure caused it. Some base runners should have a groove cut in them so they couldn't go wrong.

*Inside Stuff*

---

# THE BLACK SOX SCANDAL

October 9, 1919

**When Chicago White Sox** first baseman Chick Gandil cooked up a plot in 1919 to make some money off the World Series—that is, by throwing it—he couldn't have known that his plan would eventually become the greatest scandal to ever hit the sport.

Today, all we can say is: Thanks, Chick.

After all, the tale that grew from Gandil's audacity has all the elements of a great thriller, including villains (Gandil, Comiskey, Arnold Rothstein), heroes (Ray Shalk, "Kid" Gleason, Dickie Kerr), tension, high stakes, greed, deceit, greed, betrayal, and greed. As an added bonus, it's a coming-of-age story, with the minor twist that a nation, and not some starry-eyed adolescent, is in the end forced to grow up.

Set against a post–World War I backdrop—in an anxious, energetic nation giddy with the recent memory of having flexed its muscles on the global stage—the scandal showed the nation that even something as ostensibly pure as baseball was not immune from the vices of the real world. At the same time, a lost generation of Americans struggled with the disquieting idea of a universe in which trench warfare and chemical weapons defined what Western civilization had, for centuries, been marching toward.

In this shifting landscape, the national game was suddenly divested of much of the faith that a country had placed in it.

Of course, at the risk of belittling an American watershed, one might in fact argue that, of the two somewhat simultaneous shocks to the American system, the Black Sox Scandal had, relatively, a greater impact on the faithful than did World War I. After all, the horrors of the trenches did nothing to stop even greater carnage at regular intervals throughout the rest of the century.

On the other hand, despite, or perhaps because of, the recoil of the Black Sox Scandal, there's never been another fixed World Series. (That we know of, anyway.)

Anyhow, the story of the Chicago players who handed the Reds the championship and of the owners (especially Comiskey) whose tightfistedness drove a great team to eternal shame, and of Arnold Rothstein and Kid Gleason and Judge Landis and Shoeless "Say It Ain't So" Joe Jackson and all the rest of the imperishable characters, is a tale that's been told a thousand times, in fiction and in the history books and in movies, so there's really no need to recount it here.

What's worth recounting, though, is the tension evident in the sportswriting in the moments immediately after the final out of the eighth game (the Series being a best-of-nine affair back then). It had certainly been clear to just about anyone who knew the two teams that something was wrong throughout the Series, and there was discussion in print and on the street that a fix was, in all likelihood, in. Nonetheless, one can sense that when the Reds finally won and the writers began writing their stories, even the most hardened of insiders had trouble believing what they'd seen.

In the excerpts from both Hugh Fullerton's and James Crusinberry's stories below, for example, both writers veer perilously close to saying outright that the Series was a sham. Since he keeps bringing it up and then rejecting the notion, you half-expect Fullerton to just break down at some point and lay it bare: "It is not up to me to decide why they did such things. That all probably will come out in the wash," he writes at one point, and it's hard not to imagine him fighting hard to keep from writing, "and when it does, we'll all know *for certain* that the Sox gave this one to the Reds on a silver platter!"

Then, in Crusinberry's piece, there are the moving quotes from the seemingly bewildered, but most likely just stunned-with-rage Kid Gleason. (After the second blown game, Gleason attacked Gandil in the clubhouse, and had to be peeled off his first baseman by other players.) When, in what seems to be a moment of clarity in the midst of his confusion, Gleason admits that he wishes that "no one had ever bet a dollar on the team," it's hard to decide what's more heart-rending about the man's wish—its sincerity, or its futility.

And finally, in what might have been a reaction to the fiasco he'd just witnessed, Hugh Fullerton (who'd made his fame predicting, correctly, that the White Sox would beat the Cubs in the 1906 Series) called for the abolishment of the World Series: "Yesterday's game in all probability is the last that ever will be played in any world's series. If the club owners and those who have the interests of the game at heart have listened during this series they will call off the annual inter-league contests. If they value the good name of the sport they will do so beyond doubt."

The owners, of course, didn't listen to Fullerton (the fools!), and for the last three-quarters of a century we've had to endure one after another of the damnable Fall Classics.

# HUGH S. FULLERTON
*New York World*

Cincinnati's Reds are champions of the world. The Reds turned yesterday and gave the dope the worst upsetting it has had during all this surprising and upsetting series. They slashed away at Claude Williams's pitching and before the big crowd had settled to see the contest, it was over. The knockout punch was landed by Duncan, the kid who is the hero of the series, and Williams was driven to his defeat and elected to the office of false alarm of the series.

The close of the series was discouraging. Wednesday the dopesters all agreed that the Reds were on the run. The Cincinnati fans who have been canonizing a lot of mediocre athletes turned upon them and declared they were dogs, yellow curs and German quitters. Yesterday these same Reds swarmed upon the cocky White Sox and battered them into the most humiliating defeat of any world's series.

There will be a great deal written and talked about this world's series. There will be a lot of inside stuff that never will be printed, but the truth will remain that the team which was the hardest working, which fought hardest, and which stuck together to the end, won. The team which excelled in mechanical skill, which had the ability, individually, to win, was beaten.

They spilled the dope terribly. Almost everything went backward, so much so that an evil-minded person might believe the stories that have been circulated during the series. The fact is that this series was lost in the first game, and lost through overconfidence. Forget the suspicious and evil-minded yarns that may be circulated. The Reds are not the better club. They are not even the best club in their own league, but they play ball together, fight together and hustle together, and remember that a flivver that keeps running beats a Rolls Royce that is missing on several cylinders. The Sox were missing on several. They played the game as a team only through one game and part of another, and they deserved defeat.

Chick Gandil, Chicago White Sox

It is not up to me to decide why they did such things. That all probably will come out in the wash. They were licked and licked good and proper, deserved it, and got it.

---

## Another View

### JAMES CRUSINBERRY

*Chicago Tribune*

"The Reds beat the greatest ball team that ever went into a world's series."

That was the first statement made by Boss Gleason of the White Sox when the show was over at Comiskey Park yesterday. His next statement was about like this:

"But it wasn't the real White Sox. They played baseball for me only a couple or three of the eight days."

There was logic in the statements of Gleason to one who had followed the White Sox throughout the season. The White Sox of the world's series was not the same team that won the American League pennant. The Reds of the world's series was the best Red team of the whole summer. Pat Moran had his players up on their toes. The White Sox slumped and couldn't get into their regular stride.

"I thought the championship was as good as in after we won that third victory down in Cincinnati," continued Gleason. "I thought Lefty Williams was a cinch. But he didn't have his stuff. Anyway they started hitting him in the first inning and I yanked him in a hurry. He wasn't right. I had to do something, so I got him out of there and sent in James. James was too wild, but anyway they had a commanding lead because of what happened while Williams was in there.

"Later on I got Wilkinson on the job and he was good. Wilkinson would have won that game for me yesterday if I had started him. I wish now I had, but I couldn't start him at the beginning. It looked like our chance to win in the end was to have Williams go through. Had he gone through, we would have been soft. I congratulate Pat Moran. His team gave him everything it had. He deserved to win."

There was more discussion about the playing of the White Sox than about the peace treaty after the last game. Stories were out that the Sox had not put out their best effort. Stories were out that the big gamblers had got to them.

But all of them sounded like alibi stuff even if true, and Manager Gleason had no excuses to offer for the defeat except that the Reds had played better baseball.

"I was terribly disappointed," he continued. "I tell you those Reds haven't any business beating a team like the White Sox. We played the worst baseball, in all but a couple of games, that we have played all year. I don't know what was the matter. Something was wrong. I didn't like the betting odds. I wish no one had ever bet a dollar on the team."

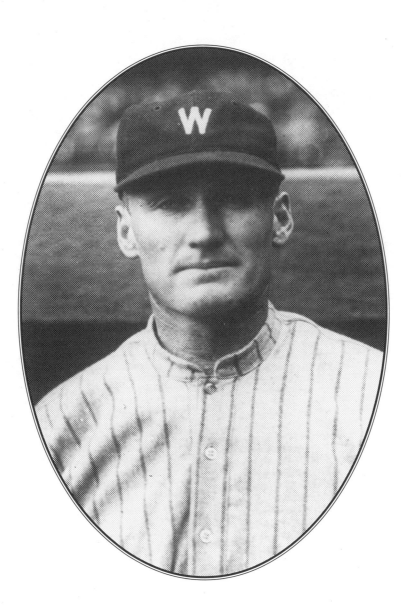

Walter "Big Train" Johnson,
Washington Senators

# The King His Crown

---

## WALTER JOHNSON FINALLY HAS HIS DAY

### October, 10, 1924

**For eighteen years,** Walter Johnson pitched for Washington teams so weak that they inspired one of the game's most enduring phrases: "First in war, first in peace, and last in the American League."

But in 1924, Walter Johnson and the Senators finally made it to the playoffs and into the Series, with Johnson, after losing two games, winning the seventh game with a gutsy, four-inning relief performance. It seemed not only as if every baseball fan in the country was happy to finally see "The Big Train" get a championship; even opposing players appeared overjoyed that the man had won it all.

The Giants' losing pitcher in the seventh game, Jack Bentley, summed up everyone's feelings pretty well when he said, "The good Lord just couldn't bear to see a fine fellow like Walter Johnson lose again." Lord or no Lord, one of baseball's best-loved figures, a gentle, sportsmanlike guy with a demonic fastball, had finally gotten his due.

Sportswriters, of course, weren't immune to the popular sentiment. One of the greatest of them all, Damon Runyon, let a bit of his own enthusiasm for Johnson spill over into his description of the celebration that erupted when Muddy Ruel crossed the plate in the twelfth for the victory:

> Hooray! Hooray! Hooroope!
>
> That's the voice of Washington as well as type can express it, screaming to the nation that the town and Walter Johnson have come into their baseball own.
>
> They've just won the world series of 1924 here—Washington, and Walter Johnson—and don't forget Stanley Harris, Earl McNeely

and "Muddy" Ruel and the rest of the boys. And they're still trying to split the eardrums of the U.S.A. yelling over it. They whipped the mighty New York Giants, by a score of 4 to 3, after twelve terrific innings in the seventh and deciding game of the series, with "Big Barney" pitching them on to glorious victory.

That's why the blood pressure of the citizens of Washington is at this moment without doubt the highest ever registered by medical science among the peoples of any race. Apoplexy is almost epidemic. Heart trouble is a common complaint.

Johnson was, by all accounts, a genuinely sweet guy who just happened to throw heat like no one before him. Of course, some of his opponent's weren't above taking advantage of the man's civility. It was common knowledge that Ty Cobb, for instance, would crowd the plate when standing in against Johnson, knowing full well that he wouldn't get any chin music from "Barney" to keep him honest.

Johnson's generosity, of course, stopped short of giving away hits, or games. He won 416 games in his career, second only to Cy Young, and dominated the American League for two decades. Stories about the speed of his fastball abound. When, for instance, Cleveland's Ray Chapman stood in against Johnson early in the 1920 season, and Johnson blew two pitches by him for strikes, Chapman walked off toward the dugout. When the umpire pointed out that he had one strike remaining, Chapman is said to have replied, "You can have it. It wouldn't do me any good." (Chapman, of course, remains the only major leaguer to ever die on the diamond, the result of a fractured skull suffered when a fastball thrown by New York's Carl Mays caught him leaning over the plate. Trivia freaks might like to note that the man catching Mays on that day in August of 1920 was none other than Muddy Ruel, the player who scored the winning run in the 1924 Series.)

Anyhow, in the '24 Series—after a regular season in which he led the league in wins, shutouts, strikeouts, and ERA—Johnson came very close to letting the title he'd sought for so long slip right through his fingers. Below, Grantland Rice comes just as close to losing control of his own account of the game, his words continually threatening to spiral off into the impenetrable sportswriting ether.

Thankfully, they're both masters, and are able to keep their priorities straight. Johnson pitches, Rice writes, reader wins.

# GRANTLAND RICE
*New York Herald Tribune*

Destiny, waiting for the final curtain, stepped from the wings today and handed the king his crown.

In the most dramatic moment of baseball's sixty years of history the wall-eyed goddess known as Fate, after waiting eighteen years, led Walter Johnson to the pot of shining gold that waits at the rainbow's end.

For it was Johnson, the old Johnson, brought back from other years with his blazing fast ball singing across the plate for the last four rounds, that stopped the Giant attack, from the ninth inning through the twelfth, and gave Washington's fighting ball club its world series victory by the score of 4 to 3, in the seventh game of a memorable struggle.

Washington won just at the edge of darkness, and it was Johnson's great right arm that turned the trick. As Earl McNeely singled and Muddy Ruel galloped over the plate with the winning run in the last of the twelfth, 38,000 people rushed on to the field with a roar of triumph never known before, and for more than thirty minutes, packed in one vast, serried mass around the bench, they paid Johnson and his mates a tribute that no one present will ever forget. It was something beyond all belief, beyond all imagining. Its crashing echoes are still singing out across the stands, across the city, on into the gathering twilight of early autumn shadows. There was never a ball game like this before, never a game with as many thrills and heart throbs strung together in the making of drama that came near tearing away the soul to leave it limp and sagging, drawn and twisted out of shape.

Washington, facing the last of the eighth inning, was a beaten team, with the dream about closed out. And then like a heavy blast from hidden explosives a rally started that tied the score, the two most important tallies of baseball lore sweeping over the plate as Bucky Harris's infield blow skirted the ground and suddenly leaped upward over Lindstrom's glove.

It was this single from the great young leader that gave Johnson his third and final chance. For, as the Giants came to bat in the ninth, with the score knotted at 3 and 3, there came once more the old familiar figure slouching across the infield sod to his ancient home in the box. Here once more was the mighty moment, and as 38,000 stood and cheered, roared and raved, Johnson began to set the old-time fast one singing on its way. With only one out in the ninth inning, Frank Frisch struck a triple to deep center, but in the face of this emergency "Old Barney" turned back to something lost from his vanished youth, and as Kelly tried in vain to bring Frisch home, the tall Giant suddenly found himself facing the Johnson of a decade ago—blinding, baffling speed that struck him out and closed down on the rally with the snap of death.

Johnson was on his way, and neither Destiny nor the Giants could head him off. He had suffered two annihilations, but his mighty moment had come and he was calling back stuff from a dozen years ago. To show that he was headed for another triumph and that young blood was coursing through his veins again, he came to the eleventh and struck out Frisch and Kelly. It was the first time in four years of world series play that any pitcher had struck out the keen-eyed Frisch. But the Fordham Flash today was facing the Johnson that used to be, the Johnson that nailed them all, the high and low alike, with a fast ball that few could see and fewer still could hit.

All this while the drama of the day was gathering intensity from round to round. Washington missed a great chance in the eleventh after Goslin had doubled, but the end was now near at hand. The human heart couldn't hold out many moments longer. The strain was too great for any team or any crowd to stand. Thirty-eight thousand pulses were jumping in a dozen different directions at the same moment as nervous systems were going to certain destruction.

For four innings now Johnson had faced Nehf, Bentley and McQuillan and two of these had been his conquerors. He was on the verge of getting his complete revenge in one sudden swirl of action. Still cool, serene and steady with the old right arm coming through with its easy and endless rhythm, Johnson again rolled back the Giant charge in the twelfth. In these four innings he had fanned five men, and most of them were struck down when a hit meant sudden death.

The long, gray afternoon shadows had now crept almost across the field. There was grave doubt that even another inning could have been played when fate in the shape of a catcher's mask intervened. With one man out and Bentley pitching, Ruel lifted a high foul back of the plate. Hank Gowdy, one of the most reliable of all who play, started for the ball, but in dancing beneath it his feet became entangled in the mask and before he could regain his balance the ball dropped safely to earth through his hands.

This was the spot which destiny picked as the place to hand "Old Barney" the long delayed crown, for Ruel on the next swing doubled to left. Johnson was safe on Jackson's error at short, and with only one out McNeely decided to follow the Harris attack. He slashed one along the ground to third, and as Lindstrom came in for the ball, for the second time in the game the ball suddenly bounded high over his head as Ruel crossed with the run that brought world series glory to Washington's game and crippled club.

The hit that tied it up and the hit that won were almost identical, perfect duplicates, as each reared itself from the lowly sod as if lifted by a watchful and guiding fate that had decided in advance that Washington must win. In the wake of this hit the ravings and the roarings again came near dislodging the rafters of the big stands. For this was the hit that meant Johnson's triumph, the hit that meant Washington's victory.

No club from the sixty years of play ever came from behind as often to break down the ramparts and get to the top. But Washington had the habit, and even when crippled and almost beaten Harris and his mates refused to waver for a moment as they formed again with what remnants were left to lead another counter charge. It was a home run by Harris that gave Washington its first score, and it was the manager's single that gave Johnson his closing chance to follow the old dream to the end of the route.

While Barnes held the winners to one hit for six innings, he weakened at last, and McGraw threw in Nehf, McQuillan and Bentley in a vain effort to save a waning cause. Washington, needing two games to win on Wednesday night, had won them both by one of the gamest exhibitions in the long span of all competitive sport.

Another perfect day with another spread of blue sky and yellow sun, the seventh in succession, helped to bring about the second $1,000,000 world series, the first being last year. This made the fourth $1,000,000 program in American sport: Dempsey-Carpentier, Dempsey-Firpo and two world series, with the former fight on top by nearly a million iron men.

The gathering around the Presidential box just before the first salvo was fired indicated the day's first excitement. When the cameramen reached the scene in the scurrying groups they discovered the President and Mrs. Coolidge, Secretary Slemp, Judge Landis, John J. McGraw, Bucky Harris and Clark Griffith all set for the last official pose of the long war's final day. With the ball park packed to the ultimate elbow, the crowd outside was even larger, as endless lines extended back around corners and alongside streets, almost blocking traffic. Inside it was a quieter and more tense gathering than the day before, with a part of the pre-game chatter stilled.

It was not until Warren Harvey Ogden, "The Sheik of Swarthmore," struck out Fred Lindstrom to start the game that rolling waves of sound indicated the amount of suppressed excitement.

After Ogden had walked Frisch he gave way to Mogridge with a string of lefty-handed hitters up, including Terry. The idea was to have Terry announced with a right-hander pitching so that if once removed with a left-hander in he was out of the series.

Great plays began to sparkle early like diamonds shining in the sun. In the second inning Hack Wilson slapped one along the ground at a whistling clip almost over second base. Here was a budding hit, if we ever saw one. But Bluege, who is remarkably fast, cut over and by an almost impossible effort knocked the ball down with his glove, scooped it up with the right and nailed his man at first from short center by a cannonball throw.

In the third inning Joe Judge started one toward right center with a rising inflection. It was on its way to gold and glory when Frank Frisch broke the high jump record and cut off a budding triple. After three innings and a half of brilliant pitching the first big crash came in the fourth. Here, with one out, came Bucky Harris reaching for another laurel sprig. His line drive over Hack Wilson carried into the stands, although Hack almost broke his massive spine in trying to pull down the drive. His impact with the low, green barricade sounded like a barrel of crockery being pushed down the cellar stairs.

Just a moment later the same Hack, having recovered his breath, came racing in for a low, rakish hit by Rice. He dived for the ball and dug it up six inches from the turf, skating along for many feet upon his broad and powerful system, stomach down. Here was another hit totally ruined by fancy fielding.

The sixth was replete with loud noises and much strategy. It was here that the stout Washington defense cracked wide open. Mogridge started the trouble by passing Pep Young. Kelly laced a long single to center, sending Young scurrying around to third. Here McGraw sent in Meusel to hit for Terry and Harris countered by removing Mogridge, the southpaw, and sending Marberry to the rifle pit. Meusel lifted a long sacrifice fly to Sam Rice, scoring Young. Wilson followed with a lusty hit, sending Kelly to third. Here the run getting should have ended.

Jackson tapped one sharply to Judge at first, and Judge, attempting to hurry the play for the plate, fumbled the ball and lost his bearings completely as Kelly scored, Jackson reached first and Wilson moved to second on a simple chance. Gowdy tapped one along the ground toward Bluege, and this brilliant infielder let the ball trickle between his feet to left field as Wilson came over with the third run. It was a pitiful infield collapse after a day of superb support up to this moth-eaten spot. The infield cave-in gave the Giants two extra runs and a tidy lead.

The eighth was the most dramatic spot of the entire series. It was full of throbs, thrills and noises. With one out, Nemo Leibold, batting for Taylor, doubled down the left field line. This started the racket with a howl and a roar. Ruel then drew his first hit of the series, an infield blow that Kelly knocked down but couldn't field. With the clamor increasing at every moment, Tate, batting for Marberry, walked, filling the bases, with only one out. There was brief lull as McNeely flied out. The vocal spasm broke loose with renewed fury when Harris rapped one sharply toward Lindstrom, and the ball, after skirting the ground, suddenly bounded high over Lindstrom's head for the single that scored Leibold and Ruel and tied it up. Harris had driven in all three runs and the gathering paid its noisiest acclaim.

It was Art Nehf who checked the Washington's assault and it was Walter Johnson who hurried in to face the Giants in the ninth with his third shot at destiny.

For a moment in the ninth he rocked and reeled on the edge of the precipice. With one out Frisch tripled to deep center. But after Johnson had purposely passed Pep Young he struck out Kelly and then led Meusel to an infield out that left Frisch stranded far from home.

Washington came within a span of winning in the ninth. With one gone Joe Judge laced a single to center. Bluege tapped to Kelly at first and Kelly whipped the ball at high speed to Jackson, the ball bounding away from Jackson's glove as Judge raced to third. A man on third and first and only one out—what a chance. But Miller rammed one sharply to Jackson at short and a crushing double play wiped out Washington's chance with Judge almost home.

Groh, batting for McQuillan, opened the ninth with a clean hit. He limped to first and gave way to Southworth. Lindstrom sacrificed, but Johnson, calling on all he had, struck out Frisch and Kelly in a row, Frisch fanning for the first time in four years of world series play.

It was Johnson's day at last.

# The Nature of His Retaliation

## BABE RUTH'S CALLED SHOT

### October 1, 1932

**There are, in all** the annals of the game, only a handful of home runs that stand out as landmarks: Mazeroski, and Fisk, and Kirk Gibson, and Bobby Thomson, of course, all hit epic blasts. Among Babe Ruth's 714 career round-trippers, there is at least one that can join those other memorable shots, and that's the one he hit off of Charlie Root in the third game of the 1932 World Series—the homer that came to be known as The Called Shot.

Controversy still dogs the event, with some folks swearing that Ruth never broadcast his intention to park one to spite the lemon-and-epithet-hurling Wrigley Field crowd, and others saying he did just that.

Either way, it's a story that won't die. In the summer of 1995, for instance, at a conference on Ruth at Hofstra University, over one thousand scholars, reporters, statisticians, and plain old ball fans came to the unequivocal position that the man . . . well, that he probably didn't call a damn thing.

But then again, maybe he did.

No less a source than the *New York Times*, via famed sportswriter John Drebinger, reported the very next morning that Ruth, in no uncertain terms, had indicated that "the nature of his retaliation [for the fans' abuse] would be a wallop right out the confines of the park." Other writers aver that Ruth was merely indicating the count with his raised fingers.

For his part, Root swore all his life that he would have knocked the Babe on his ass if Ruth had been foolish enough to insult him that way.

Ruth, who at 37 years old hit 41 home runs with 137 RBIs in 1932, was not the player he had been during the fabulous twenties. In the landmark year of 1927, for example, when he hit his epic 60 home runs, he also batted .356 with 164 RBIs. (Few fans recall that even then, Ruth was upstaged by Gehrig,

Babe Ruth in action in
the '32 World Series

who posted a modest .373 average, 47 homers, and 175 RBIs that year. Can you imagine a player today approaching two—any two—of those numbers in the same year?)

Still, Ruth was unquestionably the game's dominant player in 1932. Larger, in a sense, than the game itself, he continued to hold immense sway over the public imagination. In a terrific *Daily News* column written on the very day of The Called Shot, Paul Gallico captured the effect Ruth had on his fans:

> The Babe sat in an empty Pullman section sucking on a big black cigar. He was clad in a pair of tan pajamas, open at the throat, and over them he wore a set of green lounging pajamas, the color of Grade A arsenic, with green polka dots on them. He said: "Hello, kid. Wanna go back home Sunday night?" I said I did. He said: "All right. We'll take these fellows two straight and get back. I want to play a lot of golf and go hunting." The train pulled into Elkhart, Indiana. I got off first, got off around in back of the crowd there and watched a demonstration of warmth, affection and worship that kings might envy. There were over a thousand children of all sizes, shapes, sexes and colors waiting for the Yankee Special to pull in, their faces aglow with excitement and eagerness . . .
>
> I secured a position behind the crowd. Men in overalls, men in uniform, factory hands, railroad men, dwellers from nearby houses, excited women, old men with long whiskers, girls with babies on their shoulders or in their arms milled around, muttering excitedly. Would the Babe appear? Would the children find him? Suddenly there was a yell from a yardman in denim overalls and cap: "There he is! There's the Big Boy now. Hey Babe! O Babe," and there framed in the vestibule of the Pullman car stood the burly figure of the Babe in his green pajamas, his huge face split from ear to ear with a boyish grin. The King was ready to receive his subjects.

Maybe Ruth called his shot. Maybe he didn't. I have to admit that I don't really care whether he did or not.

The fact that, of all the men who've ever played the game at that level, there's really only one player who, conceivably, *might* have done something so ballsy, and gotten away with it . . . that possibility is, somehow, by itself, enough.

# JOHN DREBINGER
*New York Times*

Four home runs, two by the master hitter of them all, Babe Ruth, and the other pair by his almost equally proficient colleague, Columbia Lou Gehrig, advanced the New York Yankees to within one game of their third World Series sweep today.

The American League champions once again overpowered the Cubs to win their third straight game of the current classic which, for the first time, went on display in this city.

Those four blows made the final score 7 to 5. They crushed not only the National League standard-bearers, but a gathering of 51,000 which jammed Wrigley Field to the limits of its capacity and packed two wooden temporary bleachers outside the park. Included in the gathering was Governor Roosevelt of New York, the Democratic Presidential candidate.

It was by far the most turbulent and bitterly fought engagement of the series thus far. The Cubs, inspired by a show of civic enthusiasm, battled fiercely and courageously.

They even struck back with a couple of lusty homers on their own account, one by Kiki Cuyler, the other by Gabby Hartnett.

Hartnett's wallop came in the ninth inning and brought about the retirement of George Pipgrass, the first Yankee pitcher to appear in the series who had also taken part in the clean-sweep triumphs of 1927 and 1928.

But this move merely provided a setting that added still further to the glamour of the Yankee triumph. For it brought on the scene one of the greatest World Series pitchers of all time, the talented Herbie Pennock, who started pitching in these classics back in 1914. In that long interval he had recorded five personal triumphs without a single defeat. Consequently he did not mean to let this game slip from his fingers even though credit for the victory still would remain with Pipgrass.

In short, the famous squire of Kennett Square sharply halted the belated Cub rally, fairly smothering the desperate bid of the Chicagoans with consummate ease and skill.

With a Cub lurking on the base paths poised to dart for the plate, Pennock fanned a pinch-hitter and retired the next two on soft infield taps, one of which he fielded himself. The other was snared by Gehrig for the final put-out.

Thus, with three victories tucked away against no defeats, the Yankees, now skillfully piloted by Joe McCarthy, who bossed these same Cubs only two years ago, have advanced to a point where they need only one more game to clinch the world's championship. In addition, they have a chance to add still further to their remarkable world's series record. They have now competed in eleven straight series encounters without suffering a single reversal.

Both the game and all its trimmings provided a much livelier spectacle than either of the two previous encounters. In sharp contrast to the rather matter-of-fact manner in which New York had accepted the first two battles, the crowd today was as keyed up as the players, if not more so.

It was a warm day, clear and sunny, though rather windy. There was a gay, holiday spirit in the air that never forsook the gathering, for Chicago puts a great deal more fervor in its baseball than does New York. It seemed as though the fans of this mid-Western metropolis simply would not believe how severely and decisively their champions had been manhandled by the mighty Yankees in the first two games in the East.

They roared their approval of every good play made by the Cubs. They playfully tossed bright yellow lemons at Babe Ruth and booed him thoroughly as the great man carried on a pantomime act while standing at the plate.

Then they sat back, awed and spellbound, as the Babe, casting aside his buffoonery, smashed one of the longest home runs ever seen at Wrigley Field.

It was an amazing demonstration by baseball's outstanding figure, who a few weeks ago was ill and confined to his bed. It confounded the crowd, which in paid attendance numbered 49,986 and which had contributed $211,912 in receipts.

The Cubs took the field with their hopes resting upon the stout right arm of Charlie Root, but Charlie was unequal to the task. He failed to survive five rounds, retiring immediately after Ruth and Gehrig had blasted their second two homers. These came in succession in the fifth like a flash of lightning and a clap of thunder.

Both were held fairly well in restraint in the latter rounds by Pat Malone and the left-handed Jackie May. But aside from providing the crowd with a chance to give vent to boos, the earlier damage these two had inflicted proved far sufficient to carry the day.

Ruth and Gehrig simply dominated the scene from start to finish, and they began their performance early. When the two marched to the plate during the batting rehearsal they at once thrilled the crowd by uncorking a series of tremendous drives into the temporary wooden bleachers.

The Babe's very first practice shot almost cleared the top of the wooden structure, and he followed it with several more prodigious drives. Gehrig produced some more, and each time the ball soared into those densely packed stands the crowd gasped. The spectacle certainly could not have been very heartening to the Cubs.

And when the battle proper began, both kept right on firing. The Babe's two homers were his first of the current series, but they sent his all-time world's series record for home runs to fifteen. For Gehrig, his two gave him a total of three for the series and an all-time record of seven.

Fittingly enough, the Babe was the first to touch off the explosion and his opening smash sent the Yanks away to a three-run lead in the very first inning. In fact, the crowd had scarcely recovered its composure after a tumultuous reception when it was forced to suffer its first annoyance.

There was a sharp wind blowing across the playing field toward the right-field bleachers that threatened to raise havoc with the players, and it did very shortly.

Eager and tense, the crowd watched Root pitch to Earl Combs, the first Yankee batter. It at once roared approbation as Combs sent a drive squarely into the hands of young Billy Jurges who was again playing shortstop for the Cubs in place of the injured Mark Koenig.

But the next moment the throng voiced its dismay as Jurges unfurled a throw that sailed high over Manager Charlie Grimm's head at first and into the Yankee dugout.

Root was plainly flustered as Combs, under the prevailing ground rule, was allowed to advance to second base. Root strove to steady himself, but he passed Joey Sewell and faced Ruth. Cheers and jeers mingled as the great Yankee batter made his first official appearance at the plate in Chicago's portion of the setting.

Root pitched cautiously, fearful of what would happen if he allowed the Babe to shoot one high in the air with that brisk breeze behind it. His first two offerings went wide of the plate. Then he put one over and away the ball went. It was a lofty shot that soared on and on until it dropped deep in the temporary stands. Thus the Cubs, who had planned to fight so desperately for this game, already were three runs to the bad.

But desperately they fought, nevertheless, and in the lower half of the same inning they gave their cohorts the chance to do some wholehearted cheering by getting one of these tallies back.

The wind, which had annoyed Root so much, also seemed to trouble Pipgrass. He passed Herman, whereupon the crowd set up a roar as though the series had already been won. Woody English was retired on a fly to Ruth, who was performing in left field today in order to avoid the glare of the sun.

But Kiki Cuyler, who might have been the hero of this struggle had Ruth and Gehrig been playing elsewhere, lifted a two-bagger over Ben Chapman's head in right against the wire screening in front of the bleachers, and Herman scored amid tumultuous cheering.

But two innings later Gehrig, after an uneventful first inning, stepped into the picture. Leaning heavily into Root's pitch, he sent another mighty shot soaring into the right-field bleachers. That made the score 4 to 1.

At this point, however, the Cubs staged their most gallant fight of the day. With one out in the lower half of the third, Cuyler again produced a jubilant uproar by shooting a homer into the right-field stands, and this at once inspired his comrades to redouble their efforts against Pipgrass. Stephenson slashed a single to right, and though he was forced by Johnny Moore, Manager Grimm lined a drive to right that Chapman did not play any too well. The ball shot past the Alabama Arrow for a two-bagger and Moore scored all the way from first.

That left the Cubs only one run in arrears, and in the fourth they drew even amid the most violent vocal demonstration of the afternoon. Jurges, eager to make amends for his earlier miscue, slapped a low liner to left, and the crowd howled with glee as Ruth failed in a heroic attempt to make a shoe-string catch of the ball. Jurges gained two bases on the hit.

Good naturedly, the Babe doffed his cap in acknowledgment to the adverse plaudits of the fans and the play went on. Tony Lazzeri made a spectacular catch of Herman's high, twisting pop-fly back of second base. But the next moment Tony booted English's grounder and Jurges raced over the plate with the tally that tied the score at 4-all.

But it seems decidedly unhealthy for anyone to taunt the great man Ruth too much and very soon the crowd was to learn its lesson. A single lemon rolled out to the plate as Ruth came up in the fifth and in no mistaken motions the Babe notified the crowd that the nature of his retaliation would be a wallop right out the confines of the park.

Root pitched two balls and two strikes, while Ruth signaled with his fingers after each pitch to let the spectators know exactly how the situation stood. Then the mightiest blow of all fell.

It was a tremendous smash that bore straight down the center of the field in an enormous arc, came down alongside the flagpole and disappeared behind the corner formed by the scoreboard and the end of the right-field bleachers.

It was Ruth's fifteenth home run in world's series competition and easily one of his most gorgeous. The crowd, suddenly unmindful of everything save that it had just witnessed an epic feat, hailed the Babe with a salvo of applause.

Root, badly shaken, now faced Gehrig, and his feelings well can be imagined. The crowd was still too much excited over the Ruth incident to realize what was happening when Columbia Lou lifted an enormous fly high in the air. As it sailed on the wings of the lake breeze the ball just cleared the high flagpole and dropped in the temporary stands.

Grimm, the player-manager of the Cubs, called time. Consolingly he invited Root to retire to the less turbulent confines of the clubhouse and ordered Pat Malone to the mound.

Pat filled the bases with three passes but he escaped the inning without further trouble. From then on the game, like its two predecessors, passed on to its very obvious conclusion with the exception of a final flurry in the ninth.

---

## Another View

# PAUL GALLICO
*New York Daily News*

. . . The New Yorkers perished in an orderly manner, one—two—three, to start the fourth inning, but the Cubs sent the 49,986 addicts into hysteria when they tied the score on a long double by Jurges and an odiferous error by Master Lazzeri at second base.

Jurges pasted the ball out to Ruth who came in like a charging bull in an attempt to take it off his shoe tops. He missed but carried the ball along with him and finally wound up sitting on it, after sliding along a few yards on his face.

When he finally extracted it from beneath his person, Jurges was on second. English, next up, slapped a grounder to Lazzeri who fielded it, dropped it, kicked it, lost it and finally stood there just being ashamed. Crosetti ran up behind him and made a wild throw to Dickey, pulling him so far from the plate that Jurges had no trouble scoring the tying run.

However, two were already out and when English tried to steal second, Dickey cut him down with a perfect throw to Lazzeri.

Well, we now come to the creme-de-la-creme. This is what you have been waiting for. This is how the ball game was won. Sewell grounded out to open the fifth and the Great Man came to bat again. Root wound up and pitched. Strike one, the crowd booed. Babe Ruth held up one finger to the Cub dugout to indicate that but one strike had passed.

Again Root threw. Ball one. Another windup. Another pitch. Strike two. The crowd roared, yelled and cat-called. The Babe merely held up two fingers to the Cub dugout to show that there was still another pitch coming to him. He also did a little plain and fancy leering and then faced Root again with the bat clutched in the end of his fingers.

Windup. Pitch. Flash of ball! Crack! Goombye! The pellet sailed high, wide and handsome straight out for the flagpole to the right of the scoreboard in center field, where it sank into the clutching hands of customers seated in the extreme left end of the right field bleachers.

The Babe ran around the bases gesticulating at the Cub dugout, mocking them, teasing them and holding up three fingers. Oh, my New York constituents, how your hearts would have warmed had you seen the Babe, thus confounding his enemies, thus making his run.

The hubbub had not yet died away. The crowd had not yet settled down. The senses had not yet had time to digest the Great Man's latest miracle, when there came another sharp "crack" and Lou Gehrig, next up, had smashed his second home run of the day over the right field fence but just inside the foul line.

It blew Root right out of the game. Two home-run balls in succession was too much . . .

Is that fun or isn't it?

# The Young Dutchman

## JOHN VANDER MEER'S CONSECUTIVE NO-HITTERS

June 15, 1938

**When I was a** kid, certain baseball names held an almost totemic significance for me. Lou Gehrig was probably at the head of that list, if only because of the man's nickname. Iron Horse? How strong would a guy have to be in order to be called that?

Hack Wilson was another name that I couldn't hear without wishing it were mine. Playing kickball on the playground, I'd sometimes imagine my fellow fourth-graders shouting, "C'mon Hack! Let's go Hack!," and I'd picture myself booting that blood-red rubber ball over the heads of all those kids who (poor suckers!) weren't named Hack. Oddly, I don't remember wishing to be called Hack when I played baseball in my youth.

Nowadays, when I'm called Hack, I try not to take it too personally.

But of all baseball names, none rolled so easily off the tongue or looked so great on the printed page as Johnny Vander Meer. That a guy with a name like that held one of the "unbreakable" records of the big leagues seemed, somehow, just another perfect mystery in the endless string of mysteries of baseball hagiography.

Vander Meer was only 22 years old when he threw his second consecutive no-hitter. A fastballing southpaw with control problems early in his career, Vander Meer garnered the improbable deuce in the first-ever night game at Ebbets Field, four days after he'd no-hit the Boston Braves. In Brooklyn on June 15th, Vander Meer's wildness almost cost him his bid for legendary status when he walked eight Dodgers, including three in a row in the ninth, but he managed to hold it together long enough to nail the door shut.

Like DiMaggio's 56-game hitting streak, Vander Meer's is a record most ball fans can not really envision being broken. Honestly, though, it's a bit easier to conceive of a player hitting safely in 57 straight games than of a pitcher hurling *three* no-hitters in a row. It just can't happen. It won't happen. Will it?

One last note. At the end of the Lou Smith piece that follows, it's pointed out that Bill Terry, scheduled to manage the National League All-Stars three weeks after Vander Meer's Ebbets Field feat, had decided that Vander Meer was "now his No. 1 choice to open against Gehrig, DiMaggio and company." In that All Star game, played in Vander Meer's Cincinnati, the kid pitched one-hit, shutout ball for three innings.

# LOU SMITH
*Cincinnati Enquirer*

Johnny Vander Meer, sensational twenty-two-year-old fireballing portsider from Midland Park, N. J., made baseball history tonight by pitching his second no-hit game in a row while turning back the Brooklyn Dodgers 6 to 0, before a capacity crowd of 38,748 in Larry MacPhail's inaugural mazda opera here.

Last Saturday afternoon the young Redleg southpaw set down the Boston Bees without a hit, while allowing only three men to reach first on passes. Tonight he was a trifle wilder, handing out eight passes, but he didn't allow anything that even faintly resembled a hit.

Only five balls were hit out of the infield off the newest pitching sensation in the majors as he turned in his sixth straight win and seventh of the season.

His work enabled our boys to climb within one and one-half games of the second-place Cubs, and four and one-half games of the pace-making Giants.

Vandy has now pitched 26 consecutive scoreless innings, while turning in three shutouts in his last five starts. He also set seven of the Dodgers down on strikes to maintain his lead as the champion strikeout artist of the league with 65 for the season.

It was the first time in the history of organized baseball that a pitcher ever turned in two no-hitters in a row, and only the fourth time that a pitcher has blasted his way into the no-hit coterie.

Theodore Breitenstein pitched a no-hitter for the Cincinnati Red Stockings back in 1898 and again for St. Louis in 1901.

Cy Young turned the trick for Cleveland in 1897 and again for the Boston Red Sox in 1908, while the great Christy Mathewson hurled no-hitters for the Giants in 1901 and 1905.

Johnny Vander Meer,
Cincinnati Reds

While Vander Meer was turning back the Dodgers with the greatest of ease his mates teed off on a quartet of Flatbush hurlers, Max Butcher, Tot Presnell, Luke Hamlin, and Vito Tamulis, for 11 hits, including a game-clinching homer by Frank McCormick with a pair of mates aboard in the third round.

The demonstration accorded by the capacity crowd of haughty Gothamites, including Johnny's proud mother and father and 500 of his neighbors from Midland Park, N.J., was one of the greatest ever witnessed in the East.

Not a single person of the capacity crowd left the park until Leo Durocher skied out to Harry Craft for the final out with the bases loaded.

Then bedlam broke loose. It looked like a college flag rush as the frenzied fans streamed through the exits and vaulted over the railings to pay tribute to baseball's newest No. 1 hero.

They encircled the dog-tired youngster before he could cross the left-field foul line. And for a minute it looked as though he was going to pass out. He appeared to be in a haze. But he quickly recovered, and with the aid of his team-mates and several dozen of New York's finest, managed to make the dugout.

Even there he was not safe from the autograph hunters, who pushed his teammates and the cops away like they were so many corn husks. But the young Dutchman had recovered his equilibrium and beat a hasty retreat to the dressing room, where he received the congratulations of his teammates behind closed doors.

Johnny said that he had more stuff tonight than he had in setting down the Bees without a hit Saturday.

"I was much faster tonight than last Saturday," he said when on the rubbing table while trainer Doc Rhode massaged baseball's mightiest arm.

"My curve ball also was breaking sharper. I realized after the fifth inning that I had a splendid chance to turn in another no-hitter, and after that just kept fogging 'em in. I felt a little tired in the final two heats, and it was certainly a relief to me when I turned around and saw Harry (Craft) circling under Durocher's fly."

Vandy retired the Dodgers in four of the nine rounds. Five of his eight walks came in the final three rounds. In the seventh he walked Lavagetto and Camilli with one gone, but then settled down to breeze the third strike past Ernie Koy and make Durocher hit into a force play.

He sailed through the eighth with the greatest of ease, sailing the third strike past pinch hitter Woody English. Cuyler hoisted to Goodman, and Hudson hit nothing but the cooling breezes with three mighty swings.

Vandy appeared a trifle jittery as he took his place on the firing line in the final round. He handed three balls to Hassett before making the Brooklyn crooner ground out to him along the first-base line.

He then walked Phelps, Lavagetto, and Camilli, the heart of the Dodger batting order—in a row on 18 pitched balls.

This brought Manager McKechnie and the Redleg infield out to the mound for a conference with Vandy. After a few reassuring pats on his broad shoulders, the Deacon told Vandy to take his time, relax, and not to worry.

And he did just that by making Koy hit to Riggs, who fired the ball home ahead of Goody Rosen, who ran for Phelps, and then getting Durocher on a skier to center.

Outside of these two rounds the only Dodgers to dig their spikes into the initial hassock were Camilli and Cuyler. The former drew the first of Vandy's eight passes and Cuyler his second and third in the third and sixth.

The Reds not only supported Vandy in excellent style, but also drove their jinx of the past two seasons, Big Max Butcher, to cover in the third with a four-run splurge after two men had been retired.

They added another off Tot Presnell and Hamlin in the seventh, and scored their sixth and final off the latter in the eighth.

Berger's scratch single and a wild throw by Lavagetto and a walk to Goodman, followed by McCormick's line homer into the lower deck of the left-field stands started Butcher on his way to the showers.

Another walk to Lombardi and singles by Craft and Riggs completed the job while adding the fourth run before Presnell breezed the third strike past Myers to retire the side.

Presnell retired the Reds without them scoring until Goodman floored him with a hot bounder in the seventh. A stolen base by Goodman, an intentional walk to Lombardi, and Craft's third straight single scored the Redleg gardener.

Myers's infield single and Berger's triple to right center field, his second extra-base blow of the game and his third hit, accounted for the sixth and final Red tally in the eighth.

But this all ran second to Vander Meer's second straight pitching master-piece. So, again, Johnny, we salute you.

The scene following the game, according to veteran sports scribes at the game, was one of the wildest demonstrations ever witnessed in New York.

Fans rushed onto the diamond by the hundreds in an effort to pump the hand of the husky hall of fame hero.

But big Jim Weaver and Paul Drebinger, two of Johnny's pitching mates, along with a flock of New York cops, rescued him from the hero worshippers and led him to the safer confines of the dugout.

Meanwhile, folks in the milling mob discovered the pitcher's parents seated behind the dugout, and the proud parents were besieged by admirers who demanded their autographs. They started out to oblige some of the fans, but when the latter started pushing them around and pulling on their clothes, the elder Vander Meers appealed for police protection. They had to be escorted to their car by police.

Johnny remained in the peaceful confines until almost an hour after the game was over.

But he failed to outsit thousands of Flatbush fans who remained outside of the park until long after midnight for a glimpse of the newest hero in civvies.

The young Dutchman was all smiles as he drove away with his parents and No. 1 sweetheart.

He will make his next start against the Boston Bees in a double-header at Beantown next Sunday. And you can bet that the eyes of the baseball world will be focused on him then.

Bill Terry, who will manage the National League all-star team when it clashes with the American Leaguers at Crosley Field Wednesday, July 6, said after the game that Vander Meer is now his No. 1 choice to open against Gehrig, DiMaggio and company. Nice of Bill, don't you think?

# Strong Men Weep

---

## LOU GEHRIG'S FAMOUS FAREWELL

### July 4, 1939

**Cal Ripken breaking Lou** Gehrig's streak of 2,130 consecutive games might have been the best thing that could have happened to the old Yankee captain's reputation.

For months and weeks leading up to that great night in September 1995, when Ripken finally passed Gehrig, a disturbing thread began to weave through the endless discussions surrounding The Streak.

Among all the factions that had formed as it became clear that Ripken was going to just keep on going (factions that seemed to dissolve—along with everyone else who cared at all about the record—into a mass, warm embrace of the man the moment he began his spontaneous, lump-in-the-throat jog around the field at Camden Yards), there was, it seemed, a small but nonetheless significant group of voices that appeared bent on pointing out the questionable discrepancies in Gehrig's original record.

Gehrig played first base, as opposed to Cal, who played a far more demanding shortstop. Gehrig often played only an inning or two when he wasn't feeling 100 per cent—or when he was on the road, in order to keep the streak going—while Ripken played in something insane, like eight and two-thirds of every nine innings during his streak. Gehrig never had to deal with coast-to-coast airplane travel or Astroturf or blah blah blah. The point, it seemed, was that Gehrig's legendary streak, while kind of impressive, was really nothing compared to Ripken's *more genuine* streak.

And I'll buy that. Ripken's is the more amazing streak. By far. Hands down. No question.

With his streak broken, though, perhaps Gehrig can be fully appreciated as the great, great ballplayer that he was, the ballplayer whose career was cut short

Lou Gehrig,
July 4, 1939

when he still had some good years left in him, rather than as the guy whose tainted consecutive-game streak Cal Ripken finally obliterated.

But no matter how Gehrig is remembered as a player, no matter how fine or fearsome a hitter the man was (a .340 lifetime average; a .632 slugging percentage; the career mark for grand slams; 1,990 RBIs), or how loyal a team-mate, or how worthy a leader as the captain of the awesome Yankee teams of the 1920s, he will always be most-readily associated with July 4, 1939, when 60,000 fans, old teammates, and Gehrig's own words filled Yankee Stadium for the game's most famous farewell: "Today I consider myself the luckiest man on the face of the earth."

Gehrig didn't speak for long, but not too many baseball fans are unfamiliar with what he said. No words ever uttered by another athlete have resonated for so many years in the hearts and minds of so many fans, most of whom weren't even born at the time the words themselves were echoing around the far reaches of the park.

Gesturing to the "grand men," his teammates and friends, standing beside him, Gehrig asked: "Which of you wouldn't consider it the highlight of his career just to associate with them for even one day?" He went on to thank the fans, his managers, the groundskeepers, his father and mother, and his wife, in an elo-quent and tremendously moving few minutes that ended with Gehrig breaking down and Babe Ruth stepping foward to lend his old teammate support.

Gehrig's words that day might not have been recorded verbatim by Shirley Povich in his memorable *Washington Post* piece on the tribute, but no newspa-perman present when Gehrig walked to the mike better captured the esteem and affection Gehrig seemed to elicit from all who knew him—esteem and affection which, on that Tuesday afternoon, was finally given full voice.

## SHIRLEY POVICH
*Washington Post*

I saw strong men weep this afternoon, expressionless umpires swallow hard, and emotion pump the hearts and glaze the eyes of 61,000 baseball fans in Yankee Stadium. Yes, and hard-boiled news photographers clicked their shut-ters with fingers that trembled a bit.

It was Lou Gehrig Day at the stadium, and the first 100 years of baseball saw nothing quite like it. It was Lou Gehrig, tributes, honors, gifts heaped upon him, getting an overabundance of the thing he wanted least—sympathy. But it wasn't maudlin. His friends were just letting their hair down in their earnestness to pay him honor. And they stopped just short of a good, mass cry.

They had Lou out there at home plate between games of a double-header, with the 60,000 massed in the triple tiers that rimmed the field, microphones and cameras trained on him, and he couldn't take it that way. Tears streamed down his face, circuiting the most famous pair of dimples in baseball, and he looked chiefly at the ground.

Seventy-year-old Ed Barrow, president of the Yankees, who had said to newspapermen, "Boys, I have bad news for you," when Gehrig's ailment was diagnosed as infantile paralysis two weeks ago, stepped out of the background halfway through the presentation ceremonies, and draped his arm across Gehrig's shoulder. But he was doing more than that. He was holding Gehrig up, for Big Lou needed support.

As he leaned on Barrow, Gehrig said, "Thanks, Ed." He bit his lip hard, was grateful for the supporting arm, as the Yankees of 1927 stepped to the microphone after being introduced. Babe Ruth, Bob Meusel, Waite Hoyt, Herb Pennock, Benny Bengough, Bob Shawkey, Mark Koenig, Tony Lazzeri, all of the class of '27 were there. And Gehrig had been one of them, too. He had been the only one among them to bestride both eras.

Still leaning on Barrow, Gehrig acknowledged gifts from his Yankee mates, from the Yankee Stadium ground crew, and the hot dog butchers, from fans as far as Denver, and from his New York rivals, the Giants. There was a smile through his tears, but he wasn't up to words. He could only shake the hands of the small army of officials who made the presentations.

He stood there twisting his doffed baseball cap into a braid in his fingers as Manager Joe McCarthy followed Mayor La Guardia and Postmaster General Farley in tribute to "the finest example of ball player, sportsman and citizen that baseball has ever known," but Joe McCarthy couldn't take it that way, either. The man who has driven the highest-salaried prima donnas of baseball into action, who has baited a thousand umpires, broke down.

McCarthy openly sobbed as he stood in front of the microphone and said, "Lou, what else can I say except that it was a sad day in the life of everybody who knew you when you came to my hotel room that day in Detroit and told me you were quitting as a ball player because you felt yourself a hindrance to the team. My God, man, you were never that."

And as if to emphasize the esteem in which he held Gehrig though his usefulness to the Yankees as a player was ended, McCarthy, too, stepped out of the fringe full into the circle where Gehrig and McCarthy stood and half embraced the big fellow.

Now it was Gehrig's turn to talk into the microphone, to acknowledge his gifts. The 60,000 at intervals had set up the shout, "We want Lou!" even as they used to shout "We want Ruth"—yells that they reserved for the only two men at Yankee Stadium for which the crowd ever organized a cheering section.

But Master of Ceremonies Sid Mercer was anticipating Gehrig. He saw the big fellow choked up. Infinitesimally Gehrig shook his head, and Mercer announced: "I shall not ask Lou Gehrig to make a speech. I do not believe that I should."

They started to haul away the microphones. Gehrig half turned toward the dugout, with the ceremonies apparently at an end. And then he wheeled suddenly, strode back to the loud-speaking apparatus, held up his hand for attention, gulped, managed a smile and then spoke.

"For weeks," said Gehrig, "I have been reading in the newspapers that I am a lucky fellow who got a tough break. I don't believe it. I have been a lucky guy. For 16 years, into every ball park in which I have ever walked, I received nothing but kindness and encouragement. Mine has been a full life."

He went on, fidgeting with his cap, pawing the ground with his spikes as he spoke, choking back emotions that threatened to silence him, summoning courage from somewhere. He thanked everybody. He didn't forget the ballpark help; he told of his gratitude to newspapermen who had publicized him. He didn't forget the late Miller Huggins, or his six years with him; or Manager Joe McCarthy, or the late Col. Ruppert, or Babe Ruth, or "my roommate, Bill Dickey."

And he thanked the Giants—"The fellows from across the river, who we would give our right arm to beat"—he was more at ease in front of the mike now, and he had a word for Mrs. Gehrig and for the immigrant father and mother who had made his education, his career, possible. And he denied again that he had been the victim of a bad break in life. He said, "I've lots to live for, honest."

And thousands cheered.

Ted Williams, 1941

# Of Ted We Sing

---

## TED WILLIAMS HITS .406
### September 28, 1941

**"All I ever want** out of life," Ted Williams once memorably remarked, "is that when I walk down the street folks will say, 'There goes the greatest hitter who ever lived.'"

The greatest *all-around hitter?* Ever? Fans will argue about that title as long as the game is played. Was it Cobb? Hornsby? Ruth? Aaron? In the end, it's really an impossible assessment to make. After all, considering the variables one has to take into account when gauging a batter's career statistics, including the caliber of the pitching he had to face, the quality of the players batting around him in the lineup, whether he played in night games during his career, the number of . . .

Ahhh, forget it. Williams was the greatest.

The only player in the last 60-plus years to hit over .400, a .388 average when he was *39 years old*, 521 career home runs—all this while missing several seasons at the height of his career (translation: a few hundred more hits, a few hundred more RBIs, a whole mess of home runs, and probably a higher career batting average) when he served in both World War II and the Korean War. He hit for power and for average, and he did it year after year after year. He studied, practiced, slept, dreamed, and breathed hitting.

The title of the man's autobiography? *Hitter.*

In 1939, Williams won Rookie of the Year honors in the American League, hitting .327 with a league-leading 145 RBIs. A mere two years later, the slender, cocky 23-year-old had established himself as perhaps the finest all-around hitter in either league.

He had also managed to alienate fans, the press, and his teammates with what some folks perceived as his unpardonable arrogance and immaturity. One teammate, the great Jimmie Foxx, once told reporters that "Teddy" was "a spoiled boy. How long it takes him to grow up remains to be seen. But he'll have to grow up the hard way now."

Twenty years later, John Updike's classic *New Yorker* piece on Williams's last-ever at-bat beautifully captured the man's pride, and the strained, agonizing relationship between the hitter and the famously fickle and vocal Boston fans. Williams homered, of course, on that cold September day, and as the fans stood and cheered him as he circled the bases for the final time, he came close to tipping his cap in acknowledgment. But he didn't.

"I thought about tipping my hat, you're damn right I did," he said later, "and for a moment I was torn, but by the time I got to second base, I knew I couldn't do it."

Burt Whitman's *Boston Herald* piece below addresses the friction between Williams and the other Sox players in the early stages of his career, but there's little argument that Williams's end-of-the-season performance in 1941 helped ease some of that tension by setting the standard for grace—and power—under pressure. The story is familiar to most fans: Williams was hitting .39955 on September 28, when the Red Sox were scheduled to play a doubleheader against the Philadelphia Athletics. If he sat out the twin bill, he was guaranteed to end the season hitting exactly .400 (rounding off his .39955). If he played, he was guaranteed nothing.

He played, of course. Looking back now on the fierceness with which he competed over the course of his entire career, it's hard to imagine there was ever any doubt that Ted Williams would play that amazing season out to the very end. The notion that he might not have done so is, after all this time, somehow unseemly. An insult.

All he did on that cold Sunday afternoon was get four hits in the first game, one of them a home run, and two hits in the second, including a scorching double that would have gone for a homer had it not caromed violently off the loud-speaker in right. He went six for eight on the day, bumping up his average six points.

Still, Williams had to wait a few years for his first MVP award. Nineteen forty-one was also the year that Joe DiMaggio had a pretty good season. Does the number 56 ring a bell?

# BURT WHITMAN
*Boston Herald*

Ted Williams put on one of the most spectacular last-day batting splurges in the history of major league baseball today to raise his season's average to .4057, and he made this big jump from just below .400 by getting six hits out of eight times at bat in the doubleheader the Red Sox split with the A's. He smashed his 37th homer in the opener, in which he also got three singles, and he got a sizzling double off the horn in high right-center in the second game.

The Splendid Splinter is the first Boston major leaguer to amass a .400 or better average since the immortal Hughey Duffy put across his legendary .438 in 1894, and as everybody knows, the last American Leaguer to hit the .400 society was Harry Detroit Heilman, with .403 in 1923. The last National Leaguer to force his way into the select group was Bill Terry with .401 in 1931.

At the start of the games today Ted was below .400, actually .39955, and you can imagine the turmoil in the Kid's heart, and also Joe Cronin's, when this morning had all the appearance of rain, which might wipe out the day's proceedings.

But the weatherman relented and the Sox won the first game, 12 to 11; then the A's took the eight-inning grand finale, terminated by darkness, 7 to 1.

Yet it is of Ted we sing today. There were more than 10,000 customers out today and they started cheering for the Kid when he first came to bat, and they never stopped. He certainly gave them a batting show they'll have as a talking point as long as they live.

Gone today were that strain and sense of rigidity which Ted showed yesterday and in Washington, during the time of his great slump. Manager Cronin ordered his players to refrain from giving Ted advice. "I really don't see any batter who can qualify as a coach for Ted's hitting," reasoned Joe.

The Kid solved his own problem. He returned to his best late-August form at bat, loose yet argus-eyed and potent. He knew just how many hits he needed for the day to regain the .400 circle.

First time up, in the second inning, as lead-off man and against Dick Fowler, up from Toronto, Ted had two balls on him when he swished a fierce, low grounder to the right of first-sacker Bob Johnson.

Second time up, in the fifth, he hammered the second Fowler pitch clear over the right-field wall, out on to 20th Street, a smash good for at least 440 feet on the level, his 37th homer of the year, and it came with one ball and no strikes to his account.

His third straight safe hit came in the sixth, off Lefty Porter Vaughan, when there were two balls to his tally, and this time it was a harsh grounder on the right side of the first-sacker again.

His fourth safety in a row in that opener was in the seventh, off Vaughan again, with the count three and two this time, and was a clean drive over the first-sacker's head well into right field.

Up in the ninth, for his fifth time in the opener, Ted reached first when the second-sacker made an error on his harsh grounder. Fair scoring.

He finished the first game with the surety he'd finish up better than .400. We heard veteran baseball men suggest that Ted ought to call it a season and camp on his colossal batting average. But several days ago Cronin and Ted talked things over and Ted and Joe agreed that the Kid would go right down to the finish, except only for darkness in the second game today, and spurn safety-first tactics.

He got a big hand when he came up as lead-off man in the second inning of the finale, and there were two balls on him when he pulled a grounder safely between the first and second-basemen, and you should have heard the crowd applaud.

Ted made this hit off Fred Caliguiri, up from Wilmington, a pretty slick righthander.

One of the most wicked liners we've seen Ted make in the three years he's been with the Sox was his double in the fourth. The first two pitches to him were balls. He fouled the next one off. Pitch No. 4 was to his liking and he lashed the sphere to right-center. The ball streaked out with high velocity. Had Ted raised his sights a trifle, it easily would have cleared the rightfield wall and gone 460 feet on the level. But it was on a low trajectory. The ball plunked into the loudspeaker horns on the wall, high up, punched a clean hole in one of them and fell back on the playing field, just a two-bagger, but a tremendous clout all the same.

The seventh inning of the finale saw Ted up for his last official 1941 at-bat, and it was getting dim, even murky, in the crater which is Shibe Park. This time he had the count one and one when he lofted a fly to left field, of all places, where it was caught.

The batting figure is .4057, which means .406 for all practical purposes. He's batted in 126 runs, has scored 135 times, walked 151 times, fanned only 26 times, being "called" out only four times, and the best part of it is that he's so young he's almost sure to stay up in the rarefied Olympic heights of slugging, as did other immortal batters like Rogers Hornsby, George Sisler and Tyrus R. Cobb, all repeaters as better than .400 batters over the season's route.

You'd better believe, too, that the Red Sox players were overjoyed at

Ted's success in finishing over the .400 mark. He's now like a favorite younger brother with most of them. They no longer consider him somewhat like a necessary evil. Now they have a strong affection for him, because he's certainly grown up from the problem child he was a year ago.

# History

—•◦•—

## JACKIE ROBINSON BREAKS THE COLOR BARRIER

### April 15, 1947

**Among baseball fans,** 1947 is a cherished year for two reasons: an amazing World Series (in which Gionfriddo, Lavagetto, and Bevens entered Series lore), and Jackie Robinson.

Today, the fact of Robinson stepping on to Ebbets Field for the first time is studied, discussed, and celebrated as a defining moment, not only in sports, but in American history. It's a watershed that somehow feels, at once, like ancient history, and like it happened yesterday. The game of baseball was changed utterly, and wholly for the better; and, in a very elemental way, the nation itself would never be the same again.

To go back and see how the event played at the time it happened, however, is a bit disconcerting. The newspaper coverage of the moment—opening day, 1947, Ebbets Field—was cursory. In most papers, Robinson's major league debut (after he'd played in a couple of exhibition games against the Yanks) earned a paragraph, perhaps two, and that was all. Arthur Daley in the *New York Times* was fairly unique among major daily writers, dedicating substantial parts of his "Sports of the Times" column to Robinson's position as a pioneer.

Of the way Branch Rickey "quietly" announced Robinson's signing with the Dodgers (during the uproar over manager Leo Durocher's suspension, ostensibly for hanging out with gamblers, before the start of the '47 season), Daley wrote:

> It is merely an attempt to lighten the pressure on Robinson's shoulders . . . Yet nothing actually can lighten that pressure, and Robbie realizes it full well. There is no ordinary way of disguising the fact that he is not an ordinary rookie and no amount of pretense can make it otherwise . . .

Jackie Robinson, in a familiar
situation—stealing home

But Robinson almost has to be another DiMaggio in making good from the opening whistle. It's not fair to him, but no one can do anything about it but himself. Pioneers never had it easy and Robinson, perforce, is a pioneer . . . It's his burden to carry from now on and he must carry it alone.

If Robinson was carrying his burden alone, and if the major newspapers were not exactly falling over themselves covering the man's struggle, the black newspapers were certainly taking up the slack.

Wendell Smith—the *Pittsburgh Courier*'s sports editor, one of the century's greatest black newspapermen, and a man often described as the Jackie Robinson of sports journalism—dedicated no fewer than four front-page stories to Robinson's debut, all of them written by Smith himself. (Two of those pieces are reprinted in this chapter. Note the capitalization of Robinson's name in the first article.) The *Courier* also featured a huge spread of photos from the game.

Other black papers also ran multiple stories and commentaries on Robinson's debut, including Joe Bostic in the *New York Amsterdam News*. Bostic, who wrote the "Scoreboard" column for the *News*, reflected on the opening day ceremonies in light of the sensation he felt upon hearing of Robinson's signing with the Brooks in the first place:

> SCOREBOARD wasn't present in the pressbox when the message came around. We had come a-cropper of some cantankerous "mushrooms" in a Harlem eatery the day before. A flinthearted sawbones had ordered us to bed. We were obedient up to a point. Listening to Red Barber's descriptions of the goings on, we stood it as long as we could . . . jumped up, grabbed our duds and made a bee line to Ebbets Field.
>
> [Arriving at Ebbets Field, Bostic was handed, by none other than Wendell Smith, a copy of the famous announcement of Robinson's signing by the Dodgers.]
>
> There wasn't anything you could say. What words could be adequate? You just felt a warm glow inside.

The warm glow that the vast majority of black Americans and sympathetic white Americans felt as Jackie Robinson broke the color barrier was not, over the course of the year, shared by the man himself. Anxiety, rage, and, above all, pride battling one another in one body rarely produce a warm glow.

The incessant, horrific indignities Robinson suffered in that first year are well recorded, and there's no question that, as he stepped out on to Ebbets

Field on that April day 50 years ago, he must have known what was in store. Branch Rickey had chosen him to represent his race not only because of his enormous talent, but because he felt Robinson had the courage and the self-control to withstand the brutally racist verbal (and often physical) assaults he would be subjected to throughout the season.

And, of course, he did withstand them. He was called "nigger" to his face. He was taunted, heckled, and generally abused. At one point during Robinson's first year with the Dodgers, the Cardinals' Enos "Country" Slaughter deliberately sliced open Robinson's leg with his spikes. But he somehow survived it all, not by ignoring the disgust and anger that he felt at the rabid bench jockeys, but by never allowing them, either, to keep him from playing brilliant baseball. By the end of the year, he had helped lead the Dodgers to the pennant, and was named the National League Rookie of the Year.

So, maybe opening day was a bit more exciting, more enjoyable, for those who weren't playing in it than it was for Jackie Robinson. Maybe the pessimistic, but far-from-negative tone of Daley's words better reflect the state of Robinson's mind and heart than the upbeat lines of Wendell Smith.

Still, if you're a ball fan, and Jackie Robinson's a hero to you, and you're feeling particularly imaginative (say, maybe, in the first few weeks of April), it's sometimes possible to close your eyes, and find yourself there, in his shoes, as he stepped in for the first time against Johnny Sain. Behind the plate is Babe Pinelli, who nine years later will call his last pitch as a major league umpire—the legendary third strike to Dale Mitchell in the 1956 World Series. The sun is shining. You're in a Dodger home uniform. The stands are filled with fans, and they're all yelling, and they all seem to be pulling for you. They really seem to want you to do well.

Sain's in his windup, and an April breeze is just lightly blowing, and just as Sain turns toward home, just before he lets go of the ball and sends it hurtling through the sun-filled Brooklyn air, you're struck by the sensation that no one in the entire park—absolutely no one, and least of all, you—would rather, at this instant, be anywhere else in the world.

# WENDELL SMITH
*Pittsburgh Courier*

History was made here Tuesday afternoon in Brooklyn's flag-bedecked, sun-kissed Ebbets Field when smiling JACKIE ROBINSON trotted out on the green-swept diamond with the rest of his Dodger teammates and played first base in the opening game of the 1947 National League season against Boston's battling Braves.

It marked the climax of a long and determined battle on the part of the fleet-footed, agile athlete from Pasadena, Calif., who just three years ago was playing the whistle stops and traveling up and down the country with the Kansas City Monarchs . . .

When Jackie galloped out to his position at first base, attired in a snow white uniform with Brooklyn scrolled across the chest, it marked the highlight of Branch Rickey's campaign to put a Negro player on the Dodgers.

It took a lot of hard work on the part of the Brooklyn owner to make this ambition a reality. He fought many forces in the inner circles of baseball, as well as handling the difficult task of putting ROBINSON on his team without affecting its morale. But he did it. And here Tuesday afternoon he sat in his special box seat and saw his dream come true . . .

Once again ROBINSON was the "photographers' darling." No less than fifteen photographers surrounded him before the game and clicked his picture from every position imaginable. Civic officials and dignitaries from all walks of life reached over the box seat rail near the Dodgers dugout to shake his hand and offer him hearty congratulations.

Jackie, wearing a big number forty-two on his broad back, smiled happily and accepted the greetings modestly.

He was given a rousing ovation his first time at bat. He hit the second pitch from Johnny Sain and it turned out to be an easy bounder to Bob Elliott at third who threw Jackie out by five steps.

There was more significance to this opening tilt than usual. It was of more historical significance than any opening game in the majors. And the crowd seemed to sense it. There was tenseness in the spring air and the fans were keyed for a real battle. Most of them wore topcoats, only to remove them when the sun, like the opposing pitchers, bore down intensely.

It was a great day. It was a great day for Brooklyn. It was a great day for baseball, and, above all, a great day for JACKIE ROBINSON!

# WENDELL SMITH
*Pittsburgh Courier*

Playing his first big league game of the 1947 National League season, Jackie Robinson came romping home from second base here Tuesday afternoon with what proved to be the Brooklyn Dodgers' winning run while 26,623 fans roared hilariously and the Boston Braves went down to defeat, 5 to 3.

Playing in perfect baseball weather and before a colorful opening day crowd, Robinson made his major league debut at first base and in the seventh inning was responsible for the play that upset pitcher Johnny Sain and paved the way for a hard-earned and well-deserved victory.

At that point, the "Bums" were trailing the Braves, 3 to 2. Ed Stanky started the fireworks by walking. Robinson then strolled to the plate and the applause from his loyal fans here had hardly died when he laid down a tantalizing bunt along the first base line. Stanky was off like a flash for second as Sain charged in to get the ball. Robinson was in high gear, zooming down the first base line. The frantic Sain grabbed the ball and threw.

Robinson and the ball arrived at first at approximately the same time. First baseman Torgeson was apparently confused as Robinson came storming in his direction. In the confusion, Torgeson missed the throw and the ball rolled into foul territory along the right field line. Stanky kept right on to third and Robinson high-tailed it to second.

Then little Pete Reiser put the game on ice by slapping one of Sain's fast balls high up on the right field screen, scoring Stanky with the tying run and Robinson with the fourth and winning marker. Reiser eventually scored, too, but the damaging run as far as the Braves were concerned was that first run carried across the platter by Brooklyn's bronze-colored first baseman.

Jackie was at bat officially three times. And, although he failed to come through with a base hit, he looked good at the plate. He was also "on the job" in the field, handling eleven chances perfectly as the "Bums" started the long grind up the pennant road.

# ARTHUR DALEY

*New York Times*

. . . The muscular Negro minds his own business and shrewdly makes no effort to push himself. He speaks quietly and intelligently when spoken to and already has made a strong impression. "I was nervous in the first play of my first game at Ebbets Field," he said with his ready grin, "but nothing has bothered me since."

A veteran Dodger said of him, "Having Jackie on the team is still a little strange, just like anything else that's new. We just don't know how to act with him. But he'll be accepted in time. You can be sure of that. Other sports have had Negroes. Why not baseball? I'm for him if he can win games. That's the only test I ask." And that seems to be the general impression.

# Pop-Eyed Maniacs

---

## BOBBY THOMSON'S SHOT HEARD 'ROUND THE WORLD

### October 3, 1951

**"Now it is done.** Now the story ends. And there is no way to tell it. The art of fiction is dead. Reality has strangled invention. Only the utterly impossible, the inexpressibly fantastic, can ever be plausible again."

With those words—comprising probably the best-known lead in sports-writing history—Red Smith immortalized one of the single most famous moments in the history of American sports.

People remember exactly where they were when it happened. Maybe they were in a bar. Maybe they were watching it on TV in their living rooms. Maybe they were standing on a street corner with a bunch of friends and strangers, listening to a radio.

Thirty-four thousand people saw it happen before their unbelieving eyes, down, in the words of Mr. Smith, "on the green and white earth-brown geometry of the playing field." That those 34,000 didn't suffer a mass, simultaneous heart attack at the sight speaks volumes about the ability of New Yorkers to withstand the sudden, the shocking, and the mind-boggling, all at once.

We're talking here, of course, about the Shot Heard 'Round the World. The Miracle at Coogan's Bluff. Bobby Thomson's bottom-of-the-ninth, one-out, one-strike, three-run, pennant-clinching home run. For those who somehow missed it at the time, or who were too young to have known what the hell all the excitement was about, or who weren't yet born, and came to the tale years after the fact, Thomson's shot has about it something of the irreclaimable.

It's not only as if those who missed it missed perhaps the most dramatic game-ending homer ever, it's almost as if they (we) missed the instantaneous, inconceivably dramatic end of an era, after which all game-winning, heart-stopping home runs will be judged by how they measure up to Thomson's

Bobby Thomson, with some
appreciative teammates

impossible blast . . . and found lacking.

Or am I just distressed that I wasn't there? That's probably it.

Anyway, here are some varied takes on the deathless moment, including Russ Hodges's and Gordon McClendon's wonderful radio calls. Anyone who has heard these calls knows that both are as exciting as any in sports. McClendon's voice, in particular, sounds as if he's in the grip of a religious vision when he shouts—in a strangled, hair-raising echo of Hodges—"The Giants win the pennant!"

We might never see many moments like Thomson's shot again, but at least we have the following stories—and the announcers' words—to know what it must have been like, for both Giants and Dodgers fans, to see that Branca pitch, and that Thomson swing, and that low line drive of the ball sailing over Andy Pafko's head, into history.

## BOB STEVENS
*San Francisco Chronicle*

With one swift swing of his mighty bat, Bobby Thomson today broke up one of the greatest baseball games ever played.

With one of the most timely blows of all time, the slender slugging Scot turned seemingly certain defeat into the most incredible New York Giant pennant triumph in history and earned for Manager Leo Durocher's crew the right to meet the New York Yankees in the World Series tomorrow.

There were runners on second and third. There was one out. The Brooklyn Dodgers were leading, 4–2, in the last inning of the last game of the playoff for the National League title. The Polo Grounds stands were rumbling and rocking when Thomson strode to the plate to face pitcher Ralph Branca from Flatbush.

The 34,320 here and millions throughout the world watched or listened and waited, asking either for an out or a miracle.

Thomson took a called strike, a dazzling fastball inside and letter high. Another fastball, equally wicked, sizzled toward the plate. With all the power and rhythm at his command, Thomson went after it, met it squarely. It never came back. It rode high into the lower deck in left field—50 feet down from the third base foul line and between the 315 and 360 foot signs, there to land in the midst of furiously groping hands.

That was it. Clint Hartung scored from third base for 3–4; Whitey Lockman scored from second for 4–4, and Thomson scored from where he started it all.

That was it, 5–4, and tomorrow into the Series and Yankee Stadium across the Harlem River go these unpredictable battlers for the first time since 1937 to challenge the champions of the American League.

It will be anti-climactic. It is inconceivable that the mere World Series, the reason behind all this pressure-bulging struggling, can approach, let along surpass, the dramatics that today turned the Polo Grounds into a house of screaming, leaping, hat-throwing, neighbor-kissing, pop-eyed maniacs.

Until Thomson's shattering blow, baseball had not seen the equal of the 1914 Boston Braves, who came from last place on July 4 to the National League pennant. But today that memory met a match. Some say the Giants gripping stretch run surpasses the histrionics of the pre–World War I team from Boston.

Statistics provide solid ground for argument. On August 11 these Giants trailed Brooklyn by 13 games. Twice in the late evening hour of the race they won afternoon battles to forge ahead by half a game only to be drawn back into a deadlock by Brooklyn victories at night. Last Sunday they prematurely celebrated the realization of their miracle until Jackie Robinson hit his shattering 14th-inning home run to force the N.L. into its second playoff in the past six seasons.

These Giants, who leave you groping unsuccessfully for words to describe, then rode over the confident Bums in Ebbets Field, 3–1, only to suffer terrible embarrassment yesterday when the insolent, sneering, battling Flatbushers shredded them, 10–0, in the Polo Grounds.

Today, the cause looked hopeless and only the brave indulged in reckless prayer when the Bums broke a 1–1 tie in the eighth, shattered the calm of the great Sal Maglie and assumed an awesome 4–1 lead with a gallant rally that had people dancing in the streets of Flatbush as the last of the ninth frame opened.

But these Giants don't know how to quit, and Alvin Dark, the former Louisiana State football star, tied into massive Don Newcombe for a single that Gil Hodges kept from rolling into the outfield by sprawling full length toward second base to knock the ball down.

Big Newk, as great an iron man as ever brought a heart to the pitching slab, was fading. He had reasons to weary, for it was he who beat Boston 15–5, last Thursday; Philadelphia, 5–0, last Saturday and contributed 5 ½ innings of shutout baseball against the Phillies in the tremendous Sunday game that made the playoff a necessity.

It was big Newk who had run his scoreless innings of intense pressure pitching to 20 before the Giants broke through his defense to tie today's fantastic story at 1–1 in the seventh. But the fire was rapidly leaving his arm. He was pitching purely by memory now.

Don Mueller crashed another single past the embattled Hodges and into right on the first pitch and Dodgers for miles around, including the apprehensive Charley Dressen, converged upon Newk, who stood a tragic, worried-looking figure upon the mound. The Bums decided to go along with Don, and once more he sent his weary arm into a long high windup eventually to get Monte Irvin, the NL's runs-batted-in champion, to pop feebly to Hodges 20 feet foul behind first base.

Next came Lockman, the former centerfielder converted into a first baseman. He swung furiously at the first Newcombe cast and sent it crashing into the screen behind the plate, high and wide. The second pitch was like the signal of doom over Flatbush. Lockman reached across the plate and shot the ball into left field for a double as Dark scored and Mueller pounded to third, there to crack up and add more unbelievable drama to this already emotion-loaded game.

His ankle severely wrenched as the result of the crashing slide, Mueller was carried off the battle grounds in a stretcher.

That was all for Newcombe. Little Charley came and got him and put in his stead Branca, the same right-hander who ran afoul of Thomson over in Brooklyn two days ago. The Scot beat him with a fourth inning home run.

Ralph found reason to hate him just a little bit more. His first pitch was over, a called strike. His second was over, too . . . over the wall and into the grandstand as recorded and the Giants went mad.

Durocher fell to the ground and kicked his heels in the air. Thomson was nearly pounded to death when he reached home and fell into the arms of his teammates.

Branca? A pathetic sight. He must have thought he was going to get that baseball back, for he leaned over, picked up the resin bag, and then watched Thomson's blow sail away. He slammed the bag to the ground, looked unbelievingly around him and turned slowly to the clubhouse, a lonesome, heartbroken man lost in a swarm of insanely screaming Giants.

Pandemonium, as they say, reigned. Tears cascaded from eyes that even then couldn't believe what they saw. Thousands of fans hand-fought their way free of a police blockade to storm the delirious Giants and to stand, huddled closely together, for over an hour in front of the clubhouse away out there in deep center field.

# Other Views

Associated Press

Ralph Branca sat on the steps, eyes wet, his head buried in his arms. Manager Charley Dressen paced the floor like a nervous lion. Big Don Newcombe moved around, silently and aimlessly as if trying to figure out a reason for it all.

The others sat on the short three-legged stools in their dressing room, eyes boring holes through the floor. None spoke. The room had a funereal quiet about it.

These were the men of Brooklyn, wondering what they had done against destiny to make destiny treat them so.

"We are three runs ahead going into the ninth," said Jackie Robinson, the Dodgers' brilliant second baseman. "We see ourselves in the World Series. And then—boom—five minutes later we're sitting in the clubhouse."

"It wasn't a bad pitch," said Branca in a low, smothered breath. "It was a high curve ball. I didn't think he hit it too well. It was sinking when it went into the stands."

The big right-hander was disconsolate because he was charged with both of the defeats in this best-of-three playoff for the National League pennant.

Asked if he had wanted to stay in the game, Newcombe said:

"The manager is paid to think. He can think better than I can. He makes the decisions. I'll stand by them."

———◦◦◦———

Associated Press

The Giants came back today. Came back to a thunderous roar such as the staid old Polo Grounds, or any other ball park, never experienced before. Came back to a scene of such wild-eyed, hysterical madness the very din reverberated from the cold gray walls of Yankee Stadium across the river, where tomorrow Leo Durocher's team of destiny engages the Yankees in the first game of the World Series.

Scant minutes before Bobby Thomson's mighty game-winning homer, it seemed that midnight had most surely arrived for the Cinderella team. Sal Maglie, the great competitor to whom Durocher had entrusted this most crucial of all his team's 157 games, suddenly had disintegrated. Three runs had crossed the plate to give the elated Dodgers a 4 to 1 lead, and probably not a spectator among the 34,000-plus but had already buried the New York club.

It couldn't happen. The way Don Newcombe was pitching, the idea that the Giants could make up that three-run deficit was preposterous. That happens only in fiction.

When Alvin Dark singled to right there was a faint glimmer of hope for long-suffering Giant fans. The corpse had blinked. Then Don Mueller singled to right, and the Dodgers held a club meeting at the mound.

Whitey Lockman doubled to left, scoring Dark, and time was called as a stretcher was brought out and Mueller, who had suffered an injured ankle sliding into third, was toted gently to the distant clubhouse. The Dodgers huddled nervously about the mound during the recess. This wasn't the funeral they had anticipated. Something had gone wrong. When play was resumed, Newcombe had departed, Ralph Branca was on the mound, and Thomson was the batter.

The first pitch was a strike just above the knees, and then came the pitch that Branca will forever remember in his nightmares. There was the swing of powerful arms, the sharp crack of a solidly hit ball, and a fleeting moment of breathless tension, a calm before all hell broke loose.

Before Bobby had rounded third base, his long face creased by a tremendous grin, the whole Giant bench was milling at the plate in a wild, inarticulate reception committee.

The loudspeaker had announced that spectators would not be permitted on the field until the players had reached their dressing room. It was like trying to stem Maglie's native Niagra Falls with a fish net.

Giants' Announcer
# RUSS HODGES

Bobby hitting at .292 . . . He's had a single and a double and he drove in the Giants' first run with a long fly to center . . . Brooklyn leads it 4 to 2 . . .

Hartung down the line at third, not taking any chances . . . Lockman without too big a lead at second but he'll be running like the wind if Thomson hits one . . .

Branca throws . . .

There's a long drive! . . . It's gonna be, I believe! . . .

The Giants win the pennant! The Giants win the pennant! The Giants win the pennant! The Giants win the pennant! . . . Bobby Thomson hits into the lower deck of the left-field stands! . . . The Giants win the pennant! . . . And they're going crazy! . . . They're going crazy! . . . Woooaaahhooohhh! . . .

I don't believe it! I don't believe it! I do not believe it! . . . Bobby Thomson hit a line drive . . . into the lower deck . . . of the left-field stands . . . And the place is going crazy! . . .

---

# GORDON McCLENDON
## on the Liberty Radio Network

And now the sacks all but saturated with two New York Giants. At second, Lockman, who singled down the left-field line . . . At third, Hartung. Ralph Branca from Mount Vernon, New York, 21-game winner in 1947, a New York University graduate, is going on the mound to throw for the Brooklyns, and try to turn the Giants back here at the door of disaster in the last half of the ninth inning.

Ralph Branca throwing . . . Ralph's victory record, 13 and 11. This is Newcombe's game, still, to win . . . The runner at second, a tying runner, is his responsibility . . . Should he win, it'll be 21 and 9 . . . It's Maglie's game, obviously, to lose . . . His record would be 23 and 7 . . .

Well, what more can anyone say about this, what could you possibly say, to tell you about the drama? It's like the fella who tried to write a lead for a great sporting event, and he sat there, he sat after the game was all over at his typewriter, and he just couldn't think of anything . . . He finally turned around to an old-time sportswriter there, and he says, "Fella," he says, "I'm trying to think of something . . . Maybe I can dramatize it by tellin' 'em something about the setting here." And he turned around and he looked over there and he says, "Let's see, is that the sun setting over there in the west?"

And the old sportswriter says, "Son, if that sun ain't settin' in the west, you got the greatest scoop of the century."

Boy, I'm telling you, what they're gonna say about this one I don't know . . . Bobby Thomson the batter . . . The outfield deep and very much to the left . . . Ralph Branca on the hill in favor of Newcombe . . . Rube Walker catching . . . The pitch to Bobby . . .

A strike called, off the knees . . . A quick curve that Branca ripped right in . . . Branca has that tremendous, overarm sinker curve that drops down, then he has a roundhouse hook curve to right-hand batters by way of third . . . Extremely effective against right-handers . . .

Two pitchers in the Dodgers bullpen, now . . . I think one of them's Roe . . . Here's Bobby, waiting . . . Branca throws . . .

Bobby swings, a long drive to left field! . . . Going! . . . Going! . . . Gone! And the Giants win the pennant! . . .

*(Absolute pandemonium . . . )*

I don't know what to say . . . I just don't know what to say . . . It's the greatest victory in all baseball history . . . The greatest come-from-behind triumph in the history of the game . . . Bobby Thomson, a two-on-base home run in the last half of the ninth inning, and the new National League champions are the New York Giants, who came back from the brink . . .

# Lightning in a Bottle

---

## DON LARSEN'S PERFECT GAME

October 8, 1956

**The names. It's difficult,** if you're a baseball fan, to read an account—any account—of Don Larsen's perfect game, and not marvel at the names blithely tossed about by the sportswriters of the time.

Pee Wee Reese. Duke Snider. Jackie Robinson. Roy Campanella. Gil Hodges. Sal Maglie. Carl Furillo.

And that's just the Dodgers, fer chrissakes. On the New York side, there's "Brash Billy the Kid" Martin. Yogi Berra. Hank Bauer, whose game-face and legendary glare make Will Clark, even in his eyeblack and tight-lipped stare, look downright cherubic. Mickey Mantle, still young enough to be pegged a "precocious youngster" by the *Times*' Arthur Daley. And, of course, there's Don Larsen, whose pitching feat in the '56 World Series has never been matched. In fact, as far as World Series performances are concerned, Larsen's jewel has barely been approached in the 40 years since he dropped 27 Dodgers in a row.

On another level, it's sobering to consider what today's sportswriters would make of Larsen's bad-boy reputation; for example, the coy references in the following pieces to Larsen wrapping his car around a telephone pole (or, as Curley Grieve had it, a tree) would likely be fleshed out with a bit more information on Larsen's private life. And, in that spirit, we might make note here that, as Larsen was carving a spot for himself in baseball history, his estranged wife, Vivian, was filing a court complaint for non-support of her and their one-year-old daughter. So, added to the pressure of a Series game and an opposing lineup filled not just with talent, but Hall of Fame talent, things obviously weren't going too well at home for Larsen.

*Now* think about him throwing a perfect game.

At any rate, the following two pieces on Larsen are, perhaps alone among the back-to-back pieces in this book, solid examples of two highly disparate schools of sportswriting. Curley Grieve's piece in the *Examiner* manages to provide an inclusive summary of the game, while relying on a sort of strained elegance to convey the day's drama ("Sal, too, received amazing support from his still unbowed teammates.").

Arthur Daley's piece in the *Times*, on the other hand, combines some downright cornball humor with striking imagery, and Daley's wonderful mixing of the poetic and the conversational ("Out from the stands swept a low murmur of excitement, almost like surf rumbling against a distant shore.").

What comes across clearly in both pieces is the obvious sense of gratitude both men feel for having been allowed to witness Larsen's performance: after reading them, it's impossible to begrudge Daley, Grieve, or anyone else the privilege of being there.

# CURLEY GRIEVE

*San Francisco Examiner*

Don Larsen, a 27-year-old Californian, chipped himself a big hunk of baseball immortality today. With ninety-seven quick, sure shots from his rifle arm, he pitched a perfect no-hitter to stifle the Brooklyn Dodgers, 2–0, in the fifth game of the World Series.

It was the first no-hitter in all the history of this hallowed classic, stretching back to 1902, and the ghosts of preceding heroes must have joined with the 64,519 present to acclaim the unprecedented deed.

Twenty-seven up—twenty-seven down:

Gilliam, Reese, Snider.

Robinson, Hodges, Amoros.

Furillo, Campanella, Maglie.

That was the order, inning after inning, until the ninth when left-handed Dale Mitchell came on to bat for Sal Maglie, who had pitched magnificently himself. The tension that had mounted with each rise and fall of Larsen's arm seemed on the verge of explosion when Umpire Babe Pinelli's right hand shot up in the shadows of the stilled horseshoe arena to signalize a third strike, which made the twenty-seventh consecutive out.

Then pandemonium broke loose.

Yogi Berra was the first to reach Larsen as the rafters of this steel and con-crete baseball cathedral shook under the roar of the crowd. He leaped upon the six-four frame of the 225-pound hurler and clutched him with both hands. Then, in a true Croix de Guerre ritual, he kissed him on both cheeks.

By this time, the Yankees from field and bench were pounding and shaking those two big paws, one of which should be cast in bronze and placed in the Hall of Fame at Cooperstown.

It was not until minutes after Larsen and his agitated mates had stormed into the dugout that sanity returned to a crowd that jubilantly threaded its way out convinced that this was the greatest since the game was invented by Abner Doubleday in the dim past.

This was one to see, one to tell about.

It was the one to make you thank your lucky stars you were here and had a ticket stub to frame and prove it.

Larsen, his quick ones, sliders, curves and control a cocktail of perfection, fanned seven and, of course, didn't issue a single walk as he mowed down the National League champions to give the Yankees a 3–2 edge in the series.

So unerring were Larsen's slingshot serves that only Pee Wee Reese in the first inning carried him to a 3–2 count. Of his ninety-seven pitches, only twenty of them were called balls by eagle-eyed Pinelli, who umpired his last game of baseball behind the plate today.

But Larsen, despite the incredible accuracy and amazing mystery of his pitches, could never have achieved his perfect no-hitter—no hit, no run and no man on base—without at least one run and perfect support.

He got the one imperative run from Mickey Mantle, who broke Maglie's own no-hitter in the fourth with a 330-foot home run into the stands that curve out into right field. He got an insurance run in the sixth when Andy Carey led off with a single, advanced on the pitcher's own perfect third-strike bunt, and scored on Bauer's safety.

The Yankee support for a striving mate, who had been knocked out in the second inning of that nightmarish second series game in Brooklyn, was spec-tacular.

In fact, the defensive work of both teams was so sensational that it could have made its mark in history in that department alone.

There's a story behind the fielding legerdemain of Handy Andy Carey, Alameda's gift to the Yankees.

So miserable had he looked in preceding games that Manager Casey Stengel was toying with the idea of putting him on the bench. In fact, early afternoon editions today had Bill Hunter at short and Gil McDougald at third.

Before the game, Stengel shuffled three lineups, as if they were a deck of cards. Finally, at the last minute, he handed in the one with Carey at third.

Andy, as if to repay this show of confidence, twice saved the no-hitter for Larsen with unbelievable plays.

Jackie Robinson in the second inning fired a cannonball along the ground in his direction. He couldn't make the stop. But he got his glove on it long enough to deflect it into the hands of Gil McDougald, San Francisco product, who threw to first for the putout. Andy noted after the game this was not the first time they had combined in such a maneuver.

It had happened three times in regular season play.

In the eighth, when the crowd was rooting Larsen home and even had booed Robinson for delaying the game when he got a speck in his eye, Carey delivered again.

This time the dangerous Gil Hodges, Brooklyn's bat leader in the series,

Don Larsen . . .

smashed a liner that was labeled a left-field single.

Andy moved with the crack of the bat and stuck out his glove. The ball hit, popped up and settled back. Even though the umpire signaled it was not a pickup, Carey threw to first to make sure of his putout.

Mantle and McDougald also contributed outstanding plays. Mickey made a terrific run and one-handed catch of a ball in left center that sailed nearly 400 feet, also off the bat of Hodges.

McDougald made a fine, one-hop pickup of Junior Gilliam's hard line drive in the seventh.

Other plays might have been less difficult. But they were executed with faultless precision. And such support must have served to inspire Larsen, the New York hero of the day, whose father lives in Berkeley and works in Hinks' Department Store on Shattuck Avenue.

Of all the hundreds of pitchers in the fifty-three preceding World

. . . finishes . . .

series, Bill Bevens came closest of all to achieving a no-hitter. He, too, was a Yankee and he, too, was facing the Dodgers. Only the setting was Ebbets Field, not Yankee Stadium.

Bevens went down to the last out in the ninth only to be frustrated in the end when Cookie Lavagetto bashed his unforgettable double. It robbed the heartbroken Bevens, who never did recover, not only of a no-hitter but victory as well. However, Bevens walked ten men in that game so it can hardly be compared with today's brilliant exhibition.

The last perfect no-hitter in the majors was hurled by Charlie Robertson of the Chicago White Sox in 1922.

Larsen may have set a pattern for pitchers with his magnificence performance today.

The big, broad-hipped Yankee, who couldn't control the ball last Friday, discarded his windup completely.

. . . perfectly

He just aimed and fired, there was no flapping of wings or intricate footwork, no coiling and uncoiling.

"Bobby Feller would have lasted ten years longer if he had never wound up," Tommy Henrich, old Yankee hero, observed in the dressing room afterward.

Known as a gay blade who distinguished himself in spring training by wrapping a car around a tree in a wild ride at St. Petersburg, Larsen was born in Michigan City, Indiana, but has resided in San Diego for the last thirteen years.

"He's a prune picker like the rest of us," Jerry Coleman laughed in the dressing room.

Even tempered, easy going, Larsen caught fire during the tail end of the season and entered the World Series hailed as the "toughest Yankee pitcher to hit." He was 11–5 for the season.

Maglie, who beat the Yankees in the series opener and got an extra day of rest before facing them again today, pitched superbly. The 39-year-old known as Sal the Barber allowed only five hits himself and wound up the day by fanning the side in the eighth—Larsen, Bauer and Collins. He received a warming ovation as he completed his hopeless task with such dramatic finality.

Sal, too, received amazing support from his still unbowed teammates. Reese made a great running catch in left field on Berra's fly in the second, Snider made a sparkling shoelace, diving catch of Berra's low liner to center in the fourth and both Hodges and Robinson contributed to a fine double-play in the sixth.

In that frame Bauer and Collins hit back-to-back singles. Mantle blasted a grounder down the first base line that Hodges somehow stabbed. Gil touched the bag and threw to Campanella at home. Bauer was trapped. But Campy's throw to third in the rundown was wide.

Robinson made a dive and retrieved it. Sprawled on the turf he still managed to throw from a sitting position and Bauer eventually was tagged.

Mantle's homer was his third of the series and eighth in twenty-five World Series games. It came with Brooklyn using a shift on the infield, placing Reese alongside Gilliam between first and second and Robinson at short.

It didn't work as Mickey lofted the low, inside-breaking pitch out of the lot, and Manager Walter Alston didn't try it again.

Charlie Silvera, another of the Yankee San Franciscans, insists on getting into the act in respect to Larsen's no-hitter.

"Don't forget," said the catcher who has the unenviable job of playing second fiddle to Yogi Berra, "I warmed him up."

## Another View

# ARTHUR DALEY
*New York Times*

YOGI BERRA jerked up his right arm, the glistening white ball held triumphantly in his chubby fist. "Yippee!" he screamed, but his cry of exultation was swallowed by the roar from the stands. Then the stumpy catcher raced to intercept Don Larsen near the foul line, flinging himself upward into the arms of the huge pitcher and wrapping his legs around Don in bear-hug embrace.

Yogi got there first, but the other Yanks joined the mob scene, as well they might. The unpredictable right-hander from California had just performed the rarest of all baseball feats. He pitched a perfect game against the Dodgers yesterday, an achievement that's practically akin to catching lightning in a bottle.

Larsen faced twenty-seven men. He retired twenty-seven men. It's impossible to improve on such a performance. That's why they call it a perfect game. There hasn't been one since Charlie Robertson did it in 1922 and never before has there been one in a World Series. In fact there never before had been a no-hitter in the post-season festivities. This was the big one, doubled in spades.

The first two games of this World Series were such horrors that baseball authorities were concerned the Little Leaguers watching on television would get some wrong ideas as to how our great national pastime was supposed to be played. The authorities need worry no longer.

For almost four innings wily Sal Maglie had matched Larsen putout for putout. Folks were beginning to wonder if this would be the first double no-hitter since Fred Toney of the Cincinnati Reds and Hippo Jim Vaughn of the Chicago Cubs tangled almost forty years ago (Vaughn lost in the tenth).

But then that precocious youngster, Master Mickey Mantle, tagged the ancient Barber for a homer in the fourth. Another run trickled in later. But the Barber, pitching far better ball than he had in the opener, was left holding an empty bag.

Somewhere in the middle of the game the crowd seemed to get a mass realization of the wonders that were being unfolded. Tension kept mounting until it was as brittle as an electric light bulb. The slightest jounce and the dang thing might explode.

Or perhaps it was more like a guy blowing air into a toy balloon. He keeps blowing and blowing with red-faced enthusiasm. But every puff might be the last. Larger and larger grew Larsen's balloon. It was of giant size at the start of the ninth.

Out from the stands swept a low murmur of excitement, almost like surf rumbling against a distant shore. Carl Furillo fouled two pitches, took a ball and fouled two more. He flied to Hank Bauer and Bauer clutched the ball tenderly—but firmly—in his glove.

Larsen took his cap off and shook his head, apparently to dislodge any cold sweat on his brow. Roy Campanella was a faster victim. He pulled a long foul ball to left and then dribbled an easy bounder to Billy Martin. Brash Billy the Kid scooped the ball up and aimed carefully as he pegged to Joe Collins. The surf no longer was pounding on a distant shore. It was close at hand, a mighty roar.

And then, big Don fanned Dale Mitchell, a pinch hitter. Those staid Yankee fans went nuts in an unrestrained ovation that was far more indigenous to Ebbets Field. They saw history being made because the odds are at least a million to one that any eyewitness ever will see another perfect game in his lifetime.

There has to be an element of luck to any no-hitter, and Dame Fortune has to outdo herself for a perfect game. This is something that's beyond the control of any pitcher. If one of his teammates fumbles and a base runner gets aboard, the perfection is destroyed. But the Yankees fielded slickly behind their big guy. Don did the rest.

———◆———

There is a sign behind the Stadium bleachers that offers a substantial threat. It says: "Anyone interfering with play subject to arrest." The joint was alive with cops, but none put the arm on Larsen. He interfered with Dodger play in the most blatant fashion imaginable.

———◆———

The key blow of the game, if anyone is interested in anything except Larsen, was Mantle's homer. He pulled one right down the line, not his normal style, because he's more inclined to blast down the middle alley or slightly to the right of it. For a change, though, he didn't use Bauer's bat.

"He's quit on me," said Hank at the cage before the game. "Now he's using Joe Collins's bat, ain'tcha, Mick?"

"Nope," said Master Mickey. "I'm using Jerry Lumpe's bat today."

"You're nuts," said Bauer good-naturedly. "All a guy on this team has to say is, 'Hey, Mickey, I got a good bat,' and Mickey will say, 'Let me try it.'"

So Lumpe, a World Series ineligible, gets an assist on Mantle's homer.

———•◦•———

By the ninth inning, the most nervous persons in the ball park, bar none, were the three official scorers, Lyall Smith of Detroit and his two assistants from New York, Jerry Mitchell and Gus Steiger. They were terrified that a questionable decision would confront them, and ruin Larsen's performance for posterity. But this one could have been scored by a cricket player watching the first baseball game of his life. It was a breeze.

———•◦•———

The feat of Larsen demonstrates the value of patient managerial handling of a problem child. Casey Stengel never fined the big fellow when the sprightly Larsen curved his automobile around a telephone pole in St. Pete last spring at 5 A.M. one dawning. Ol' Case reasoned that the massive Californian had been so well behaved up to that point that he should be permitted one fling. Nor was Larsen abashed about it.

"Not only did I get the telephone pole," he joshingly related afterward, "but you should have seen what I did to the mailbox."

# BOB WOLFE
## on Mutual Radio

Dale Mitchell will bat for Sal Maglie.

Be sure to stay tuned for Bill Corum's wrap-up of today's game. Bill's one of the country's top sports authorities. He knows baseball inside and out. You'll enjoy his slant on today's highlights.

Dale Mitchell comes up with two out in the ninth inning. Here comes the pitch, and it's ball one. Ball one to Dale Mitchell.

With two away in the ninth . . . here comes the next pitch . . . a strike called! That is one and one, and this crowd just straining forward at every pitch.

One and one to Mitchell . . . he's a left-handed batter. Dale Mitchell up there with two away in the top of the ninth. They're playing him almost straight away.

Here it comes . . . a swing and a miss! Two strikes, ball one to Dale Mitchell. Listen to this crowd! Two strikes, ball one to Mitchell with two away in the ninth. Larsen looks in . . . here comes the pitch . . . fouled off to the left.

Two strikes and a ball the count remains to Mitchell. Babe Pinelli motions for some more baseballs to the batboy. I'll guarantee that nobody, but nobody has left this ballpark. And if somebody did manage to leave early, man, he is missin' the greatest.

Two strikes and a ball. Mitchell waiting. Stands deep, feet close together. Larsen is ready . . . Gets the sign . . . Two strikes, ball one . . . Here comes the pitch . . .

Strike three! A no-hitter! A perfect game for Don Larsen! Yogi Berra runs out there, he leaps on Larsen! And he's swarmed by his teammates . . . Listen to this crowd roar!

Man oh man, how 'bout that? A perfect game for Don Larsen. There's never been a no-hitter in Series play before. There've been three one-hitters . . . you'll find all that in the Encyclopedia of Baseball . . . But the first World Series no-hitter, a perfect performance by Don Larsen. Man! What a thrill this is!

# 36 Men in a Row

HARVEY HADDIX'S TWELVE-PERFECT-INNINGS LOSS

May 26, 1959

**Of the tens of** thousands of big league baseball games played prior to the night of May 26, 1959, only seven had been perfect.

Plenty of Hall of Fame pitchers had played out their careers without ever retiring 27 batters in a row. Christy Mathewson, Walter Johnson, Grover Cleveland Alexander, Bob Feller (who threw three no-hitters)—none of them ever threw a perfect game.

On that May night in 1959, suffering from a cold and a cough, Harvey Haddix took the mound in Milwaukee for the Pittsburgh Pirates, and proceeded to join and then surpass the seven previous members of the perfect club. Through the ninth, and into the tenth, and the eleventh, and the twelfth innings, Harvey Haddix baffled every hitter he faced, sending Milwaukee players like Eddie Mathews, Joe Adcock, and a young outfielder named Henry Aaron back to the bench without so much as a base on balls.

But it wasn't only the 36 batters retired in a row that made this perfect game unique. What also separated this contest from the majors' seven previous perfect games was the way it concluded: when the game was finally over, after the thirteenth inning, Harvey Haddix had pitched the greatest game in major league history, and he had lost.

Although he knew he had a no-hitter going, Haddix wasn't aware that he was working on a perfect game. He thought he might have walked someone earlier in the game, but there was no way for him to find out. If you're throwing a no-hitter, you don't ask anyone about it. You don't mention it. You just keep throwing.

Incidentally, baseball superstitions are great things. Dick Groat, the Pirates' captain, said after the game: "We had a green Planter's peanut on the bench and we used this as a good luck charm. We passed it among various players to hold. Once we laid it on the dugout steps, hoping it might help to start a rally."

It didn't.

Haddix was far from a one-game wonder. He pitched brilliantly for the Pirates in their 1960 World Series triumph over the Yankees, for example, winning two games, including the finale in which Mazeroski clouted his game-winning shot.

But really, now . . . victories, shmictories. Let's hear about the twelve perfect innings, and the 36 straight outs, and the confused ending to the game (When is a home run not a home run?), and the secure spot in the record book, and the suddenly famous 33-year-old man, exhausted in the clubhouse after the game, reflecting on the feat as "just another loss, and that's no good."

## OLIVER KUECHLE
### *Milwaukee Journal*

No Hollywood scenario was ever like this. They wouldn't dare. Harvey Haddix, a 33-year-old southpaw with the Pittsburghs, pitched the greatest game in the history of all baseball here Tuesday—and lost it. The greatest game? Exactly. The greatest game—and lost it. Harvey Haddix retired 36 men in a row through 12 innings—no hits, no walks, no errors, no runs, no nothin'— 36 men in a row. And then in the 13th inning he lost this game.

How do you write of something like this? Where do you begin? The immensity of this pitching feat, the drama, the weird climax in which the winning home run with two men on base was not a home run at all, in which the score was not 3 to 0 or 2 to 0 but 1 to 0 befuddles the mind.

It is not a matter of opinion that this was the greatest game ever pitched, it is a matter of record, and let's begin there. The record.

Nobody in all baseball has ever retired 36 men in a row before—period. John Richmond of Worcester back in 1880 retired 27 men in a row and won, 1–0. John Ward of Providence in the same year did it and won, 5–0. Cy Young of the Boston Red Sox did it in 1904 and won, 3–0. Addie Joss of Cleveland did it in 1908 and won, 1–0. Ernie Shore of the Red Sox did it in 1917 and won, 4–0. Charlie Robertson of the White Sox did it in 1922 and won, 2–0. Don Larsen of the Yankees did it in the 1956 World Series and won, 2–0.

Harvey Haddix, ninth inning,
May 26, 1959

These are the only men who ever pitched nine innings of perfect ball.

But wait—that isn't all the records show.

Sam Kimber of Brooklyn pitched 10 innings of no-hit baseball in 1884, but not perfect ball. The scoreless game was called in the 11th because of darkness.

Harry McIntyre of Brooklyn pitched 10 and two-thirds innings of no-hit ball in 1906, but not perfect ball. He lost in the 13th, 1–0.

George Wiltse of the Giants pitched 10 innings of no-hit ball in 1908, but not perfect ball. He won, 1–0.

And Fred Toney of Cincinnati pitched 10 innings of no-hit ball in 1917, but not perfect ball. He won, 1–0. Hippo Vaughn of the Cubs in the same game pitched nine and one-third innings of no-hit ball, but not perfect ball.

Harvey Haddix? Harvey Haddix pitched 12 innings of perfect ball. Harvey Haddix retired 36 men in a row—and Harvey Haddix lost.

They'll talk of this game as long as baseball is played, not because of its weird finish in which Joe Adcock's home run out of the park was ruled a double, but because of Haddix's pitching.

Only an amalgamate of those words baseball writers like to use so well—incredible, astounding, fantastic, fabulous—can properly describe his pitching. He had a scythe in his hands and methodically cut down 36 men.

This was no run of the mill big league team he put the blade to, either. This was a team with five .300 hitters in the line-up and one .298. This was a team with a team average of .290—the best in the league by almost twenty points. This was a team whose eleven men on the field held a composite average of .315.

As inning after inning of Haddix's perfect pitching passed, as one fine fielding play after another helped him out of momentarily tight spots, the loyal Braves crowd of 19,194 slowly became a Haddix crowd. At the finish they were almost solidly Haddix.

They couldn't help themselves.

Lost in the high drama and confusion of the game's climax was still a second superb pitching performance, not a one-hitter as Haddix's ultimately turned out to be, but a 12-hitter—and what a 12-hitter.

Lew Burdette, obviously, did not match pitch-for-pitch with the man he faced. But he did a job that except for Haddix's phenomenal work through 12 innings would be in the headlines itself today.

Burdette did not walk a man. In only two innings, the third and ninth, did the Pirates get two men on base. And only twice, for all of their 12 hits, did they get a man as far as third.

Burdette, too, was a master, and if Haddix didn't deserve to lose, which is just a matter of sentiment for his 12 innings of perfect ball, neither did

Burdette. Under pressure, which Haddix because of his perfection didn't face, Burdette never wavered.

The unlucky guy in all that happened on this tingling night was Joe Adcock. Here was a man who hit a home run to break up the game, but who got only a double, and worse, who because of someone else's careless base running (Aaron's failure to touch all of the bases ahead of Adcock) might thoughtlessly be considered by some to be to blame himself. It wasn't his fault. It was Aaron's.

Suppose something like this had happened in the last game of the season with Adcock in position, say, to break the home run record. Would there be an uproar or would there be an uproar? The rules of baseball, it seems, might well be changed to credit the man who hits a ball out of the park with a home run regardless of what base runners ahead of him do.

In a case like this, Aaron's run wouldn't count because he did not continue beyond second base. Mantilla's would because he went around third and touched home. Adcock's would because he hit the ball out of the park. Why penalize Adcock in his personal record for somebody else's mistake?

That's what happened tonight. Adcock was penalized. But that's the kind of game this was. Everything happened. How do you write about it? Where do you begin? This all seems so inadequate for one of the great games of all time— the very greatest in pitching.

<hr />

## Another View

### CLEON WALFOORT
*Milwaukee Journal*

Harvey Haddix had achieved baseball immortality by pitching the greatest game in major league history at the stadium Tuesday night. All it had gotten him, after retiring 36 batsmen in order for an all-time record, was a 1–0 licking.

"Just another loss, and that's no good," the 160-pound southpaw said sadly. But it was impossible for a 33-year-old man who had blazed his name indelibly in the baseball books to be completely disconsolate. It was a bittersweet sort of experience in which his pitching performance would be remembered long after the score, or even the outcome of the game. In fact, the feat may be enhanced in enshrinement, at least sympathetically, by the heartbreak of his defeat.

On the Pirates bench the players had traditionally avoided mentioning anything about a no-hit game to Haddix, although they had discussed it among themselves as they exhorted each batter to go out and break it up for the skinny veteran.

But Haddix had known as early as the third inning.

"Then, somewhere in the extra innings, I sort of lost track and wasn't quite sure whether I might have walked a man earlier in the game," he said.

When had the pressure really begun to tell? He had repeatedly taken off his cap and brushed his hair with his pitching hand in the last five innings but that mannerism was an exaggeration rather than a novelty for him.

"I was tense late in the game," Haddix admitted. "Once, I think it was in the tenth inning, I almost got my feet tangled up getting ready to pitch. But I snapped out of it. In the last couple of innings I was more tired than nervous.

"Burgess (his catcher) came out to talk to me just three times that I recall. Once he wanted to check signals on a batter. Then he asked me how I felt and I told him, I was getting tired. In the last inning, when there were men on base, he came out to make sure I knew what I was going to do with the ball if it was hit to me . . .

"I made a few mistakes, but not many. I got away with them until I got that slider too high on Adcock on the last pitch . . ."

The hardest hit ball until Adcock connected was a line drive by Johnny Logan to shortstop in the third inning, but the Braves were hitting some lusty flies in the extra innings.

"Schofield (shortstop) and Virdon (center fielder) both helped me out with some good plays," Haddix said. "Did Hoak apologize for his error? No, why should he? 'I've booted 'em before and I will again,' was all he said as we drove to the hotel after the game. He's that kind of guy and I admire him for it . . ."

Did anyone on his club say anything during the game?

"Nope, not a word."

How about the Braves?

"Only once. When I came to bat in the ninth, Del Crandall said, 'Hey you're pitching a pretty good game.'"

Haddix answered the barrage of questions patiently between interruptions by newspaper photographers and long distance telephone calls.

"No, I haven't had a chance to call my wife," he said. "She's back in Pittsburgh with our 17-month-old daughter."

Burgess, who called the pitches and caught the balls the Braves couldn't hit, also described it as "the best game ever pitched."

"Harvey had the greatest stuff he's ever had, and pinpoint control of all four pitches—fast ball, curve, slider and change-up," Burgess said. "He wasn't behind a single batter until he got a 2–0 count on Andy Pafko in the 12th inning. He hadn't walked a man in his last three games until he was instructed to pass Aaron in the 13th . . ."

(Pirate manager Danny) Murtaugh had played second base for the Pirates when Cliff Chambers no-hit the Boston Braves in 1951. How did Haddix's game compare with that one?

"What could compare with the kind of game Haddix pitched tonight?" Murtaugh demanded.

(Braves' manager Fred) Haney was with Detroit when Charlie Robertson of Chicago pitched not only a no-hitter but a perfect game against the Tigers in 1922.

"Haddix's was better, of course," the Braves' boss said. "He went three innings farther than Robertson and Robertson was hit harder. Haddix pitched the greatest game I ever saw."

Umpire Vinnie Smith, who played with the Pirates for six years before breaking his leg in 1946, had never seen a no-hit game in the majors but he had caught Bob Feller in one when they were both in the Navy.

"I was working pretty hard myself tonight," the umpire said. "I knew what he had going and I had to bear down on balls and strikes. I don't remember a squawk from Haddix or Burgess and there were very few from the Braves."

This was, of course, Haddix's first no-hit game, but he came close when he was with St. Louis in 1954. He had not allowed a hit until Richie Ashburn and Granny Hammer singled in the ninth inning.

"The difference was that I won that one (2–0)," Haddix said.

A native of Medway, Ohio, who makes his winter home in Springfield, Haddix is known as both the Kitten, from the way he fields his position, and Wheels, from his speed afoot.

He is properly called Harvey Haddix, Jr., and at the moment is the most famous player in baseball.

Bill Mazeroski brings it home

# The Welkin Rings in Old Forbes Field

## BILL MAZEROSKI'S WORLD SERIES—WINNING HOME RUN

### October 13, 1960

**How many millions of** kids have lain in bed at night, picturing themselves up against a Feller or a Koufax or a Gibson or a Maddux, in the bottom of the ninth inning, in the seventh game of the World Series, with the game on the line? How many kids have dreamed of hitting that homer that's going to give their team the championship?

I sure did. And for that very reason, Bill Mazeroski was one of the first ballplayers to take up residence in the mind of this fledgling fan. Maz, after all, had really done it. He'd stood up in front of thousands of people and, with one swing, had given the Pirates the World Series title. It was years after the fact when I first heard or read about Maz's feat, and I didn't even really like the Pirates that much; but I honestly can't think of any other ballplayer who held, for a few years at least, a more prominent place in my imagination than Bill Mazeroski.

Part of it, as with my appreciation for Vander Meer, was the man's name.

Mazeroski. Maz. It was a great baseball name, and, for a kid growing up in a small, fairly homogeneous town in Connecticut, it was also vaguely exotic. (Of course, if I found "Mazeroski" exotic, just imagine how excited I was when, for instance, Cassius Clay changed his name to Muhammad Ali. I thought my head would pop off when I heard that one.) For years, I really didn't know anything about Mazeroski—whether he was an exceptional player, or who had pitched the ball he'd hit, or any of that stuff—and I didn't want to know. I just knew that some guy named Bill Mazeroski had somehow been able to do exactly what I had begun to dream of doing—and that alone, in my eyes, made him sufficiently larger-than-life.

The 1960 Series was pretty weird. The Yankees scored more than twice as many runs as the Pirates over the seven games, but when it was all over the Pirates had their first title in 35 years, and the Yankees had a lot of explaining to do. They were heavily favored to blow the Pirates away and throughout the first six games had piled up individual and team records for runs and hits in Series play. Their team batting average of .341 going into the seventh game reflected how hard they'd been pounding the Pirate pitching. But the Bucs refused to die.

"So far as I know they haven't changed the World Series rules," Pirate manager Danny Murtaugh said after the sixth game. "This thing still goes to the team that wins four games, and not to the club that makes the most records."

And so the seventh game rolled around, and the fact that the Bucs had been outgunned by almost 30 runs over the previous six games meant nothing. With only one home run in the first six games of the Series (and that one by Mazeroski), the Pirates finally unloaded on the Yankee pitching, with three crucial blasts in the finale. A little luck played a part, too, of course, when a Bill Virdon grounder took a crazy hop on the Forbes Field "alabaster infield" and slammed Yankee shortstop Tony Kubek in the throat, opening the door for a five-run rally in the bottom of the eighth.

But when it came down to that last inning, there was Mazeroski standing in at the plate, and all the runs and records that the Yankees had been accumulating over the course of the series must have seemed like a bunch of fool's gold when Ralph Terry let loose with an 0 and 1 fastball, just about waist high, and Maz turned on it, and in an instant, it was all over except for the loud and ceaseless shouting.

# BILL LEE
*Hartford Courant*

This is a city gone wild—the wildest it has been since V-J Day.

The Pittsburgh Pirates won the baseball championship of the world this warm Indian summer Thursday by beating the New York Yankees, 10 to 9 on a dramatic ninth inning home run by Bill Mazeroski.

The towering smash far over the fence in left-center field came when Mazeroski started—and finished the ninth inning. It touched off a mad celebration that made the welkin ring in old Forbes Field and filled the downtown streets inches deep in torn paper that came streaming down from office windows.

Horns honked madly and traffic became quickly and hopelessly snarled, but no one seemed to care. Cars loaded to overflowing rolled through the streets of Pittsburgh, their tops down and their occupants cheering the victorious Bucs. It was like New Year's Eve in broad daylight, although twice as noisy and more spontaneous than any New Year's celebration could possibly be.

New Year's comes every year right on schedule, but this was Pittsburgh's first World Series victory in 35 years.

Apparently beaten by a surging Yankee four-run rally in the sixth inning that overcame an earlier Pittsburgh 4–0 lead, the battling Bucs were beaten to their knees by two more Bomber runs in the eighth that made it 7 to 4 with Bobby Shantz squeezing the life blood out of the Pirates with a masterful pitching job.

But the Bucs got up from their knees to fight back with a four-run rally in the eighth that rocked the city of Pittsburgh to its strongest smokestack. This was the inning in which Hal Smith, a former Yankee, had blasted a three-run homer far over the left field fence that restored Pittsburgh to the lead. It was 9 to 7, Pirates, an inning after the Yankees had seemed to roll the Pittsburgh baseball body into a morgue refrigerator.

Then the 36,683 nerve-frazzled spectators died all over again when the Yankees rebounded for two tying runs in their half of the ninth. By this time Pirate fans had walked so close to disaster so often they were sick with fear of the worst.

But Mazeroski, a home town boy who plays second base for the Pittsburghers, strode to the plate in the leadoff spot in the Pirate ninth and put a storybook finish to what may be the zaniest World Series on record in the 57 years the classic has brought the baseball season to its conclusion.

Mazeroski circled the bases and somehow reached home plate in the midst of one of the most joyous finishing celebrations the series has known.

Wild-eyed fans raced across the field to greet the Pirate hero as he came churning toward third base and hundreds more poured from the stands and tore toward home plate, where jumping Pirate teammates were waiting for the third and ultimate Pittsburgh hero of an unbelievable afternoon.

Hundreds of police had been standing in readiness for the finish but they were engulfed by the excited and overjoyed throng of fans who wanted to pound Bill Mazeroski on the back. It took a late rally by Pittsburgh's finest and a cordon of state police to rescue Mazeroski and the other Pittsburgh players from the jumping throng and shepherd them to the Pirate clubhouse.

The roar of a winning crowd filled Forbes Field a half hour after the game. Thousands remained in the stands, but eventually the celebration erupted into the streets outside the ballpark and then mushroomed into an even madder demonstration in the business section.

Trolley cars and buses came to standstill and one trolley car was pulled off the tracks in the heart of downtown Pittsburgh, bringing a swarm of police cruisers to the scene. Mostly, however, it was a good-natured, overjoyed mob scene which every man, woman and child in the streets of the city seemed to be enjoying with equal abandon.

They whooped it up around normally quiet hotel lobbies, and a pretty girl jumped into a beautiful fountain at Gateway Center, the heart of the Golden triangle.

Pittsburgh hadn't won a pennant since 1927 and hadn't won a World Series since 1925, when they rallied from a 1 to 3 deficit to win the last three games and beat Walter Johnson in the decisive seventh contest.

Last time they had met the Yankees in the World Series of 33 years ago, the hated New Yorkers had swept four in a row. Pittsburgh never got off the ground.

This time they were knocked to the ground, bruised, battered, and bloodied by Yankee victories by such horrendous scores as 12 to 0, 10 to 0 and 16 to 3. Every time, though, the mauled Bucs climbed up and fought back. The Yankees had clubbed them to death Wednesday in the 12 to 0 sixth game that brought the teams even and made it—finally—a "one game" World Series.

Everything rode on this one.

The Pirates started Vern Law, their best pitcher who had beaten the Yankees twice last week. The Pirates rushed off to two runs each in the first two innings and a 4 to 0 lead fashioned on a two-run homer by Rocky Nelson in the first and a two-run single by Bill Virdon in the second.

The Pirates chased Bob Turley in the second, but the Yankees got a run in the fifth on Bill Skowron's home run blast into the right field stands and four in an explosive sixth in which Bobby Richardson and Mickey Mantle singled, Tony Kubek walked and Yogi Berra homered into the right field seats.

Suddenly the leading Pirates were 4 to 5 behind, Vern Law had been knocked out and Bobby Shantz was making the Pirates eat crow right out of his little old left hand.

Shantz came in after Bill Stafford had given way to a pinch-hitter in the second and the veteran southpaw had strung together five of the handsomest World Series innings on record. Only one man reached first in the third, nobody at all in the fourth, fifth and sixth. Burgess singled in the seventh for the second hit off Shantz since he had entered the game, and it now appeared that the Yankees had their 19th world's championship in their pocket and 70-year-old Casey Stengel the honor of becoming the first baseball manager ever to lead seven world championship teams. But fate had different things in store for the Yankees and a happier script written out for the seemingly beaten Pirates.

In their half of the eighth, the Yankees had scored twice and made it 7 to 4, getting their runs after two were out. By this time the unbeatable Elroy Face had come in to pitch for the Pirates, and when he was an out from retiring the Yankees in the eighth, Berra walked and Bill Skowron's high bounder to third was more than Hoak could handle in time for a force at second.

Blanchard scored Berra and sent Skowron to third with a looping hit to right, and Cletis Boyer lined the first pitch to the left-field corner scoring Skowron with the second run.

Now the tide turned in the Pirate eighth and the National League champions got what Manager Danny Murtaugh afterward described as the biggest break of the game.

Cimoli, batting for Face, dropped a single in front of Maris. Bill Virdon, the next batter, drove a sharp ground ball straight at shortstop Tony Kubek. It had double play written all over it. Suddenly the ball took a bad hop and hit Kubek squarely in the larynx. The Yankee shortstop went down like a felled log.

Both men were safe. For a moment it seemed as though Kubek might be badly hurt. Gamely he tried to tell Casey Stengel he could remain in the game, but he was too badly hurt for this. He went to a hospital instead, and the Pirates, grabbing their lucky bull by the horns, responded like true champions.

Groat rammed a single through the hole into left field, scoring Cimoli. Stengel removed Shantz at this point and brought in fastballing Jim Coates. Skinner advanced both men with a flawless sacrifice bunt. Nelson flied to Maris, the runners holding. Clemente, with two strikes, beat out a dribbler toward Skowron, Virdon scoring and Groat racing to third.

This set the stage for Hal Smith, one of Pittsburgh's trio of home run heroes. On a 2 and 2 count, the reserve catcher and one-time Yankee hammered a Coates fastball far over the left-field fence into Schenley Park. Groat and Clemente scored ahead of Hal, Clemente doing a wild, leaping dance on his way to the plate. Terry replaced a pitifully crestfallen Coates and the Pirates whooped it up over a newfound lead of 9 to 7.

But the Yankees weren't beaten—not quite yet.

They got two to tie it in their ninth. Richardson singled off Bob Friend, who had just come in to pitch. Dale Long, batting for DeMaestri, did likewise. Murtaugh replaced Friend with the left-handed Harvey Haddix, and "The Kitten," as Haddix is called, got Maris on a foul to the catcher, but Mantle drove Richardson home with a single to right and put Long on third.

McDougald ran for Long and Berra bounced one down over the first base bag that Rocky Nelson scooped up, tagging the bag. This took the force off and Nelson couldn't immediately find Mantle to complete a double play. Mickey slid back safely and McDougald scored the tying run.

The Pirate ninth was much more simple and history-making.

Mazeroski, a Pittsburgh citizen, no less, was the man the fates chose to cap the climax with the most wondrous home run in Pittsburgh's baseball history.

Harvey Haddix was the winning pitcher by the skin of his teeth and young Ralph Terry the loser. Rocky Nelson, Hal Smith and Mazeroski were the big heroes in the most thrilling finish the World Series has known within the memory of the oldest inhabitant.

Pittsburgh is going madder by the minute as these lines are being written. Milling crowds are filling the streets with noise and a small army of teenagers just stomped through the lobby of the Pittsburgh Hilton, where the Yankees had been staying.

## BOB PRINCE
### from the Pirate Clubhouse

Prince: Here's Bill Mazeroski, who got the game-winning blow . . . Heeeeeyyy, wasn't that somethin', Billy?

Mazeroski (Laughing giddily): Oh, I can't even talk I'm so tired! . . .

P: What did you do, ya didn't have to run very far, did ya, boy? . . . (Mazeroski laughing) . . . What was the pitch you hit, Bill?

M: It was a high fastball.

P: A high fastball . . . That did it, and the Pirates are the world's champions for the first time since '25 . . .

Here's our general manager, Joe Brown . . . What a great job you did as general manager of this fine team . . .

Brown: It was these guys around you who did it, Bob, God Almighty, it was just wonderful! . . . I think it was just sheer guts against power, and the guts . . . the guts came through. . . . This is . . . I'm . . . I'm speechless . . .

P: I know you are . . . I know how you feel. . . . Here's Dick Groat . . . We're going coast to coast, Dick. I know you're real happy about that one . . .

Groat: Aaahhh, I feel wonderful, Bob, this is the greatest ball club in the world! . . .

P: World's champion Dick Groat . . . How's it sound?

G: Wonderful! . . . It's the greatest feeling in the world to be a world's champion . . . They thought we were dead, but we fought back, didn't we, Bob?

P: Yes, you did . . . Wonderful, thank you very much, Dick Groat . . . And the commissioner of baseball, ladies and gentlemen, Mr. Ford Frick . . . Commissioner, without question one of the most exciting World Series of all time . . .

Frick: Well, this is my 39th, and I never saw a finish like that one, Bob. . . . Never.

P: Did you ever see a World Series where we got . . . where the Pirates got beaten so badly and then turned right around and came on to take it like they did?

F: Well, you know the World Series, like everything else, it's only one that counts . . . That's that last run, that wins the final game . . .

P: Well, it was a thriller, and Commissioner Frick, thank you very much . . . Here's Danny Murtaugh . . . You Irishman, you! You did it! . . .

Murtaugh: By golly, Bob, what a finish . . . But, we've been doing that all year, and I think the fans were looking forward to it.

P: Thank you very much, Dan . . . And I'll just say thank you to everybody . . . I hope you fans have enjoyed hearing from these very happy world champion Pittsburgh Pirates . . .

# Sunny, with a Gale Blowing to Right

## STAN MUSIAL'S LAST GAME

September 29, 1963

**Emerson once remarked that** "a foolish consistency is the hobgoblin of little minds." It's a shame Ralph Waldo never saw what an inspired consistency like Stan Musial's could do.

In Musial's first game with the Cardinals, in 1941, he got two hits, and the Cards won, 3–2. In his last game with the Cardinals, in 1963, at the age of 42, he got two hits, and the Cards won, 3–2, prompting a sportswriter at the time to joke, "Twenty-two years in the majors, and Musial hasn't improved at all."

He was known, of course, as The Man, and for those 22 years, exhibiting what Jimmy Cannon called his "serene dependability," he did it all.

He won seven batting titles, drove in 1,950 runs, and hit 475 home runs. He won two MVP awards. He cranked out 3,630 hits (1,815 on the road; 1,815 at home), and by the time he retired, he held or shared sixteen major league records and more than two dozen National League records. Like all of the game's great ones, he inspired great lines from other players—as when Preacher Roe described how he liked to pitch him: "I throw him four wide ones, and then I try to pick him off first"—and he contributed a few of his own ("I don't think Warren Spahn will ever get into the Hall of Fame. He'll never stop pitching.")

He never trash-talked. He never showboated. He never disrespected the fans. All he did was tear up National League pitching year after year, and win the respect and love of fellow players and the fans, and then, when it was time to retire, he did it with grace and dignity and, of all things, a sense of joy.

In other words, he earned his nickname.

The piece by Ed Wilks on Musial's last game is one of a handful in this book that deal with events that the writers knew were going to occur. Like Ripken breaking Gehrig's record, or Rose breaking Cobb's, it became, after a while, only a matter of time. Which, of course, doesn't exactly detract from the moment's drama; on the contrary, it simply places a burden on the writer to make the inevitable dramatic.

Wilks, I think, manages to do just that. But he also catches, in the locker room, the minutiae of Musial's life—the clubhouse details, the gentle ribbing with teammates and the press—that Musial himself might well have been trying to absorb, and remember, after 22 years of playing the game.

In the end, Wilks offers us a sense that Musial is leaving the game not a moment too soon, and not an instant too late; and that, too, is a measure of The Man: you simply don't accomplish the sort of things that Musial did without a finely-honed, Hall of Fame sense of timing.

# ED WILKS

*St. Louis Post-Dispatch*

By 11 o'clock yesterday morning a crowd had gathered at the Dodier Street gates at Busch Stadium. Around the corner on Spring Avenue, another line formed at gate 23, while ushers and concessionaires checked in at a private entrance.

Upstairs, in the Cardinals' dressing room, clubhouse man Butch Yatkeman thumbed through slips of papers and told players how much they owed for tips and minor expenses through the season.

Sitting on a stool in front of his locker, Stan Musial thumbed through his memories, answering questions as he chatted with reporters and photographers.

Out on the field, other reporters and photographers walked on the newly seeded grass behind home plate as the Cincinnati Reds took batting practice. The Reds' Eddie Kasko, a rookie with the Cardinals in 1957, waited his turn to bat.

"After the tremendous career he's had, you knew it had to end on a day like this," he said. "Sunny, with a gale blowing to right and a hard-throwing right-hander pitching."

A guy walked through the dugout, up the steps to the clubhouse and inside. "The wind's blowing to right, Stan," he said.

"Best news I've heard yet," Musial answered, beaming and laughing.

Now it was 12:10, less than an hour and a half before the pre-game ceremony for Stan's farewell as a baseball player. Musial was out by the batting cage, posing for pictures, signing autographs for reporters, chatting and joking.

Suddenly, the batting cage was empty, but Musial, his back turned, continued to talk. On the other side of the cage, the Cardinals hooted. "Where's Stan?" Curt Flood asked mockingly. Hey, Stan, you going to hit?"

Musial hit. Lloyd Merritt, a one-time Cardinal, was pitching batting practice for Stan's swings. A high pop-up. A ground ball to first base. A fly ball to right. Another to center. A ground ball to the right side of the mound.

Then a long drive to right, off the screen. The early crowd cheered and applauded.

Then, another pop-up.

"One more," Musial yelled to the mound.

Merritt ("I wanted to give him something good.") came down the middle. Musial put the ball on the pavilion roof. The early crowd was an old crowd, cheering, stamping, applauding for a batting-practice homer as much as any crowd ever responded to a Musial home run.

Frank Robinson and Joe Nuxhall of the Reds walked toward The Man self-consciously. Each carried a baseball, thrusting it toward Stan as they asked for an autograph.

"To Frank, one of baseball's greatest players. Best wishes, Stan Musial."

"To Nick, best wishes, Stan Musial."

To Nick?

"He's a fellow back home (Hamilton, OH)," Nuxhall explained. "He's always telling us how great a hitter Musial is, as if we don't know. But we always try to aggravate him. We keep saying Ted Williams was the greatest.

"I'm going to give him the ball for Christmas."

It was 12:40 now. Stan was in the clubhouse, signing autographs while Sad Sam Jones sprayed sneezing powder. Sam's a gagman.

Mike Shannon and Gary Kolb passed Musial's locker. "Wait a minute," he said, putting an arm around each of the young Cardinals. "These are my proteges," he said. "They're going to take over for me—aren't you?" The young outfielders blushed. Cameras clicked.

Musial returned to writing his name—on slips of paper, on programs, on a bat for Shannon, on baseballs, on the color photo of him that was distributed to the crowd. He sat as he has batted: In a crouch.

Photographers shifted around him, taking candid shots of the best-known player in baseball.

"You fellows are all my friends," Stan said. "Don't take any pictures of me with a cigar in my mouth."

His friends obliged, granting this small request to protect an image for kids.

Stan Musial,
September 29, 1963

Now, suddenly, it was almost time. He patted down his hair, slipped on his cap. "Let's go."

Out the door and down the steps, across the ramps—as a crowd cried, "Here, Stan!" "Sign mine, Stan!"—and down the steps to the dugout.

Musial stepped out into a roar. He smiled, waved, and strode toward folding chairs set up between the mound and home plate. The Cardinals, out of habit, followed him, stopping at the third-base line as Stan The Man greeted baseball—commissioner Ford Frick, National League president Warren Giles, American League president Joe Cronin, Sid Keener, keeper of the Hall of Fame—as baseball greeted him.

The ceremonies began. It was 1:30. On the nose.

It was 2 when Stan stepped to the microphone. For a minute and 15 seconds he stood, shifting his feet humbly, listening to a standing ovation.

His speech—"There are so many I want to thank, I've made notes," he said apologetically—was made to background "pops" of balls smacking mitts as Bob Gibson and Jim Maloney, the starting pitchers, warmed up.

At 2:37, Stan Musial stepped to the plate against Maloney, 23-game winner. The first pitch was a called strike. Umpire Al Barlick plucked the ball from catcher John Edwards's mitt, and handed it to Stan.

Musial jogged toward the edge of the Cardinal dugout and flipped the ball to Giles. It is to go to Cooperstown, N.Y., and the Hall of Fame. Musial jogged back to the plate, then had to return to the box seat railing to re-hand the ball to Giles. The photographers had blown the real thing.

On the mound, Maloney waited, playing catch with Edwards. His second pitch to Musial was fouled into the upper deck. Strike two. The third pitch was a curve. Musial let it go by. Barlick's hand went up. Strike three. ("I don't call 'em the way I'd like to call 'em, but the way they are," Barlick explained later.)

When Musial came to bat a second time, Maloney had not allowed a hit. Of ten outs, six had been strikeouts. With one out in the fourth inning, Maloney's first pitch was a ball. His next was a called strike. His third was a fastball. Stan put it just beyond the reach of second baseman Pete Rose's glove for a single to center. The time was 3:22. The noise from the stands was tremendous.

The next time Stan came to bat was in the sixth inning, one out, score 0–0. Flood on base with a double. Stan swung viciously at the first pitch, fouled it back of the plate. The next two pitches were balls.

The third pitch was a curve ("A pretty good pitch, inside," said Maloney). Stan lined it past a sprawling Gordy Coleman into right field, driving in Flood for a 1–0 Cardinal lead.

The stands erupted, but the cheers were mingled with boos as Kolb replaced Musial as a pinch-runner.

Stan jogged off the field, followed to the dugout steps by an ovation that was a goodby. At 3:48 yesterday afternoon, September 29, 22 years of baseball with the Redbirds came to an end.

Two minutes later, Stan was striding up the steps to the clubhouse for the last time as a player. He stepped, smiling, into the dressing room, where cameras and reporters waited.

He brought with him a wave, a laugh, and 3,630 major league hits—and 1,950 runs batted in.

"That's what I like," he said. "Even numbers!"

There was talk of a final home run that was missed on his final day. "Everyone was telling me to hit one out of here," Stan said. "I'd just as soon settle for a little single—something I could be noted for. I'm not a home run hitter."

Now it was 4:06 and Stan hung up his uniform shirt for "the last time" at the request of photographers. "One more," they said, and he hung up his shirt for the "last time" twice more.

Stan patted the "MUSIAL" lettered above the red 6 on the back of the shirt. "If I do say myself, pal," he said, laughing. "You're all right."

Now there were TV interviews and questions and autographs. Then the wait began for the game to end, for a final farewell by Stan to the Cardinals. The wait was quiet. Too quiet.

"Come on, you guys," Stan joshed. "This is a happy occasion! Butch! How about a beer!"

Maloney, removed for a pinch-hitter, walked into the Cardinal clubhouse, hand outstretched for a handshake with Musial. "Congratulations," said Maloney.

"This is a guy who's tough," said smiling Stan, an arm around the enemy.

"I was glad to see him go out hitting," Maloney said. "It may cost me the game, but I was glad to see him do it."

The wait dragged on. The Reds tied the score in the ninth. A radio informed the group that Tim McCarver was at bat. "Hit it on the roof, Tim," Musial said. The game went into extra innings.

"Nothing like giving the fans something for their money on the last day," cracked Stan.

In the eleventh, Carl Sawatski batted as a pinch-hitter. "Hit one out of here, Carl," Musial said. The game went into the twelfth.

In the thirteenth, Musial pleaded. "Come on, gang," he said to his Cardinals, who couldn't hear him. "Let's go."

Musial stretched out on a rubbing table. He was there when the game ended. It was 6:16. Two hours and twenty minutes after he left the field, Musial was on hand for last clubhouse goodbys and a final radio interview as the "star of the game."

He was dressed in a business suit now, charcoal, with black shoes and socks. And a dark striped tie on his white-on-white shirt.

Then it was down the stairs. Autographs. Out gate 23. Autographs. Across the street. Autographs. Into a sleek, blue-gray Cadillac parked behind a refreshment stand. Autographs.

Finally, at 6:50 yesterday evening, Stan Musial drove away from the ballpark. Behind him were photographers, kids with programs. "One more! One more!"

The Man had said goodby.

# His Greatest Stuff

## SANDY KOUFAX'S PERFECT GAME

September 9, 1965

**For six seasons in** the early 1960s, Sandy Koufax simply dominated the hitters of the National League. He threw as hard as anyone has ever thrown, and after conquering a streak of wildness early in his career, he threw with astounding accuracy. When, in 1963, he struck out 306 men, he only walked 58.

The praise of his contemporaries speaks volumes. When Gene Mauch, who managed Philadelphia against Koufax's Dodgers, was asked whether Koufax was the best left-hander he'd ever seen, he said, "He was the best right-hander, too."

Casey Stengel, who had seen Koufax win two games against the Yankees in the 1963 World series (including the Series opener, in which he struck out a record 15 Yankee batters), said of the Dodger ace: "Forget the other fellow (Walter Johnson). Forget (Rube) Waddell. The Jewish kid is probably the best of them."

The Pirates' great slugger Willie Stargell claimed that trying to hit Koufax was "like drinking coffee with a fork." (Then again, Stargell is also credited with having said that trying to hit Steve Carlton's slider was like "trying to eat soup with a fork." Since most folks will probably agree that drinking coffee with a fork is a bit tougher than eating soup with a fork, we'll assume that Stargell had a harder time with Koufax than with Carlton, or anyone else for that matter.)

The stats bear it out. Four no-hitters in four successive years. Leading the league in ERA for five years. Three-time Cy Young Award–winner, at a time when the award went to the best pitcher in *either* league.

And then there was the look of the man. There are photographs of Sandy Koufax that are as beautiful as any sports pictures ever taken. They capture an

Sandy Koufax: "There was a bow and
arrow feeling about the way he used
his body," Roger Angell observed.

artist in complete control of an awesome instrument—his own body—and one can't help but wonder how anyone hitting against him could concentrate on the ball, and not simply marvel at the man's form. Roger Angell portrayed the man's delivery perfectly when he said that "there was a bow and arrow feeling about the way [Koufax] used his body."

It was, it seemed, not so much that he was throwing the ball, but that he was slinging it at the batter out of some wonderfully-designed contraption specifically built to confound hitters.

He was also, of course, an exemplary sportsman. For example, in the infamous Johnny Roseboro–Juan Marichal incident, when Dodger catcher Roseboro tossed a ball back to the mound, barely missing Marichal's head, and Marichal proceeded to beat on Roseboro's head with his bat, Koufax was the Dodgers' pitcher.

Roseboro later said that if any other pitcher had been out there, Marichal probably would have received retaliation from the pitcher for having thrown at Dodger batters all day. But with Koufax—a guy who "was constitutionally incapable of throwing at anyone's head," according to Roseboro—on the mound, the Dodger catcher felt he had to take it upon himself to sanction Marichal.

In 1965, Koufax was at his peak. He would lead the Dodgers that fall to the World Series title (a Series in which he declined to pitch the opening game, as it fell on Yom Kippur), and would pitch his masterpiece: a perfect game against the Chicago Cubs, during which, as Koufax himself later said, he had moments that were "the best I've ever pitched." In other words, in light of how well he threw on even an average night, the Cubs had no chance.

The monetary reward for the best pitcher in baseball's finest night? A $500 raise.

Perhaps the most astonishing performance of Koufax's career, however, came in the off-season. In 1966, after winning 27 games and leading the Dodgers into the Series against the Orioles, Sandy Koufax retired from baseball. Arthritis in his pitching elbow, and the painkillers that had to be pumped into it to allow him to pitch, seemed like too great a price to pay for the pleasure and privilege of hurling a baseball for a living.

At a press conference called a month after the Series, Koufax said that "to take a shot every other ball game is more than I wanted to do and [to] walk around with a constant upset stomach because of the pills and to be high half the time during a ball game because you're taking painkillers . . . I don't want to have to do that."

He was 30 years old.

# BOB HUNTER
*Los Angeles Herald-Examiner*

Baseball's Golden Arm fashioned one of baseball's golden-and-finest hours last night.

It was a dual storybook and record-book spectacular by Sandy Koufax.

The heavily-muscled Dodger left-hander became the first man in history to pitch four no-hit games, and by not permitting a Chicago player to reach first base, Koufax became only the 10th ever to record a perfect performance.

The classic 1–0 score was almost incidental in the dazzling delirium, as was the remarkable performance of Sandy's opponent, Bob Hendley.

The Chicago left-hander surrendered just one hit which, oddly, did not occur in the inning the hunt-and-peck Dodgers scored the lone, but winning run.

Until the solitary hit of the night came with two out in the seventh, the 29,139 fans had visions of witnessing the second double no-hitter ever pitched.

That was almost a half-century ago, in 1917, when Chicago's James (Hippo) Vaughn lost to Cincinnati's Fred Toney when the Cub hurler surrendered two hits in the 10th inning.

Koufax's performance was impeccable. Only one batter—Billy Williams—got as many as three balls. Sandy struck out 14 and grew stronger and tougher as the splendid game blossomed into a sports spectacular.

He struck out the last six batters to close out a classic among classics, with Sandy himself describing his ninth-inning march through the Cubs as "the best I've ever pitched."

Walter O'Malley sent down a bottle of champagne, which the 29-year-old Koufax stuck in the ice box in exchange for a beer.

"There'll be more rewards to follow," said the Dodger owner.

This will undoubtedly be a $500 raise. But it won't match two other benefits—the big boost given the Dodger pennant hopes, and Sandy's enhanced chances at earning once again the Cy Young Award.

Maybe they should rename it the Cy Koufax Award.

Young's long-standing and honored space in the record book has now shrunk to agate type compared with the big, bold entry made by Koufax.

Until last night four great pitchers—Koufax, Young, Bob Feller, and Larry Corcoran of the Cubs back in 1880–84—topped the pitching immortals with three no-hitters apiece.

Adding even more fantasy to the feat is that Sandy accomplished his in successive seasons.

Harvey Kuenn, one-time American League batting king, put last night's cliff-hanger in the record books by striking out on a fastball to end the game.

Kuenn also was the final out of Sandy's Giant conquest, three years ago.

"Without Sandy's no-hitter," said Walter Alston, "we'd have lost another game, probably.

"But that's been our story. Someone has picked us up each time we've been down."

Then as he went over to shake Sandy's hand once again he added:

"But they haven't all been this sensational. It came at a good time. I've seen all his no-hitters and I'd have to say he had his greatest stuff in this one.

"We had no right to win this game, but because of Koufax we did. Remember that other guy (Hendley) pitched a helluva game, too."

The victory left the Dodgers in a second-place tie, a half-game behind San Francisco.

As the classic neared its climax, Sandy was throwing everything at the Cubs—including his cap.

Three times it flew off as he put an extra zing on the ball that was almost inhuman.

You had to see it to believe it, which is why the Cubs don't believe it yet.

Someone asked Koufax what he threw in that last inning and he replied, "Everything I had."

It was in the seventh inning, Sandy explained, that he realized the no-hitter was almost in his grasp. Then he began concentrating on strikes.

"I really wanted that no-hitter," he said. "I didn't think so much about the perfect game—but I really wanted that no-hitter."

It was a quick and colossal conquest of an hour and 43 minutes from the time of Sandy's first pitch, which bounced in front of the plate and hit the backstop, until Kuenn swung and missed.

"That's harder than I've ever seen him throw before," said Ron Santo, one of the Cub stars.

Ernie Banks, who struck out three times for the only time this season, said: "He was trying to throw the ball by us—and he did."

"I think the way Hendley was pitching gave him a bigger incentive," suggested Ed Bailey, who has been in uniform during five no-hitters.

"But Koufax didn't give me a bit of trouble."

Bailey didn't play.

Santo, dressing next to Bailey, retorted almost under his breath: "That guy (Koufax) will drive you to drink."

Every player in the Cub box score, including two ninth-inning pinch hitters, Joey Amalfitano and Kuenn, struck out at least once.

"Don't they want Sandy in Japan along with Drysdale?" asked Amalfitano.

Two Cubs—Don Young and Byron Browne—had just played in their first major league game.

One of the Chicago veterans walked up to them and asked: "Are you SURE you want to play in the National League?"

Actually, there were few close calls for Koufax last night.

In the first inning Glenn Beckert hit one that landed just foul along the left field line, and in the second Browne lined to center for the only actual threats to the no-hitter.

However, in the seventh, when there was a three-ball count on Williams, and in the sixth when Wes Parker dug up a bouncing throw by Maury Wills, the perfect game seemed briefly in jeopardy.

The run came on a copyright Dodger "homer" in the fifth when Hendley, a beautiful mound artisan himself, issued his only walk to Lou Johnson.

Ron Fairly sacrificed him to second. Johnson promptly stole third, and when Chris Krug fired the ball into left field, the run scored.

With two out in the seventh Johnson hit one of Hendley's slip pitches off the end of his bat for a double over first base.

Jeff Torborg, who caught the masterpiece, was as jubilant as Koufax.

"These don't come along too often," cracked the rookie, when asked if it was his first perfect game.

Then he took a ball and asked Koufax to autograph it.

All that was left was to think up something for an encore.

Someone remembered then that Koufax will be making his next start Tuesday—against the Cubs in Chicago.

What next in this wild National League script?

# VIN SCULLY
## on the radio

Sandy fussing . . . Looks in to get his sign . . . 0 and 2 to Amalfitano . . . The strike two pitch to Joe . . .

Fastball, swung on and missed, strike three! . . .

He is one out away from the promised land . . . And Harvey Kuenn is coming up . . .

So Harvey Kuenn is batting for Bob Hendley . . . The time on the score-board is 9:44 . . . The date, September the 9th, 1965 . . . And Koufax working on veteran Harvey Kuenn . . . Sandy into his windup . . . And the pitch . . . Fast-ball for a strike! . . .

He has struck out, by the way, five consecutive batters . . . And that's gone unnoticed . . . Sandy ready, and the strike one pitch . . . Veeerrry high . . . And he lost his hat . . . He really forced that one . . .

That's only the second time tonight where I have had the feeling that Sandy threw instead of pitched . . . Trying to get that little extra . . . And that time he tried so hard his hat fell off . . . He took an extremely long stride to the plate, and Torborg had to go up to get it . . .

1 and 1 to Harvey Kuenn . . . Fastball, high . . . Ball two . . .

You can't blame a man for pushing just a little bit now . . . Sandy backs off, mops his forehead . . . Runs his left index finger along his forehead . . . Dries it off on his left pants-leg . . . All the while Kuenn just waiting . . .

Now Sandy looks in . . . Into his windup, and the 2–1 pitch to Kuenn . . . Swung on and missed! . . . Strike two! . . .

It is 9:46 P.M., 2 and 2 to Harvey Kuenn . . . One strike away . . . Sandy into his windup . . . Here's the pitch . . .

Swung on and missed! A perfect game! . . .

On the scoreboard in right field, it is 9:46 P.M., in the city of the angels, Los Angeles, California . . . And a crowd of 29,139 just sitting in to see the only pitcher in baseball history to hurl four no-hit, no-run games . . . He has done it four straight years . . . And now he capped it . . . On his fourth no-hitter, he made it a perfect game . . .

# Swatting at Invisible Moths

## BOB GIBSON'S SEVENTEEN STRIKEOUTS
### October 2, 1968

**If there was ever** a fiercer competitor than Ty Cobb, it must have been Bob Gibson.

How else do you describe a man capable of pitching—and winning—three complete games in one World Series, as Gibson did in '67? Or a man who, in a famous instance of being wholly true to himself, drilled his former roommate, Bill White, with a pitch the very first time White stepped in against him for an opposing team.

Roger Angell called Gibson "terrifying," and even though he was one of my heroes when I was a kid (I had a big Bob Gibson poster over my bed for years), I'm not sure I would have liked to have met the guy on a day when he was pitching, and certainly not on a day when he was pitching and I had to face him with a bat in my hand.

As Angell once put it, "He was never pleasant . . . And the way he threw—with that extraordinary last finishing flourish as he stepped over and his right leg crossed over his left leg and he fell off the mound to the left—[it] looked as if he was jumping at the batter." Bob Gibson *jumping* at me, a split second after he's *thrown the ball?* Call me old-fashioned, but that just doesn't sound like a fun way to spend an afternoon.

That anyone ever got a hit off the man still strikes me as kind of hard to believe, especially in that amazing year he had in 1968. Consider the numbers: a 1.12 ERA over 305 innings, 28 (!) complete games, 13 shutouts (and 11 other games in which he gave up only one run), and only 62 walks over the course of the entire regular season.

So, going into the first game of the World Series that year against the Tigers, Gibson looked pretty formidable.

Bob Gibson,
October 2, 1968

Nine innings and a World Series–record 17 strikeouts later, he looked absolutely unstoppable.

After Gibson's masterpiece, Denny McLain, the Tigers' 31-game winner during the regular season and the losing pitcher in the opening game match-up, said, "That was the greatest performance I've ever seen by anybody on a ball field."

Asked what he thought of Gibson's game, Tiger manager Mayo Smith put it a bit more poetically: "That's like asking Mrs. Lincoln how she enjoyed the play. What the hell, he just ate us up. I've seen that guy pitch a lot of times, but that's the best I've ever seen him. That's the whole story," he told the reporters jammed into the locker room. "I don't see why you even came in here."

The Tigers, of course, bounced back to win the Series, with big Mickey Lolich pitching three victories of his own, and the Tiger bats—Kaline, Cash, Horton and the rest—finally finding the power they'd shown all year.

Still, it was Gibson's numbers during the season, and his astonishing opening-game performance in the Series that caught the imagination of most writers in 1968. As Bob Stevens wrote in his *San Francisco Chronicle* story on Gibson's Game 1 tutorial, "You sort of got the idea in this one that if you went to the laboratory to make a pitcher you'd come out with Bob Gibson."

## JOHN HALL
*Los Angeles Times*

The Bullet and the Organ Player met here in broad daylight Wednesday and the outcome was medically predictable. The Organ Player died.

Pierced through the heart, Denny McLain, baseball's first 30-game winner in 34 years, was laid to rest quietly as Bob Gibson and the St. Louis Cardinals humbled the Detroit Tigers, 4–0, to step to the front in the 65th annual insanity known as the World Series.

Game No. 1, performed before a record Busch Stadium mob of 54,692, was advertised as the classic pitching match-up of the century—and that, at least, was half-right. It was a half-classic.

Gibson, 32, tall, dark, and human (maybe), completely mastered McLain, completely mystified the Tigers, and completely surprised hardly anybody at all.

Ho, hum. It was Gibson's 14th shutout of the year.

Ho, hum. It was Gibson's sixth straight triumph in World Series action, a record, spanning three different classics dating back to 1964.

Ho, hum. Gibson struck out 17, shattering a Series record of 15 set by Sandy Koufax against the Yankees in 1963. Ho, hum. He breezed home on a five-hitter.

Ho, hum. It was murder in the first degree.

With his dancing slider and burning fastball blazing through the St. Louis sunshine, Gibson struck out the side in the second, he struck out the side in the ninth, he struck out every regular in the line-up at least once, and he struck out for the Hall of Fame with every effortless, majestic delivery.

And Gibson's reaction to it all? Ho, hum.

"I've thrown better," he allowed in the midst of the jam of the Cardinal dressing room. "I was up quite a bit, but it was mostly the fact that the Tigers haven't seen me. I was pretty much of a surprise to them."

Gibson said he wasn't aware of the strikeout record until he saw it flashed on the stadium message board.

"It's always nice to have a record, but I never think about them," he said in a tone which could have been accompanied by a yawn.

Well, it was that yawningly easy. Going into the final inning one shy of the Koufax record, he mowed down Al Kaline (for the third time), Norm Cash (for the third time), and Willie Horton (for the second time)—the heart and soul of the Detroit attack.

"I wouldn't say it was one of the best games I've ever pitched, but it was one of the most important," he said. "My breaking pitch helped a lot. I don't think they expected me to throw anything but fastballs. No, McLain didn't say anything to me and I didn't say anything to him. What would there be to say?"

Thus ended the pitching classic of the ages. Another yawn, another ho-hum and another ah, shucks. It wasn't anything special, pal.

And it doesn't rain in Indianapolis in the summertime.

Good Lord. For a human, Bullet Bob Gibson is some kind of inhuman machine.

He left the American League just where it came in and went out in 1967.

McLain, 31–6 in his remarkable regular season, was a shambles. While Gibson fanned them, Denny walked them and it was all over in a wild and weary fourth inning.

Denny walked Roger Maris on four straight pitches to open the fourth. He walked two men. He once threw six straight balls. He threw a total of 15 balls before the fatal frame was finished.

It was no ball for the Tigers. After Maris walked, Orlando Cepeda (hitless again in a new Series) popped out. Then, the second walk to Tim McCarver.

Then, the knockout. Third baseman Mike Shannon bounced a single to left to bring Maris racing all the way home from second.

Willie Horton kicked Shannon's single in left field, McCarver winding up at third and Shannon at second on the error. Julian Javier rifled a single past first basemen Cash to drive in both. That was it, bingo. Just like that.

McLain, walking a total of three and tagged for three hits (one a McCarver triple) and two earned runs, retired for a pinch hitter in the top of the sixth, trailing 3–0.

Lou Brock slammed a seventh inning homer off reliever Pat Dobson to round out the first game scoring, but the TKO sign had long been up in lights by then.

As they return for game No. 2 here today, the loose and laughing Tigers know now they are in serious trouble.

Whatever happens next, there is Gibson just around the corner.

But Mickey Lolich, the left-handed motorcycle jockey, will try to get Detroit even against the pride of Santa Clara, Nellie Briles.

Topping off the humiliation, the Tigers committed three errors in the field, the Cards swiped three bases, and Gibson even outclassed McLain in a bunting duel. McLain bunted foul for a third strike trying to advance a runner to second in the third.

Gibson coolly sacrificed a man to second in the same inning.

There was only one mild Detroit scoring threat—when Kaline doubled Dick McAuliffe to third with two out in the sixth. Can you imagine what happened next? Cash, one of the best of the Tiger clutch hitters, went down swinging.

It was futile from the start. Gibson fanned seven in the first three innings. Jumping at shadows, the Tigers looked like they were swatting at invisible moths.

All the while, Gibson worked smoothly. No fuss. No muss. Up the pitches came. No strain. So easy. Another strike. It was a big deal to touch him for a foul.

Another strike. Is it the seventh inning already? Or is it the 27th? Gibson never changes.

Of the record 17 strikeouts, 10 were swinging, six were called by plate umpire Tom Gorman and one was McLain's foul bunt.

And that just about told it all regarding McLain's day of days, the day he confronted Bob Gibson with the sun shining and the stadium rocking and the world waiting.

For Denny the dashing, Denny the music man, Denny the darling of Detroit and Denny the new Dizzy Dean, it all turned into a foul bunt.

## Another View

# BOB ADDIE
*Washington Post*

It was, as St. Louis manager Red Schoendienst said, just like a no-hitter. Nobody on the Cardinals' bench was saying a word about a World Series strike-out record today when Bob Gibson was moving through the Detroit Tigers like wind on a prairie.

Gibson struck out 17 batters, two more than Sandy Koufax did in the 1963 Series opener against the New York Yankees when he was pitching for the Los Angeles Dodgers. Koufax is an announcer now and ordinarily he would have been on hand to see his strikeout record erased. But Koufax was unaware of the smaller drama. He was at a temple praying on Yom Kippur, this the day of Atonement.

The spectacular confrontation between Gibson and Denny McLain, the cool cat of the Tigers, was no contest after the fourth inning. The suspense drifted through like sand in an hourglass until excitement built up—not over the pitching duel but over Gibson's run at the strikeout record.

Records are the meat and potatoes of the game for baseball fans. These are the deeds enshrined in another time and another day. These are the "immortal" deeds, and Gibson's performance today will give him another line in the Series record book, in place of the one that reads: "Most strikeouts, one pitcher, game—15, Sanford Koufax, Los Angeles, NL Oct. 2, 1963."

McLain seemed bemused by the fact he was playing a supporting role this time to Gibson. On the eve of the Series, the pitching musician (he plays the organ) entertained himself and his teammates and their wives with a two-hour concert in the cocktail lounge of their hotel. He played until 11:50 P.M., then cut out and hit the pad. If he didn't get much rest Tuesday night he made up for it today because he was out of the game after the fifth inning.

The pitching duel between Gibson and McLain struck classic poses. McLain is a nervous pitcher—something like Camilo Pascual of the Senators. He paws the ground like an annoyed bull trying to unravel the mystery of the taunting red cape. Gibson was the cold-eyed matador, today—the man who likes a challenge and meets it head-on.

Gibson is not one to gloat. He thinks his professional skills are such that he can meet any emergency. But there is a little bit of boy in every man, and the Cardinal pitcher could not help getting some satisfaction over how he upset the Detroit scouting reports. All week long Gibson has been insisting the scouting reports were for the birds, not the Cardinals.

"I'm a case in point," he said happily. "I was reading what our scouts gave in their report on the Tigers. I think I know what the Tigers said about me—I was a power pitcher who couldn't throw the breaking stuff."

Gibson was right. The Tigers didn't think much of his slider or curve. "I crossed them up," Gibson said in a delighted tone . . .

Gibson said he heard "a lot of hollering" in the ninth after he struck out Kaline. "Then I looked around and saw the scoreboard. But I wanted to keep pitching. I wasn't aware of any record. Records don't mean anything. Winning is the thing."

McLain calmly parried all questions after the game, drinking his inevitable bottle of soda pop. "Why are you guys in here?" he asked the reporters. "Gibson is the glamor boy, isn't he? Maybe you're in here to see me because I have more funny lines. I come all the way to the World Series and pitch my lousiest game. I couldn't get the ball where I wanted it to go. What was wrong? I didn't have any rhythm.

"Those walks killed me. Imagine giving a walk to (Dal) Maxvill. That's like walking Mark Belanger (of the Orioles). What did Maxvill hit this year—around .200?"

McLain was told that Maxvill had hit .253 for the Cardinals this season.

"I take it all back," McLain said. "If he hit .253 he'd be a star in the American League. I wish I could print the one-word description I have for myself today. But you can't. Just say 'lousy.' That's close enough."

# Born to Laughter

## THE AMAZING METS WIN THE WORLD SERIES
### October 16, 1969

**I remember it as** a great World Series, and I don't think that's only because it was the first World Series that I was really excited about as a kid. There was, it seemed, something really electrifying about it, and that probably had to do with a great cast of characters—and especially the Mets characters—taking the stage.

Cleon Jones. Donn Clendenon. Jerry Koosman. Tom Seaver. Tommie Agee. Bud Harrelson. Jerry Grote. Ron Swoboda. Even old Gil Hodges. These weren't the Yankees, or the Dodgers, or the Cardinals; these weren't the sort of folks you expected to see playing deep into the post-season. These guys were different. These guys were a little weird. These guys were playing like their lives depended on it. These guys were New York *Mets*, of all people, and they were a blast to watch.

The Orioles, of course—led by the inscrutable, combative Earl Weaver— weren't exactly a dull team, either. With folks like Frank Robinson, Boog Powell, Don Buford, and Brooks Robinson pounding the ball, and Jim Palmer, Mike Cuellar, and Dave McNally pitching other teams silly, the O's were favored to beat, if not downright embarrass, the upstart Mets in the '69 Series.

Funny how things turn out, isn't it? Behind brilliant pitching by Koosman and Seaver (and a Game 3 victory on the arms of Gary Gentry and Nolan Ryan), clutch hitting by Jones and Clendenon, and remarkable fielding by Agee and Swoboda, the Miracle Mets took the Orioles in four staright games after dropping Game 1.

When the Mets finally won it, a fan at Shea Stadium waved a sign reading, "There are no words."

But, of course, there were, and the *Knickerbocker News*' Ralph Martin and

The Mets win it all

the *Star-Ledger*'s Jerry Izenberg were there to make certain of that. Both pieces are well done, but there are two elements of Izenberg's, in particular, that are worth noting.

First of all, early in his piece, Izenberg writes of the Mets fans after the final out: "(T)hey ran in great circles . . . they slammed their bodies together like great two-legged cymbals, wiped off the blood and slammed again."

Of course, anyone who has spent any time in a punk club in the last fifteen years will find in Izenberg's words as succinct and evocative a description of a mosh pit as one could hope for. Just another illustration that everything old is, eventually, new again.

Then there's the description late in the piece of Boog Powell booting a ground ball at first. Powell, Izenberg says, played the ball "like a man trying to cross the Gobi Desert on ice skates," and then "looked at the sky in embarrassment" after blowing it.

The careful reader (that is, someone who might approach this book sequentially, which I don't necessarily recommend) will find that Izenberg's words faintly echo Paul Gallico's description of a Tony Lazzeri error in the 1932 (Called Shot) World Series: "Lazzeri . . . fielded it, dropped it, kicked it, lost it and finally stood there just being ashamed."

Just another illustration that everything old is new again. Again.

# RALPH MARTIN
*Knickerbocker News* (Albany, NY)

"We're No. 1, best in the National League, American League, and best in the world. And, man, if you don't believe it now, you never will."

The speaker, Donn Clendenon, sagged gently against a locker in the Mets dressing room and tried to remain calm in a scene of utter chaos.

All agreed with Clendenon that the Cinderella Mets or Destiny's Darlings or the Amazing Ones were, indeed, No. 1. Who would argue after the brash New Yorkers confounded the experts again by dumping the favored Orioles, 5–3, to win the 1969 World Series championship before a record crowd of 57,397 in Shea Stadium yesterday?

No one would contest Dandy Donn's words that the Mets, those once comical, inept performers, were now No. 1. But, in all due respect to the series most valuable player it's hard to believe this joyful ending to the impossible dream.

"I know it's true, but I can't believe it, I really can't," said J. C. Martin, whose remarkable restraint may have been due to an advanced state of shock.

Martin, the former White Sox catcher, was calm—outwardly, at least. So were Clendenon, who hit three home runs in the series, and infielder Ken Boswell, caught in a moment of disbelief as he sat and silently gazed toward the floor.

But elsewhere in the packed room emotions spilled out as freely as champagne.

Caught up in the joy of the moment were Ed Kranepool, who splashed the bubbly juice over anyone within range and Ed Charles, the old veteran who gyrated to the beat of soul music that tried in vain to compete with the laughter and shouting.

There was winning pitcher Jerry Koosman, who in a statement that surprised absolutely no one, said: "This is my greatest thrill."

Elsewhere, a group of Mets sang "East Side, West Side" with a flair that hardly will get them on TV commercials.

Then there was Tommy Seaver, the 25-game winner who lost the series opener only to come back strong and take Wednesday's 4th game.

"Unity," he said, his voice cracking with emotion, "that's what we have is unity."

Each of the Mets reacted in his own way, some with shouts, some with laughter, and yes, some with tears. The joy was multiplied by fans outside the locker room, fans who had finally seen their darlings become winners after seven years of feebleness and frustration.

Youngsters, many not far removed in age from the mod Mets, gleefully pranced on the field, sending up orange flares and shouting, "We're No. 1."

Horns blared, people waved and cheered and it's safe to say there was shouting from the rooftops. Mayor Lindsay, thoroughly doused with champagne, got into the act by pronouncing Monday "Met Day," a move that will undoubtedly get him more votes than a dozen debates over garbage removal.

There was joy everywhere as the Mets' victory has to be one of the most exciting sports stories of our time—or any time.

Laughed at, ridiculed, downtrodden, born to laughter—the club has risen from the ashes of defeat to smite the lordly kings of the game and become champions.

And the Amazin' Ones did it an unpredictable (make that unbelievable) way. They never ceased to astonish. Take yesterday as an example.

Dave McNally appeared to have the New Yorkers on the ropes for six innings. The pitcher, just to show that the Baltimorians can be amazing, too, staked the Orioles to an early lead with a two-run home run in the third. It was only his second homer of the season. Slugger Frank Robinson, perhaps to show that homers are his department, then belted a solo shot to deep left center to make it 3–0.

McNally continued to tame the Mets as the crowd lapsed into a hushed state that well could have prompted an uninitiated passerby to believe that the stadium was being used as the site of a prayer meeting. Only a rhubarb in the sixth with the ump over players hit by pitches broke the silence.

In the seventh, Clendenon narrowed the margin to 3–2 with a two-run homer. Then in the eighth—surprise of surprises—banjo-hitting Al Weis evened things with a clout over the left field fence.

"I was just trying to meet the ball and get a single," said Weis. "And what do you know, the thing went out."

These words came from a man who had only two homers this season and a total of five his first four years in the majors.

The unexpected heroics of Weis and other Mets are what fans have come to expect.

In the series, for example, the club bounced back to win four straight after being soundly beaten in the opener. There was hurler Gary Gentry, who usually just gives a pitch a passing wave, shocking the world by hitting a two-run double to spark the third game win. And Gentry had a pretty good buddy in that contest in Tommy Agee, who committed larceny on a couple of well-hit balls. Ron Swoboda, sharpening his skills as time goes on, was the man of the fourth series game, staving off an Orioles rally with a circus catch.

But then that's the way it was practically all season long—a hero a day.

The fans grew to love this dashing group of players, all of whom bubble with talent and play the game with a captivating flair.

But the love goes deeper than the 1969 champions. It goes back to their entrance into the league in 1962, to the comical flair of Casey Stengel, to the classic ineptness of Marvelous Marv Throneberry and to the catcher who dubiously boasted that "I caught more 20-game losers than anyone in baseball."

The love grew as the Mets struggled year after year, finishing a total of 288½ games out of first place the first seven seasons.

Why did fans take to the Mets? For the same reason fans take to all underdogs, be it a likable kid who is having his first ring match, an outclassed football team, or—the Mets. And the Mets were not only the underdogs, but they had the laughs to go with it. That was an unbeatable combination in New York, which never really took to the Yankees even in the Bombers best years.

The Mets were the Dodgers of Flatbush reborn.

The Mets had their same underdog tag going into the 1969 season. It was a brave writer who picked them to finish higher than third. Odds at their taking the pennant ran as high as 100–1.

But the Mets had a surprise in store for their followers. Mostly a young, swinging group, they started playing the game with a zest and talent under the firm but knowing hand of Gil Hodges. And they became winners.

Despite their Eastern Division playoff title, they were underdogs both in the National League playoffs and against the highly respected Orioles in the series. But they pulled some more wonders out of their bag of tricks and went all the way.

And in going their merry way, they provided the sports scene with a moving and memorable event.

It's little wonder Mrs. Joan Payson, the club's owner, was too choked up to talk for a while after the victory. A lot of emotions can spill out after seven years of frustration.

## Another View

### JERRY IZENBERG
*Newark Star-Ledger*

At 3:16 they came pouring over the waist-high restraining walls . . . uncles and cousins and Mets' fans by the dozens. Gently, like a falling safe, they flung their bodies at the pitcher's mound. Guys who wouldn't get off their rumps to take out the garbage if their wives mailed them written requests came busting into that sea of humanity. Kids who wouldn't walk a block to mail a letter as long as there was gas in the family car crawled across the infield on their bellies and hacked out pieces of turf. Things being what they are today, it was unclear whether they were going to save them or sell them.

They stole home plate . . . they stole the pitching rubber . . . they ran in great circles . . . they slammed their bodies together like great two-legged cymbals, wiped off the blood and slammed again. The joint had all the charm of the railroad depot in Barcelona when they announced the last refugee train in 1936.

So this is how the championship of all baseball came to the Mets of New York. Not with a whimper and not with a bang but with a wall-to-wall groan as they dragged the bleeding and wounded through the runways and off toward the aid stations.

Meanwhile, as the survivors chalked graffiti on the outfield fences, Mrs. Joan Payson, the mother of the Mets, was inside speaking to the President of the United States on the telephone. When the Mets win the World Series, baby, there is something for everyone.

And the Mets won this one yesterday. They won it without the aid of poltergeists. They won it, 5–3, and they won it because Jerry Koosman pitched magnificently despite an early stab wound. They won it because they played their best baseball of the series.

For the purposes of history, the Mets of New York began to win this thing in the sixth inning. The Orioles were then in front, 3–0, on home runs by their pitcher, Dave McNally, and their best bat, Frank Robinson. Mr. Robinson rates a second mention here in connection with the sixth inning.

This has not been a very good Series for umpires. On Wednesday, Shag Crawford exiled Earl Weaver, the Baltimore manager, apparently because he was guilty of a lack of compassion. Yesterday, on a dark gray day which looked as though it were a refugee from the dark side of the moon, home plate umpire Lou DiMuro moved stage center by default.

Robinson claimed he had been hit by a pitch. Mr. DiMuro said he hadn't felt anything. Mr. Robinson grew highly agitated and Earl Weaver rushed out of the dugout to cool him off.

After what happened to Mr. Weaver on Wednesday, this is not unlike hiring Ghengis Khan to mediate the war between the Normans and the Saxons. Mr. DiMuro won but he didn't beat anybody because Frank Robinson simply walked off the field.

So there was Lou DiMuro, the symbol of World Series authority, standing with his hands on his hips for six minutes and all but shouting into the Oriole dugout:

"Hey, Earl, can Frank come out and play?"

Which brings us to the bottom of the inning when Cleon Jones said he was hit by a pitch and DiMuro said he was not and Gil Hodges walked out of the dugout holding the ball and pointing to what he said was a shoe polish mark. DiMuro sent Cleon to first and the Orioles insisted that he couldn't tell spit from Shinola. At any rate Donn Clendenon hit one out and the Mets were just one run back.

Al Weis, who may refuse to play next year unless he can bat once a year against Baltimore, evened it all up in the seventh with a dandy shot over the left field fence.

So the world knew the Mets would win it right there.

And they did in the eighth with doubles by Jones and Clendenon and a magnificently lousy play by the Baltimores.

This last takes a little explaining because it wasn't easy. Jerry Grote rapped the ball to Boog Powell's right. Powell played it like a man trying to cross the

Gobi Desert on ice skates. Which is more than you can say for Ed Watt, who barely ran at all, arrived late, and dropped a throw which wouldn't have nailed Grote anyway. The two errors brought Swoboda all the way home from second.

Powell looked at the sky in embarrassment and a man was reminded of Brooks Robinson's words of the day before. "I don't believe they have us spooked or anything like that. If they could fly, then I'd believe it."

It was at that precise moment that a man could swear he saw Choo Choo Coleman buzz the field and dip his wings.

The rest was automatic. As the natives shuffled restlessly through the stands and began to lay siege against the restraining walls, Dave Johnson golfed a high fly to left field. Cleon Jones made a routine catch and a magnificent run. He never broke stride. With half of adoring America in loving pursuit, Cleon ran across the outfield. He ran like a man being chased by 5,000 people. He was.

As he disappeared through the haven of the bull pen fence, the cultural portion of the proceedings began with all the restraint of the mob scene from "Duffy of San Quentin." In its very vortex stood a brave soul with a sign which demanded, "What Next?"

He found out when the first pilgrim slammed into him.

# His World Series

---

## ROBERTO CLEMENTE'S WORLD SERIES MVP
### October 17, 1971

**When the plane carrying** Roberto Clemente and supplies for earthquake victims in Nicaragua crashed into the sea on New Year's Eve, 1972, baseball lost a man considered by many to be the greatest player of the previous decade.

His homeland of Puerto Rico, however, and all of the Caribbean, lost a living Latin symbol of talent, and achievement. In Puerto Rico, the governor issued a proclamation ordering three days of official mourning; a heartfelt gesture, no doubt, but also quite likely the most unnecessary proclamation ever signed.

Clemente was, for years, the most popular and highly regarded man in Puerto Rico, and one of the best-loved public figures throughout the Caribbean. Radio stations all over Puerto Rico cancelled regular programming from the moment word came that Clemente's plane was lost. Somber music filled the airwaves for days.

The day after the plane crash, in the *San Juan Star*, sports editor Tito Stevens wrote sparely and movingly of Clemente as a friend, and as a national hero:

> The last time I saw Roberto was a little over a year ago when he returned to Puerto Rico after leading Pittsburgh to the world championship. Thousands of his fellow countrymen were at the airport to greet him. They broke police barricades to be close to him.
>
> The giant Eastern 747 that brought him and his wife from New York was a madhouse as newsmen crowded around Clemente, who was more worried about his aging dad's safety in the mob. I spotted

one of his sons who was scared by the big commotion and crying. A relative asked me to take the youngster off the plane and get him into the car which would take Roberto to La Fortaleza where Secretary of State Fernando Chardon would give Clemente a plaque.

As I carried him to the car I told Roberto's son not to worry about his father—that nobody was trying to hurt him. That they all loved him and wanted to be close to him.

Back in the States, Clemente's death elicited from his friends and colleagues spontaneous tributes to the man's dignity and boundless sense of charity.

John Galbreath, chairman of the board of the Pirates, called Clemente "one of the greatest persons I knew. If you have to die, how better could your death be exemplified than by being on a mission of mercy? It was so typical of the man. Every time I was down there, someone was always saying how he contributed to the youth and needy of his island, how he was going to make that his life's work. He did these things without fanfare or anything—just what he thought was right to help somebody else."

Most everyone else echoed the sentiment that if he had to die so young, it was appropriate, somehow, that Clemente would die while helping others. It also became clear, in the tone and the profusion of tributes, that these folks weren't merely being kind or polite in their praise. Clemente, it seemed, had touched an enormous number of people in his lifetime, and no one had come away unmoved.

His teammate Steve Blass said of Clemente that "we're all better players and people for having known him. I think we all learned from him."

Baseball Commisioner Bowie Kuhn, however, might have put it best when he said, simply, that Clemente "had about him a touch of royalty."

And with that royal demeanor, of course, came an enormous, unquenchable pride.

For years, Clemente had felt that sportswriters had slighted him, that they made a fuss over players who might have been flashier than he was, or who might have put up bigger numbers, for one or two seasons, than he had—but year after year, injured and healthy, he believed himself to be the best all-around player in baseball.

Finally, in the 1971 World Series, he proved it. In that Series, in the words of Roger Angell, Clemente was "throwing and running and hitting at something close to the level of absolute perfection."

Clemente was voted the Series MVP, and even in his moment of personal triumph, proved himself a man with a remarkable sense of what, in the end, was most important to him. In the Pirates' locker room after the seventh game,

Roberto Clemente: "You call
Pete Rose 'Charlie Hustle.' He
doesn't hustle more than me."

Clemente, standing before the thicket of microphones thrust at him by the media, asked permission to say a few words in Spanish to his mother and father in Puerto Rico: "On this, the proudest moment of my life, I ask your blessings."

In the piece below—written at the moment Clemente is finally being acknowledged and celebrated as perhaps the finest all-around player of his generation—Clemente's pride is in full-blown, wonderful, shameless evidence. At the same time, the writer, Frank Dolson, basically admits that, yes, for years sportswriters had given Clemente less than a fair shake.

Dolson's piece, then, is the one article in this book that manages to be, at once, both a paean to a magnificent ballplayer and, in a small way perhaps, something close to an act of contrition.

# FRANK DOLSON
*Philadelphia Inquirer*

This was Roberto Clemente's World Series.

He was standing on a wooden platform the television people had set up. Sweat and champagne trickled down his forehead. Men with pencils and pads and tape recorders surrounded him, jostling for position, straining to hear his words.

Clemente was happy to see them. Eager to talk to them. Now they would listen. Now they would understand. Now they would find out that Roberto Clemente, the unsung superstar, baseball's most underrated player, wasn't a bad guy, after all.

The players knew that already. Wes Parker of the Dodgers thought so much of Roberto Clemente that he sent him a telegram on the morning of the seventh game. "Do it for your parents," the wire said.

And Clemente did it, just as he has been doing it all week. Just as he has been doing it through 17 years in the big league.

The Clemente who dominated this World Series, who destroyed the Baltimore Orioles, was no different from the Clemente who played 132 National League games this season.

The man who made those incredible throws from right field always makes incredible throws. The man who hit those savage line drives always hits savage line drives. The man who ran out every ball, even routine grounders, always runs out every ball.

"I've never seen a man day after day give more of himself," Pirates general manager Joe Brown said as the mob engulfed Clemente. "People see him hit a ball to the mound and run his tail off and they think he's doing it because it's a World Series. He does it every day."

But only now, after one of the great individual performances in World Series history, was the recognition his.

"You call Pete Rose 'Charlie Hustle,'" Clemente had scolded a group of writers in the Pittsburgh clubhouse two days before. "He doesn't hustle more than me."

Nobody hustles more than Clemente. And nobody plays baseball better.

"This is the best player I've ever seen," Brown was shouting over the noise. "I thought Mays was the greatest until 1966. After that, this man. I'm not saying this just today, under these circumstances. This man is the greatest I've ever seen . . . "

And never has his greatness stood out in such bold relief as in this World Series. His World Series.

"When it comes to sports the only regret I have, I feel I have been neglected," he said the other day. "Not only me. All Latin players."

But if they neglected Clemente before, they were not neglecting him now. An hour after the final out, his teammates had to fight through the crowd of writers to congratulate him.

"Excuse me," shouted Charlie Sands, elbowing his way to the edge of the platform. "I want to shake the hand of the greatest damn ballplayer in the whole world."

And then came Willie Stargell, the slugger whose bat grew so silent in this World Series. The champagne running down his face, the happiness showing in his eyes, he finally reached Roberto's side, gripped his hand and said, "Helluva job. I know you're going to be the Most Valuable Player. But if you're not, I'm going to buy you a car myself."

Not even the press that had overlooked him all these years could overlook Clemente after this World Series. He hit in every game, as he did in the 1960 World Series, and he hit for power.

It was almost as if Clemente wanted to show the world, once and for all, that he could do it all.

He is not a home run hitter because he does not choose to be a home run hitter. "I say the hell with homers," he said. "One fence is short. One is long. One is high. One is low."

But Sunday's biggest hit was a Clemente home run. "I prove to you I hit home runs if I want to," he said.

The critics bother him. They have always bothered him. When they write he can't do something, he gets angry. "The madder I get the better I play," he said.

Clemente must have been furious this World Series. He read that the Orioles would slaughter the Pirates. And he read that he was only a right field hitter, a man who couldn't pull a baseball.

So on his first at-bat in Saturday's sixth game he slammed the ball just to the left of straightaway center. "They say I can not pull the ball," he said later. "I can not pull ball, eh? So I get triple."

For the better part of two decades he has been waging this war for recognition, this struggle to prove that he is better than the stars who get all the publicity, the stars who get the TV shows and the commercials and the catchy nicknames.

"Any new player who comes up, they build him up," he said, standing on that platform with the crowd still surrounding him. "Me, I break my neck, but I'm still just Roberto Clemente."

And on this, surely the most satisfying day of his baseball career, he was the same Roberto Clemente as before. Let the others shout and laugh and douse each other with champagne. Clemente's face, through most of the post-game celebration, was serious.

"I have a serious face," he said. "Most places I go, people say, 'Smile.' It makes me mad. If occasion is for smiling, sure I smile . . ."

But if he smiled only occasionally, even now, inside he was bubbling with happiness. The 1960 World Series had meant a lot, he said, but this one meant more.

"My mother is 87, my father 91," he explained.

For them, for his teammates, for his fans, for himself, he played these seven games the way he always plays baseball.

Forget the misunderstandings. Forget the occasional displays of anger, of bitterness. Nobody plays the game harder. Nobody plays the game better. For that, Roberto Clemente deserves all the recognition this World Series can bring him.

# A Tremendous Weight

## HANK AARON'S 715th HOME RUN

April 8, 1974

**It's been played and** replayed a thousand times, but the image of Henry Aaron hitting the 715th home run of his amazing career can still take your breath away.

In retrospect, it's not so much that the sound of the bat crushing the ball, as Dave Anderson points out in his piece below, was so spectacular.

It's not the idea of Tom House racing in from the bull pen with the ball in his glove, just wanting to hand the ball to the man, and then suddenly, as he recalled later, finding Aaron "looking over his mother's shoulder, hugging her to him . . . (and seeing) what many people have never been able to see in him—deep emotion . . . I looked and he had tears hanging on his lids."

It's not even the crowd standing and cheering for minutes on end—a crowd of thousands, as Vin Scully remarked in his radio call, in Georgia, standing and cheering the monumental accomplishment of a black man.

What's really hard to get your mind around is the fact that Aaron was able to pull on his uniform, and go out on to the field, and swing a bat at all, much less power a major league fastball over a major league fence. For anyone to withstand the pressures that Aaron had to withstand, and then, on top of that, to actually *do it* . . . It's just too much.

The pressures, of course, included an enormous and incessant media entourage; the eyes of the nation watching his every swing; the constant reminders that he was chasing the most hallowed of baseball records (held by the most hallowed of baseball players); and, finally, the vicious racist threats on his own life, and the lives of his children.

But Aaron persevered. The racists had nothing but cowardice to fuel them, while Aaron had enormous talent, patience, and courage. Far more people were

Hank Aaron: "I never knew that my
mother could hug so tight."

rooting for him to break the record than were hoping to see him fail, and on April 8, 1974, he sent a rocket off into the Georgia night that made millions of folks inexpressibly glad.

## DAVE ANDERSON
*New York Times*

In the decades to come, the memory of the scene might blur. But the memory of the sound will remain with everyone who was here. Not the sound of the cheers, or the sound of Henry Aaron saying, "I'm thankful to God it's all over," but the sound of Henry Aaron's bat when it hit the baseball tonight. The sound that's baseball's version of a thunderclap, the sound of a home run, in his case the sound of the 715th home run. The sound momentarily was the only sound in the expectant silence of 53,775 customers in Atlanta Stadium and then, as the sound faded, the ball soared high and deep toward the left-center-field fence. And over it. On the infield base paths, Henry Aaron was trotting now, trotting past Babe Ruth into history in his 21st season. On his first swing in tonight's game, the 40-year-old outfielder of the Atlanta Braves had hit another home run, just as he had hit his record-tying home run on his first swing at Cincinnati in last Thursday's season opener. At home plate, surrounded by an ovation that came down around him as if it were a waterfall of appreciation, he was met by his teammates who attempted to lift him onto their shoulders. But he slipped off into the arms of his father, Herbert Sr., and his mother, Estella, who had hurried out of the special box for the Aaron family near the Braves' dugout.

"I never knew," Aaron would say later, "that my mother could hug so tight."

Moments later he was accepting a diamond wrist watch from the commissioner of baseball, Bowie Kuhn, but not from Kuhn himself. Rather than expose himself to the boos of the Atlanta populace, Kuhn had dispatched an ambassador, Monte Irvin, to the scene of the pre-game festivities in the event the 715th home run occurred. When it did, Irvin presented the watch and when he was introduced as being from the commissioner's office, the boos roared. In his jubilation, Aaron smiled.

"I was smiling from the boos," he would say later. That's all he would say because that's the way Henry Aaron is. Henry Aaron doesn't gloat. Quietly, he has resented Kuhn's attitude toward him, whether real or imagined. It began when Kuhn ignored his 700th home run last season and it simmered when Kuhn ordered Eddie Mathews to use him in the starting line-up in Cincinnati yesterday after the Braves manager had planned to preserve him for the Atlanta audience. Kuhn was correct in that ultimatum, because the Braves were defying the integrity of baseball.

But the commissioner was wrong tonight in not being here. He had stood up gallantly, but suddenly he had sat down again. Henry Aaron should have ordered the commissioner to be here.

"I thought the line-up card was taken out of Eddie Mathews's hand," the man with 715 home runs said. "I believe I should have been given the privilege of deciding for myself."

It's unfortunate that controversy somewhat clouded Henry Aaron's moment. It's also untypical. Of all our superstars, Henry Aaron has been perhaps the most uncontroversial. But time will blow those clouds away. Soon only his home runs will be important, not where he hit them, not where the commissioner was. His eventual total of home runs will be his monument, although they represent only a portion of his stature as a hitter.

With a normally productive season, in what he insists will be his last, Henry Aaron probably will hold six major league career records for home runs, runs batted in, total bases, extra base hits, games and times at bat. Ty Cobb will retain the records for hits, runs, batting average and stolen bases. Babe Ruth will hold the records for slugging average and walks. Through the years, Cobb and the Babe were the ultimate in hitting, but now they must move over.

"With a good year," Henry Aaron has said, "I'll hold six records, Cobb will hold four and Ruth two."

Perhaps that will convince the skeptics who minimize his accomplishments as a hitter. Some of the skeptics are traditionalists, some are racists. Statistically, their argument is that Henry Aaron needed 2,896 more times at bat than Babe Ruth in order to break the home run record. Those skeptics ignore Henry Aaron's durability and consistency, attributes as important as Babe Ruth's charisma. And when his 715th home run soared over the fence tonight, Henry Aaron never lost his dignity, his essence as a person.

"You don't know what a weight it was off my shoulders," he said later, "a tremendous weight."

Now the weight will be transferred to the hitter who someday challenges Henry Aaron, if that hitter appears.

## Another View

# FURMAN BISHER
*Atlanta Journal*

The flower of American sporting journalism was caught with its tongue tied. With its fingers arthritic. Its brain turned into a glob of quivering gelatine. Its nervous system drawn as tight as a banjo's strings.

It had rehearsed every move, memorized every line. Then took the stage to perform and every word stuck in its throat.

Henry Louis Aaron hit the 715th home run in the 2,967th game of his major league career, and nobody had anything left to say. I mean, there just aren't 715 ways to say that Henry Aaron hit a home run. Besides, they'd worn out all the others in a long winter's anticipation, and last week when he hit No. 714 in Cincinnati.

In fact, No. 715 was only a rerun of No. 693, also hit off Al Downing in Atlanta Stadium with a man on base. And it was nothing to compare with No. 400, which cleared everything in Philadelphia and came down somewhere near Trenton. Aaron's guest of honor that night was Bo Belinsky.

There is this to be said about it: It was the first home run he has ever hit after hearing Pearl Bailey sing the national anthem. It was also an occasion added to extensively, though witlessly, by the absence of Bowie Kuhn, riotously referred to as the Commissioner of Baseball.

It was a Louisville bat against a Spalding ball which hit a BankAmericard display sign over the left-field fence and was fielded by a left-handed pitcher named Tom House. Fifty-three thousand people saw it in person, but what they weren't going to appreciate so much was when they got home they learned that with their tickets their sellout had bought free television for the other million and a half Atlantans who stayed at home.

The Braves had thrown open the show for local consumption just before the field was turned into a riot of color, Americana, teary-eyed emotionalism, political swashbuckling and deafening fireworks.

Alphonso Erwin Downing has won a Babe Ruth World Series for Trenton, N.J., and pitched in a World Series for the New York Yankees. He has won 115 games, 20 in one season, and become known as a steady, reliable member of the Los Angeles Dodgers. But Monday night he carved his initials on America's memory. He has a new cross to bear, he won't be remembered for the 115 games, but for the inside fastball that Aaron hit over the fence.

At the same time, he assured several pitchers a place in posterity, a little hall of notoriety of their own. They all belong to the "We Served Henry Aaron a Home Run Club," senior member Vic Raschi, then on the shady side of a substantial career and serving it out as a St. Louis Cardinal.

The lineup of Aaron's victims is a procession of extremes, from Sandy Koufax, who was on his way to the Hall of Fame, to Joe Trimble, a Pittsburgh rookie who never won a game in the majors.

He hit No. 10 off Corky Valentine, who now may be seen around town as a cop. Then he was a Cincinnati Red.

He hit one off an infielder, Johnny O'Brien, one of a pair of famous college basketball twins who was trying to discover a new career with the Pirates. He hit one off a Congressman, the Honorable Wilmer Mizell (R-NC). Wilmer was then "Vinegar Bend," a bumpkin rookie with a bashful smile and the kind of "aw shucks" personality that made sports reporters look him up.

He hit another off Faul and off Law, and another off a Brewer, a Boozer, and a Barr. One off Rabe and one off Mabe. And off Hook and Nye.

He hit 'em off Morehead and Moorhead. And R. Miller and R. L. Miller, three different Jacksons, and Veale and Lamb.

With No. 715 he assured permanent attention for handservants merely passing that way. Otherwise Thornton Kipper, Herb Moford, John Andre, Rudy Minarcin, Tom Acker, Lino Dinoso, Art Caccarelli and the improbable Whammy Douglas would have passed on and been forgotten. They are now forever engraved on the marble of Aaron's record like the roll of the soldiers memorialized on a courthouse monument.

Naturally, one is supposed to feel that he has been witness to one of the monumental sports events of all history, if he were in the park. These things don't penetrate the perspective so soon. You're over-prepared. It's not like sitting there watching this flippant youth, Cassius Clay, knock a bear like Sonny Liston out of the world heavyweight title. Or Centre College whip Harvard.

There's no shock to get your attention. No. 715 was anticipated, awaited like childbirth. It's like buying a ticket to watch a bank get robbed, or a train wreck. Everybody's so thoroughly ready that nobody can appreciate the history of it all. Even the President sat in Washington with his dialing finger exercised for action.

"He invited me to the White House," Aaron said. It is suggested that he not loiter on the way.

"Magnavox gets the ball and the bat for five years, then they go to the Hall of Fame," he said. That covered several other loose ends.

I don't want to fuel another fire, but as I depart I feel compelled to leave you with another record in the line of fire: Aaron is well ahead of Ruth's pace the year he hit 60 home runs. The Babe didn't hit his second home run until the 11th game.

# VIN SCULLY
## on ABC Radio

So, the confrontation for the second time.

Aaron walked in the second inning. He means the tying run at the plate now, and we'll see what Downing does.

Al at the belt . . . delivers, and he's low . . . Ball one. (*Tremendous boos from the crowd.*) And that just adds to the pressure. The crowd booing. Downing has ignored the sound effects, and stayed a professional and pitched his game.

One ball and no strikes . . . Aaron waiting . . . The outfield deep and straight-away . . . Fastball . . .

There's a high drive into deep left-center field! . . . Buckner's back to the fence . . . and it is . . . gone!

(*Pandemonium . . . Two solid minutes of nothing but the crowd going nuts, and the explosion of fireworks.*)

What a marvelous moment for baseball . . . What a marvelous moment for Atlanta, and the state of Georgia . . . What a marvelous moment for the country and the *world* . . . A black man is getting a standing ovation in the Deep South for breaking a record of an all-time baseball idol . . . And it is a great moment for all of us, and particularly for Henry Aaron . . .

He is met at home plate, not only by every member of the Braves, but by his father and mother. He threw his arms around his father, and as he left the home plate area, his mother came running across the grass, threw her arms around his neck, kissed him for all she was worth.

As Aaron circled the bases, the Dodgers on the infield shook his hand, and *that* was a memorable moment.

Aaron is being mobbed by photographers, he is holding his right hand high in the air, and for the first time in a long time, that poker face of Aaron shows the tremendous strain and relief of what it must have been like to live with this for the past several months.

It is over.

# At 12:34 A.M.

---

## CARLTON FISK'S GAME SIX HOME RUN

October 21, 1975

**Even though I grew** up in New England, I was never a big Red Sox fan. I was, however, surrounded by those poor souls who wander through the summer, believing against all evidence that their team is finally going to win it all; and who, when the chill days and crisp nights of fall come around, seem to get that deer-in-the-headlights look in their eyes.

These are the folks you'll find shuffling along through November drizzle in Falmouth, and Portsmouth, and Hartford, muttering to themselves. You can often get close enough to them to hear what they're saying—they're usually pretty harmless at this time of year, as if they've been stunned, or are readying for hibernation—and if you take the time to decipher their eerie, whispered incantations, you'll eventually make out what they're softly and incessantly telling themselves: "Next year. Next year. Next year."

Well, in 1975, it seemed to a lot of Boston fans that next year had finally arrived. The Red Sox had an explosive, exciting team, led by three tremendous outfielders (Yastrzemski, the perpetually-crashing-into-walls Fred Lynn, and Dwight Evans); a pitching staff anchored by the ageless Luis Tiant and kept loose by Bill "Spaceman" Lee; and a cast of dozens of other weird and wonderful characters, including Bernie Carbo, Rico Petrocelli, and their solid-as-a-rock catcher, Carlton Fisk.

Of course, the Red Sox had to face somebody else in the Series—them's the rules, after all—and the team they had to face happened to be one of the strongest of all-time. Pete Rose, Joe Morgan, Johnny Bench, Tony Perez, Ken Griffey, Cesar Geronimo, Rawley Eastwick, and the rest of the Big Red Machine combined power and speed and some pretty good pitching to a degree rarely seen before. Like the Yankees of the '20s, they seemed to have no weaknesses.

So, we come to Game 6. Nowadays, folks seldom even bother mentioning the year. If you're talking to somebody about Game 6, it's just understood that you're talking about 1975. It's generally regarded as the greatest World Series game ever played, and its hero, with one swing, joined a handful of other players—Bobby Thomson, Mazeroski, Kirk Gibson—whose home runs pushed fans into paroxysms that, recalled years later, can still send a chill down the spine.

But how many heroes can a game have? There was Fred Lynn, hitting a monster three-run homer, and then almost breaking his back against the center field wall later in the game—and staying in the game, anyway; there was Dwight Evans, saving the game with his glove; there, of course, was Bernie Carbo, who took one of the pitches of Eastwick into the center field seats in the bottom of the eighth to tie up the game and ratchet up the tension just a wee bit tighter.

But, ultimately, there was Fisk, in the bottom of the twelfth, and his crazy, leaping, arm-waving hop down the first-base line as the ball caromed off the foul pole, and those strange, endearing creatures known as Red Sox fans had a reprieve of one more night before their long winter of slumber, and dreaming of next year, began again.

# PETER GAMMONS
*Boston Globe*

And all of a sudden the ball was there, like the Mystic River Bridge, suspended out in the black of the morning.

When it finally crashed off the mesh attached to the left field foul pole, one step after another the reaction unfurled: from Carlton Fisk's convulsive leap to John Kiley's booming of the "Hallelujah Chorus" to the wearing off of the numbness to the outcry that echoed across the cold New England morning.

At 12:34 A.M., in the 12th inning, Fisk's histrionic home run brought a 7–6 end to a game that will be the pride of historians in the year 2525, a game won and lost what seemed like a dozen times, and a game that brings back summertime for one more day. For the seventh game of the World Series.

For this game to end so swiftly, so definitely, was the way it had to end. An inning before, a Dwight Evans catch that Sparky Anderson claimed was as great as he's ever seen had been one turn, but in the ninth a George Foster throw ruined a bases-loaded, none-out certain victory for the Red Sox.

Which followed a dramatic three-run homer in the eighth by Bernie Carbo as the obituaries had been prepared, which followed the downfall of Luis Tiant after El Tiante had begun, with the help of Fred Lynn's three-run, first-inning homer, as a hero of unmatched emotional intensity.

So Fisk had put the exclamation mark at the end of what he called "the most emotional game I've ever played in." The home run came off Pat Darcy and made a winner of Rick Wise, who had become the record 12th pitcher in this 241-minute war that seemed like four score and seven years.

But the place one must begin is the bottom of the eighth, Cincinnati leading, 6–3, and the end so clear. El Tiante had left in the top of the inning to what apparently was to be the last of his 1975 ovations; he who had become the conquering king had been found to be just a man, and it seemed so certain. Autumn had been postponed for the last time.

Only out came an Implausible Hero, to a two-out, two-on situation against Rawlins J. Eastwick III, and Carbo did what he had done in Cincinnati. Pinch-hitting, he sent a line drive into the center field bleachers, and the chill of lachrymose had become mad, sensuous Fenway again. Followed by the point and counterpoint.

In the ninth, a Denny Doyle walk and Carl Yastrzemski single had put runners at first and third, which sent Eastwick away and brought in left-hander Will McEnany. Who walked Fisk to load the bases and pitch to Lynn.

Lynn got the ball to the outfield, but only a high, twisting fly ball down the left field line that George Foster grabbed at the line and maybe 80 feet in back of third base. Third base coach Don Zimmer said he told Doyle not to go, but he went anyway, and Foster's throw got to Johnny Bench in time for the double play. As the Red Sox shook their heads mumbling, "bases loaded, nobody out in the ninth," the Reds had their hero in Foster, who put them ahead in the seventh with a two-run double.

Then in the 11th, the Reds had it taken away from them by Evans. With Ken Griffey at first, one out, Joe Morgan crashed a line drive towards the seats in right. Evans made his racing, web-of-the-glove, staggering catch as he crossed the warning track ("It would have been two rows in"—Reds bullpen catcher Bill Plummer), then as Griffey in disbelief stopped halfway between second and third, Evans spun and fired in to Yastrzemski, who had moved to first for Carbo's entrance to left, retrieved it to the right of the coaches' box, looked up and guess who was standing on first base, waiting for the ball? Rick Burelson. Who had raced over from shortstop. So Dick Drago, who worked three scoreless innings, the Red Sox and a seventh game all had been saved.

When it was over, it was almost incomprehensible that it had begun with Tiant trying to crank out one more miracle. But it had, and for four innings, the

Carlton Fisk connects . . .

evening was all his. They had merchandised "El Tiante" t-shirts on the streets, they hung a banner that read "Loo—Eee for President," and everything the man did, from taking batting practice to walking to the bullpen to warm up to the rhumbas and tangos that screwed the Reds into the ground for four innings, brought standing ovations and the carol, "Loo—Eee, Loo—Eee . . ."

El Tiante had had a 3–0 lead from the first inning, when Lynn had followed Yastrzemski and Fisk singles by driving a Gary Nolan kumquat into the bleachers over the pitching mound of the Boston bullpen. Nolan did not last long.

And the abracadabra that had blinded the Reds before began to smudge. In the fifth, after Boston had lost two scoring opportunities, Luis walked Designated Bunter Ed Armbrister, and before he could hear his father incant Grande Olde Game No. 56 ("Walks . . ."), Pete Rose singled and Ken Griffey became the first player in three games here to hit The Wall. Not only was it the first time anyone had scored off Tiant in 10 innings, but as the ball caromed away to be retrieved by Evans, the park went silent. In his running, leaping try for the ball at the 379-foot mark, Lynn had crashed into the wall and slid down to the ground, his back hurt.

Lynn eventually was able to stay in the game, but by the time the inning was over Bench had become the second to tickle The Wall, with a single, and it was 3–3. Then when Foster sent his drive off the center field fence in the seventh, it was 5–3, and when Tiant was left in to start the eighth, and Cesar Geronimo angled a leadoff homer inside the right field foul pole, El Tiante left to his chant and his ovations. And in the press box, *Sport Magazine* editor Dick Schapp began collecting the ballots that determined which Red got the World Series hero's automobile.

So, if the honey and lemon works on the throat and the Alka-Seltzer does the same for the heads, Fenway will not be alone tonight. She has one drama, and it is perhaps sport's classic drama.

Bill Lee and Don Gullett, the Cincinnati Reds and the Boston Red Sox, and a long night's journey into morning, a game suspended in time as Fisk's home run was suspended beyond the skyline, a game that perhaps required the four-day buildup it got.

Summertime has been called back for just one more day—for the seventh game of the World Series.

. . . and exults

## Another View

# RAY FITZGERALD
*Boston Globe*

Call it off. Call the seventh game off. Let the World Series stand this way, three games for the Cincinnati Reds and three for the Boston Red Sox.

How can there be a topper for what went on last night and early this morning in a ballyard gone mad, madder and maddest while watching, well, the most exciting game of baseball I've ever seen.

But maybe my opinion doesn't count. I've only seen a thousand or so baseball games. Reds manager Sparky Anderson has been to a billion and he said when it was over, "I've never seen a better one."

It was a game with a hundred climaxes. Fred Lynn hit a three-run homer and the Red Sox were cruising. Easy stuff, take Luis Tiant out suggested the sages, and save him for the seventh game.

But then opportunities went sliding down the river—bases left loaded, two men on and no out and no production, things like that, and you could feel it slipping away, into the batbag of the Big Red Machine.

And then the magic began to disappear from Luis Tiant's wand, that seemingly tireless right arm that had been snaking the baseball past the Reds for so many innings.

Snap, crackle and pop, and there were the Reds ahead, 5–3, and King Tut's tomb couldn't have been any more silent than Fenway Park as Tiant started the eighth.

Why he was allowed to start the inning was a mystery, because it was obvious that he had tired badly in the seventh. Maybe Darrell Johnson wanted him to get a final Fenway ovation.

If so, it cost the Red Sox, because Cesar Geronimo hit Tiant's first pitch into the right field stands to make it 6–3.

And in the skyview seats, the sporting bards of America began typing the obituaries, like this:

"Death, as it must to all teams, came to the Boston Red Sox last night at 11:16 P.M. when Rawley Eastwick the 3d . . ."

Or,

"The powerful Cincinnati Reds, stretched to the limit by the tenacious Boston Red Sox, captured their first World Series championship since . . ."

Or,

"Time ran out for the marvelous Luis Tiant tonight as . . ."

Ah, yes, there were deadlines to make, so why not get the story started, because Bernie Carbo was at the plate and barely able to get his bat on Eastwick's pitches.

With the count two and two, Carbo was about to let a pitch go past when suddenly he saw it dipping into the strike zone. Carbo chopped at it like a man cutting sugar cane, barely fouling it off. The patient was still breathing. But the 35,205 relatives were gathered at the bedside and saw no hope. It was all over, as the saying goes, but the shouting.

Ah, yes, the shouting. The screaming, the dancing, the ab-so-lute bedlam as Carbo hit the next pitch into the center field seats for the game-tying home run.

I sat in on the Bill Mazeroski home run that won the 1960 World Series for the Pirates, and that has always been, for me, No. 1 among great baseball games played under great pressure. Excitement pyramided in that one to where you didn't think there could possibly be any more.

Now, the Mazeroski game is No. 2. Last night was a Picasso of a baseball game, a Beethoven symphony played on a patch of grass in Boston's Back Bay.

Here's the kind of game it was. *The Globe*'s Bud Collins was assigned to do a piece on the game's hero. At the end of the 11th inning, he said, "I've already crossed off 19 heroes. Maybe they should play a tie-breaker, like tennis."

And listen to Pete Rose, who said to Carlton Fisk in the 10th, "This is some kind of game, isn't it?", and later in the dressing room, "This was the greatest game in World Series history and I'm just proud to have played in it. If this ain't the National Pastime, tell me what is."

Rose videotapes each game so he can sit back and watch them later. He was a loser in this one, but he is the sort of competitor who can admire such things as Dwight Evans's catch off Joe Morgan in the 11th that saved the game.

Sparky Anderson called the catch "the greatest I've ever seen. You won't see them any better."

The drama piled up like cordwood. Lynn's titanic homer, the Reds come-back, Lynn slumped against the fence after crashing into it trying for Ken Griffey's triple, the Carbo homer, the Reds escaping a bases-loaded none-out situation in the ninth, the Evans catch, and finally, Fisk's game-winning homer.

As Fisk came around the bases, fans poured out onto the field and he had to dodge them on his way home.

"I straight-armed somebody and kicked 'em out of the way and touched every little white thing I saw."

At 12:34 it was over, but the people stayed. John Kiley played "Give me Some Men Who Are Stout-Hearted Men" and the fans sang along. He played the Beer Barrel Polka and Seventy-Six Trombones and they sang some more.

Next to me, Peter Gammons began to write.

"What was the final score?" he asked. In such a game numbers didn't seem to mean much.

# NED MARTIN and CURT GOWDY
## on NBC Radio

Gowdy: . . . We're going to the last of the twelfth inning . . . Carlton Fisk, Fred Lynn and Rico Petrocelli for the Red Sox against Pat Darcy . . . They've had twelve pitchers in the game, a new record . . . It's all tied, 6-all, and here's Ned again . . .

Martin: Okay, Curt . . . Now, it's Fisk up, and he hasn't had a hit since the first inning . . . He singled then . . . He has been intentionally passed twice . . . He is one-for-three officially . . .

Game tied, 6–6 . . . Darcy pitching . . . Fisk takes high and inside, ball one . . . Freddy Lynn, on deck . . .

There've been numerous heroics tonight, both sides . . . The 1–0 delivery to Fisk . . .

He swings . . . Long drive, left field! . . . If it stays fair it's gone! . . . Home run! . . . The Red Sox win! . . . And the Series is tied, three games apiece! . . .

G: Carlton Fisk hit a one-nothing pitch . . . they're jamming out on the field . . . His teammates are waiting for him . . . The ball hit the foul pole, and the Red Sox have sent the World Series into Game 7, with a dramatic 7–6 victory . . .

They had a chance to win it in the ninth, with the bases loaded, nobody out . . .

They were trailing by three runs when Bernie Carbo came up in the eighth inning and hit a pinch-hit, three-run homer . . .

What a game! . . .

# Shakespeare, Plastered

## REGGIE JACKSON: THREE SWINGS, THREE HOME RUNS, ONE GAME

### October 18, 1977

**Bill Lee, the pot-smoking,** philosophizing, rock-and-rolling pitcher for the Red Sox during the mid-seventies, was a great one for quotes. He once said that Cincinnati's Big Red Machine "is about the third-best team in fundamentals I've ever seen—behind the Taiwan Little Leaguers and the USC NCAA champions of 1968," and memorably described the Oakland A's championship teams of the early '70s as "emotionally mediocre. They remind me of [ex-con pinch-hitter for the Tigers] Gates Brown lying on a rug."

But perhaps Lee's finest line came when he described the Yankees of the mid- and late 1970s as "a bunch of hookers swinging their purses." It's perhaps a bit difficult now, in an age when fair-to-middling infielders routinely make a million bucks a year, to recall what it was like when that colossal clown, George Steinbrenner, began shelling out big money for a championship team. The Yankees seemed to be a team not only of hookers swinging their purses, but of prima donna hookers swinging fancy, expensive purses in the white-hot media glare of New York City.

The greed-is-good Reagan years were just around the corner, when pimply MBAs would be pulling down salaries that made ballplayers' look downright honorable by comparison; but at the time, such huge sums paid to athletes seemed to just about everyone as . . . well, as kind of obscene.

Reggie Jackson, of course, was *the* prima donna on the team, the richest, flashiest player on the richest, flashiest team in baseball. When, on the night of October 18, 1977, he hit one, then another, and then a third home run with three swings of his bat—in a row, in the World Series, in New York City—the title "Mr. October" no longer seemed a cheap, gaudy label plastered on

Jackson's pinstripes: it seemed instead a mantle that fit the man as if he were nobility.

Which, of course, on that night, he was.

The two articles below help capture the various features of the man—his pride, even his arrogance, but also his tremendous confidence and his eloquent, disarming candor—but most of all they capture the imponderable thrill of his performance.

In the end, both writers also succeed in bringing to life the one aspect of the game that, to this day, remains perhaps the most extraordinary element of Jackson's achievement: namely, that he made it seem inevitable. Yes, it was freakish, and unprecedented, and almost beyond belief. "Lurid," Red Smith called it, and it was that, too; not only in the sense of being shocking, and sensational, but lurid to the point where everyone seemed a bit stunned by the man's talent, his timing, and his gall. The unspoken words on everyone's lips seemed to be, How *could* he?

I remember watching the game as a sixteen-year-old Yankee-hater, being drawn unwillingly into the almost palpable mood of assuredness that he was, in fact, going to do it. He was going to knock another one, a third one, out of the park, and there was nothing anyone could do about it.

And then there he was, in his last at-bat, stepping into the batter's box, and almost before you could catch your breath, he ripped the first pitch he saw and there was absolutely no doubt that it was gone.

How *could* he?

# JIM MURRAY
*Los Angeles Times*

Excuse me while I wipe up the bloodstains and carry off the wounded. The Dodgers forgot to circle the wagons.

Listen! You don't go into the woods with a bear. You don't go into a fog with Jack the Ripper. You don't get in a car with Al Capone. You don't get on a ship with Morgan the Pirate. You don't go into shark waters with a nosebleed. You don't wander into Little Big Horn with General Custer.

And you don't come into Yankee Stadium needing a win to stay alive in a World Series. Not unless you have a note pinned to you, telling them where to send the remains. If any.

They told us these weren't the *real* Yankees. I mean, not like the genuine article of years gone past, the Murderers' Row Yankees, the Bronx Bombers. These were just a bunch of pussycats dressed up in gorilla costumes. These were the Yankees who had "take" signs in the playbook. These were the Yankees who talked of "beating you with the glove." These were "hit-and-run Yankees," not the old kind who just stood there and hit balls into the stratosphere and played "hit and walk" baseball.

That's what they told us. That's what the scouting report said.

They said these Yankees weren't even speaking to each other. You wondered why they dared show up.

Years ago, old-timers remembered, on the 1927 Yankees the right fielder in World Series used to stand there and hit back-to-back home runs out of the park. Why, he hit three in one game in World Series *twice!*

Well, the 1977 Yankees' right fielder has just hit home runs on his last four consecutive official at-bats. And he became only the second player in history to hit three home runs in a game.

You have the feeling the Dodger pitchers are longing to see Babe Ruth stand in there. He might be a welcome relief.

"If I played in New York, they'd name a candy bar after me," boasted Reggie Jackson before the season started. They may name an entire chocolate factory after him now.

Once again these were the Yanks who had your back to the wall when you were ahead only 2–0. Once again, they were head hunters. If they were fighters they'd never go to the body. Once again, they're a bunch of guys who go for the railroad yards in bombing runs or shell Paris with railroad guns.

These are the Yankees who let you store up runs like a squirrel putting nuts in his cheek. When you get them all neatly piled up, the Yankees come along and pile up more with two swings of the bat.

Reggie Jackson hits one . . .

These Yanks are store-bought. They're not home-made like a proper ball club should be, stitched at home with tender loving care. George Steinbrenner just went out and ordered them like a new car. Expense was no object. It didn't matter. With George, it was either a question of buying a ball club—or buying Rhode Island.

There's an old familiar smell in the Yankee locker room—fermenting grapes. The wine of victory spreads across the floor, the waterfall of success. Where Ruth or Gehrig once dribbled champagne across their chins, Reggie Jackson does now.

The reporters are 10-deep around Jackson's locker in this, the House That Ruth Built. It is Jackson's Yankees now. "Mr. October." The most dangerous World Series hitter since Ruth used to call his shots.

No one has ever seen more devastating home runs than Reggie Jackson ripped out of Yankee Stadium Tuesday night. Two were on so-so fastballs but the third was a knuckler down and away. "He hit a helluva pitch," Da Manager Tom Lasorda confessed later, still in some shock.

The pitchers' union is not ready to strike its colors. The pitcher who threw it, Charlie Hough, recalls it as a knuckler that didn't knuckle.

One of the homers was a line drive that would have crossed state lines and gone through the side of a battleship on its way to the seats. The other two were booming Jack Nicklaus–type tee shots, high and far, the kind that pitchers wake up screaming in the middle of the night over.

Reggie was, for him, composed as the forest of microphones was thrust under his chin and the photographers called for one more shot of a tilted champagne bottle.

How often had Ruth struck this pose for the midnight tabloids? Mantle?

The home run is to the Yankees what the Raphaels are to the Vatican and the pyramids to the Pharoahs—symbols of glory and tradition.

How many National League teams have been bludgeoned in this hallowed stadium by mighty multiple home runs?

You see a Dizzy Dean struggling manfully to hold down the floodgates of homers in 1938, a Wee Willie Sherdel, a Carl Hubbell, a Charlie Root in 1932. And now a Hooton, Sosa and Hough.

The star-of-the-day, the new Sultan of Swat in Yankee Stadium, was managing to sound more like a one-man HEW bureau. "What am I going to do?" Reggie Jackson answered slowly. "First I'm going to go out and have a few drinks and put some of this money back in circulation. Then I'm going to share my World Series money with the city of New York which did so much for me, go to Phoenix where I live and to Oakland where I come from." What did he feel on becoming the first man to hit four home runs in a row in a World Series?

"Jubilation, relief, pride, and some justification," added Reggie.

This was a team that was supposed to self-destruct before your very eyes about the seventh inning of every game. They weren't supposed to be real Yankees that they made movies about.

From what anyone could see in the wreckage of the Dodger planes, the only difference between the 1927 Yankees and the 1977 Yankees is a few million dollars in salaries.

The 1927 Yankees is the yardstick against which baseball historians measure all subsequent teams. Old-timers' eyes mist over when they say, "You should have seen that bunch!"

Today's bubblegum collectors can take the offensive, too. "Baby, you should have seen the 1977 Yankees, the Jackson Yankees. Four at-bats in a row, Reggie hit home runs—on *four swings*. Reggie hit the first pitch on all four of them. Match *that* around the Ruth Yankees."

Reggie gets unlimited champagne, a new Thunderbird and a page all his own in the record books and a free trip to Cooperstown. But the Yankees get a new mythology. This stadium will be the House That Reggie Built. He goes to join Ruth's called shot, Mantle's tape measures. It's his Series. It will be remembered as The-Year-That-Reggie-Jackson—the year that Reggie Jackson hit five home runs, the last four his last four times up. No one will remember anything else about it 20 years from now. The 1977 World Series is Reggie Jackson's fee simple. Everything that went on before he stepped to center stage was prologue. It was an opera that all led to the appearance of the star. When the scene was set and the overture over, Reggie gave 'em goose bumps.

It was one of sports' great moments, the kind of thing that will make 500,000 people who weren't say, "I was there." The homers will get longer, higher, farther in the re-telling. But nobody has to embellish the frequency.

. . . two . . .

We're not likely to see their like again.

But then, they said that about Ruth, too, didn't they?

---

## Another View

### RED SMITH
*New York Times*

It had to happen this way. It had been predestined since Nov. 29, 1976, when Reginald Martinez Jackson sat down on a gilded chair in New York's Americana Hotel and wrote his name on a Yankee contract. That day he became an instant millionaire, the big honcho on the best team money could buy, the richest, least inhibited, most glamorous exhibit in Billy Martin's pin-striped zoo. That day the plot was written for last night—the bizarre scenario Reggie Jackson played out by hitting three home runs, clubbing the Los Angeles Dodgers into submission and carrying his supporting players with him to the baseball championship of North America. His was the most lurid performance in 74 World Series, for although Babe Ruth hit three home runs in a game in 1926 and again in 1928, not even that demigod smashed three in a row.

Reggie first broke a tie and put the Yankees in front, 4–3. His second fattened the advantage to 7–3. His third completed arrangements for a final score of 8–4, wrapping up the championship in six games.

Yet that was merely the final act of an implausible one-man show. Jackson had made a home run last Saturday in Los Angeles and another on his last time at bat in that earthly paradise on Sunday. On his first appearance at the plate last night he walked, getting no official time at bat, so in his last four official turns he hit four home runs.

In his last nine times at bat, this Hamlet in double-knits scored seven runs, made six hits and five home runs and batted in six runs for a batting average of .667 compiled by day and by night on two seacoasts 3,000 miles and three time zones apart. Shakespeare wouldn't attempt a curtain call like that if he was plastered.

This was a drama that consumed seven months, for ever since the Yankees went to training camp last March, Jackson had lived in the eye of a hurricane. All summer long the spike-shod capitalists bickered and quarreled, contending with their manager, defying their owner, Reggie the most controversial, the most articulate, the most flamboyant.

Part philosopher, part preacher and part outfielder, he carried this rancorous company with his bat in the season's last fifty games, leading them to the East championship in the American League and into the World Series. He knocked in the winning run in the 12-inning first game, drove in a run and scored two in the third, furnished the winning margin in the fourth and delivered the final run in the fifth.

Thus the stage was set when he went to the plate in last night's second inning with the Dodgers leading, 2–0. Sedately, he led off with a walk. Serenely, he circled the bases on a home run by Chris Chambliss. The score was tied.

Los Angeles had moved out front, 3–2, when the man reappeared in the fourth inning with Thurman Munson on base. He hit the first pitch on a line into the seats beyond right field. Circling the bases for the second time, he went into his home-run glide—head high, chest out. The Yankees led, 4–3. In the dugout, Yankees fell upon him. Billy Martin, the manager, who tried to slug him last June, patted his cheek lovingly. The dugout phone rang and Reggie accepted the call graciously.

His first home run knocked the Dodgers' starting pitcher, Burt Hooton, out of the game. His second disposed of Elias Sosa, Hooton's successor. Before Sosa's first pitch in the fifth inning, Reggie had strolled the length of the dugout to pluck a bat from the rack, even though three men would precede him to the plate. He was confident he would get his turn. When he did, there was a runner on base again, and again he hit the first pitch. Again it reached the seats in right.

When the last jubilant teammate had been peeled off his neck, Reggie took a seat near the first-base end of the bench. The crowd was still bawling for him and comrades urged him to take a curtain call but he replied with a gesture that said, "Aw, fellows, cut it out!" He did unbend enough to hold up two fingers for photographers in a V-for-victory sign.

. . . three home runs.

Jackson was the lead-off batter in the eighth. By that time, Martin would have replaced him in an ordinary game, sending Paul Blair to right field to help protect the Yankees' lead. But did they ever bench Edwin Booth in the last act?

For the third time Reggie hit the first pitch, but this one didn't take the shortest distance between two points. Straight out from the plate the ball streaked, not toward the neighborly stands in right but on a soaring arc toward the unoccupied bleachers in dead center, where the seats are blacked out to give the batters a background. Up the white speck climbed, dwindling, diminishing, until it settled at least halfway up those empty stands, probably 450 feet away.

This time he could not disappoint his public. He stepped out of the dugout and faced the multitude, two fists and one cap uplifted. Not only the customers applauded.

"I must admit," said Steve Garvey, the Dodgers' first baseman, "when Reggie Jackson hit his third home run and I was sure nobody was listening, I applauded into my glove."

# Work to Do

---

## TOM SEAVER'S 300th WIN

August 4, 1985

**One of the most popular** sports figures in New York for a solid decade, Tom Seaver was finally driven out of the city in 1977 by an inflexible Mets management (especially the Chairman of the Board, Donald M. Grant) and a number of scathing articles by *New York Daily News* columnist Dick Young. Young went so far as to suggest that the reason Seaver was holding out for more money and a contract extension with the Mets (Can you imagine such insolence on the part of a mere future Hall of Famer?) had more to do with Seaver's wife's jealousy of Nolan Ryan's hefty contract, than with any real value Seaver might have for the Mets.

Disgusted with the Mets and their mouthpiece at the *News*, Seaver demanded to be traded; a few hours hours before the trading deadline, he was shipped off to the Reds in exchange for a pitcher, an infielder, and two outfielders. The Reds, of course, got the better of the deal.

A few years later, Seaver was again back with the Mets, but they did nothing to try and keep him in New York, so he moved along to the Chicago White Sox. Aside from the fact that Seaver and the rest of the Sox had to wear the alarming uniforms that Chicago foisted upon the world in the mid-'80s (sort of *2001: A Space Odyssey* meets the bargain hamper at Pajama World), Seaver continued to have success, and, in early August of 1985, was poised to win his 300th game.

Of course, a bunch of other pitchers have won 300 games in their careers, and certainly some of them were more gifted—but none ever worked harder to squeeze every ounce of effort and skill from the talent at hand. Some of those in the 300 Club were more consistently exciting than Seaver—but few were able to accomplish all that Seaver did over the course of his career, including

Tom Seaver and Carlton Fisk
celebrate Seaver's 300th

the 300 wins, more than 3,500 strikeouts, a no-hitter, and of course, a World Series ring.

Finally, few players have ever inspired the affection that Seaver shared with the fans in New York. As Ira Berkow recounted in his *New York Times* story on the August 4th game: "Most of the fans cheered, but there was a smattering of boos. 'I can't believe all the Mets fans out there screaming for Chicago,' said a Yankee fan in the stands.'"

"He would have been closer to the fact if he had said 'baseball fans.'"

Listening to a recording of Seaver's 300th win, it's amazing, and enormously moving, to hear the vast majority of the 54,000 fans in Yankee Stadium that day not necessarily cheering *against* the Yankees, and not even cheering for the White Sox—but definitely cheering for Seaver.

When the White Sox score four runs in the sixth, it sounds like the place is going to crumble to the ground. When Seaver finally wins the game, with the crowd cheering every strike and every out in the ninth, it seems like everyone in the entire stadium is standing and yelling and stomping. Not too many players, playing for an opposing team years after leaving town, could bring that out in a bunch of hometown fans.

Seaver was one man who could.

## JOHN FEINSTEIN
*Washington Post*

He had waited almost 19 years for this moment. In the back of his mind, it had always been one of *the* goals in his life and now Tom Seaver was one out away. One more out and he would have 300 victories in the major leagues.

All afternoon, Seaver had been fighting his emotions. He would say later he was so emotional he couldn't even feel the baseball coming off his hand for most of the day. Now, he stood on the Yankee Stadium mound, believing that he was having trouble keeping his feet on the ground.

"I felt like I was levitating out there," he said moments after he had become the 17th major league pitcher to win 300 games with a 4–1 victory over the New York Yankees. "I was so nervous today I felt like I was pitching my first major league game all over again. I had a headache, my stomach hurt, it was awful."

Harold Baines had just made a circus catch on Willie Randolph's line drive toward the right-field wall and Seaver's Chicago White Sox needed just one out. Third base umpire Terry Cooney walked past Seaver and said softly, "Congratulations, Tom, you deserve this."

Seaver was touched, but pragmatic. "Don't congratulate me until I get one more out," he said.

In the dugout, all the White Sox were on the top step. "It was so intense it was like a World Series," said second baseman Bryan Little. "I could hardly breathe."

Next to the dugout, Seaver's wife Nancy, his two daughters and his 74-year-old father leaned over the railing. They were almost alone among the 54,032 in the old stadium in that they were sitting. Most were on their feet, yelling for Seaver.

The batter was Mike Pagliarulo. Don Pasqua was on first base. Seaver, who had already thrown 141 pitches, threw four straight balls for his first walk of the game. Catcher Carlton Fisk walked to the mound to, as Seaver put it, "Give me a kick in the butt."

Fisk told Seaver he was pushing the ball and said simply, "You've waited a long time for this."

Seaver nodded and stared in at Don Baylor, pinch-hitting for Bobby Meacham. He was the potential tying run. One inning earlier, in the same situation, Seaver had struck Dave Winfield out on a 3–2 changeup that was low and away.

On another day, in another situation, Seaver might have come out. He is 40, can't throw as hard or as long as he used to and the White Sox have a lot of confidence in Bob James coming out of the bullpen. But Seaver wasn't coming out today.

The day started with ceremonies honoring former Yankee Phil Rizzuto, whose uniform No. 10 was retired before the game.

It was 6:11 P.M. when Seaver went into his compact motion one more time, rocked and threw pitch No. 146, a fastball in on Baylor's hands. Bailing out, Baylor swung under the ball and sent it very high toward left fielder Reid Nichols.

"When he hit it, I thought it was an out," Seaver said. "After 19 years, you sort of know the arch of a home run. After all, I've given up enough of them that I should know what it looks like."

As the ball floated toward Nichols, Seaver stood just off the mound, watching, waiting. Nichols cradled the ball in his glove and Seaver leaned forward, hands on his knees for a moment, and felt himself almost carried away with joy.

"It's been an awfully long time since I've been that happy after a ball game," he said. "This is truly a day I'll always remember."

So will his teammates. They pounded Seaver, shook him and hugged him. As Seaver walked toward the dugout, he saw his family. When he hugged his wife and saw she was crying, he felt a surge of tears himself.

"I think seeing those tears coming out of her eyes may have been the best moment for me," he said later, his voice choking at the memory. "I'm glad all my family was here to see it. This is a terrific feeling."

Actually, Terrific, as in Tom Terrific, the nickname hung on Seaver when he first arrived here as a New York Met in 1967. It was on April 19th of that year, on a cold, blustery afternoon with 5,379 at Shea Stadium, that Seaver got his first victory, 6–1, over the Chicago Cubs.

In the days since, Seaver had won three Cy Young Awards, pitched the once-pitiful Mets to two pennants and a World Series title, pitched a no-hitter, struck out nearly 3,500 batters and assured himself a spot in the Hall of fame. He had talked about 300 as something he wanted but kept insisting it wasn't all *that* important.

Today, he found out it was a lie. Nervous? "Almost sick," he said.

But, as he has been so many times in the past, Seaver was equal to the moment. He trailed briefly when the Yankees got a run in the third and might have been frustrated by his teammates' horrendous baserunning that stopped several early rallies.

"We did run into some outs early," Seaver said. "But I felt like if I could just keep it close that eventually we were going to score some runs."

He was right. In the sixth, the White Sox scored four runs. Greg Walker walked and was forced by Fisk, who barely beat the relay, a crucial play as it turned out. Oscar Gamble singled and Yankees manager Billy Martin replaced starter Joe Cowley with Brian Fisher.

It was a mistake. Tim Hulett doubled in a run, Ozzie Guillen singled another home and, after Rudy Law walked, Little singled in two more.

Now, it was up to Seaver. He breezed through the sixth and seventh and took a three-hitter into the eighth. But in the eighth, Meacham led off with a single. Seaver struck out Rickey Henderson (zero for four) looking and got Griffey to ground out but gave up a rocket-shot single to Mattingly. Two out, two on, and up came Winfield, whose 16th homer Friday tied a game with two out in the ninth.

He worked to 3–2. Fisk signaled for another fastball. Seaver shook him off. He wanted to throw the change-up. He did. It floated away from Winfield's lunging bat. Strike three.

Exultant and exhausted, Seaver said to nine-year-old daughter Anne, "Three more outs to go, Annie."

"Good, daddy," she answered. "Then can we go swimming?"

But first there was the ninth. After Pasqua's leadoff single, Seaver retired Ron Hassey for his 3,499th career strikeout, got Randolph on Baines's fine catch and finally reached The Moment.

"But you can't really think about moments then," he said. "You still have work to do."

"I seriously doubt if there's ever been a pitcher in baseball who's worked harder or prepared himself better to pitch than Tom," Fisk said. "He just goes out there all the time and competes."

Seaver has always approached baseball analytically and he talked this evening about staying ready and going after No. 301 on Friday. But as he blinked the champagne out of his eyes, Seaver was clearly ecstatic. "You know," he said, holding up a glass to toast his teammates, "we ought to do this more often than once every 19 years."

# FRANK MESSER
## on the Radio

Willie Randolph the batter . . . Randolph has grounded to short, been hit with a pitch, and flied to left . . . Pasqua leads away at first, Walker stays behind him . . . Infield shifts to the left side for Randolph . . . The outfield straight up . . .

Fly ball, hit deep to right field! . . . On the move, Baines . . . Baines . . . He jumps, makes the catch! . . . Baines makes the catch! . . . As he hit the wall, he held onto it! . . . He is shaken up, but he held on to the ball! . . . Baines hitting the boards, and caught it with a leaping grab at the wall in right . . . He's okay . . .

(*Pagliarulo walks*)

. . . Don Baylor will bat for Meacham . . . And pitching coach Dave Duncan trots out to the mound . . . (*Raucous, sustained boos from the crowd*) . . . Duncan out talking to Seaver . . . Fisk is out there . . . So is the shortstop Guillen . . . Second baseman Scott Fletcher wanders in . . . He'll have to stand off to the side, he can not join the meeting on the mound . . .

Seaver stays in the ballgame . . . (*Raucous, sustained cheers from the crowd*) . . .

Don Baylor will bat for Bobbie Meacham . . . Baylor is hitting .240 . . . A team-leading 18 home runs . . . 67 runs batted in . . . So it boils down to one of the top hitters of the past years, and certainly one of the top pitchers . . .

Seaver against Baylor, with two outs and two on . . . Baylor the tying run at home plate . . . Seaver sets, checks Pasqua and pitches . . .

Baylor swings, sends a fly ball into shallow right! . . . Now it's deeper, back goes the . . . left-fielder, rather, into left . . . It's caught! And Seaver has won his 300th game! . . . Tom Seaver slapping his hands together . . . He jumps into the arms of Carlton Fisk . . . Accepting high fives, handshakes all around . . . Baylor's fly ball to left field caught by Reid Nichols . . . He races in with the souvenir in his glove . . . The entire White Sox bench on the field . . . As Seaver is congratulated, the bull pen crew on a dash from beyond the left field fence . . . Everyone wanting to shake Seaver's hand . . . Carlton Fisk shaking hands with all of the players as they come in . . .

. . . And now Seaver hugging Fisk . . . His hand being shaken by his teammates . . . He waves his cap to the crowd . . . (*Huge, thrilling chant from the roaring crowd: "Sea-ver! Sea-ver! Sea-ver!" as Seaver disappears into the dugout*).

# The Big Knock

## PETE ROSE'S 4,192nd BASE HIT

September 11, 1985

**Going back and looking** into the coverage of Pete Rose's breaking of Ty Cobb's career-hits mark is, to a large degree, an exercise in unease. Hindsight, of course, is the reason for this unsettling sensation: at the time he was setting the record, there was really nothing but goodwill and praise being directed at this almost comically competitive, energetic, exuberant 44-year-old. He was still seen by many as, in the immortal words of Sparky Anderson, "the best thing to happen to the game since, well, the game."

It's impossible to look at Pete Rose today as anything less than a tragic figure—and the classic tragic flaw requisite of those destined to tumble from great heights was, in Rose, his infamous addiction to gambling.

I was never really a big Pete Rose fan, but his fall, his banishment from baseball, his disgrace—these were incredibly difficult *facts* to accept. Over the years, as other name players had come and gone, Rose continued to play the game, day in and day out, year after year, with more enthusiasm than most of the rookies who were half his age. It was heartening, somehow, to see him out there. Seeing him again every spring, even if you didn't really like the guy all that much, was exciting. He loved playing the game so much, that he helped make it very easy to love watching the game, or listening to it, or just caring about it. During a period when baseball itself seemed to be in the middle of a prolonged identity crisis, Rose's clear-eyed passion for his sport was invigorating.

So, it's a little weird to read what folks were saying about Rose on the night he broke Cobb's record; and it's even weirder to read what Rose was saying about himself: "A lot of people will remember me for tonight," he said. "There are a lot of things you can remember me for, not all of them good. You can remember me for a divorce . . . for a paternity suit . . . (but) I know what I've accomplished. I really can't worry about it."

At the same time, a lot of people were happy to contrast the old-fashioned baseball purist they thought they saw in Rose with some of the apparently tactless, halfhearted younger players coming into the league. Bob Verdi in the *Chicago Tribune*, for example, took Padres pitcher Eric Show to task for his actions and attitude after Rose's record-breaking hit:

> . . . Pete Rose, throwback, trucks on, thinking now only of his next game. What Eric Show, modern day athlete, thought about Wednesday night, who knows? Who cares? He called the Rose celebration a "media creation," then slinked into the night.
>
> Show argued in the dugout with Carmelo Martinez, loudly criticizing the Padres' left fielder for not catching Dave Parker's bloop single after The Hit. Show, in his pique, doesn't comprehend that Wednesday night probably will be his closest brush with greatness.
>
> Someday, perhaps Eric Show and his ilk will learn what it's all about. Which is the beauty of Pete Rose. He never had to be taught.

Show, of course, was one of the brainiest and most troubled people to ever don a major league uniform. An accomplished jazz guitarist and lover of philosophy, he was also a staunch John Bircher, a manic-depressive and, at the end of his short life, a man self destructing—through drug abuse and other nameless demons—before his friends' eyes. Rather than a foil for Rose, in retrospect Show seems instead a kind of bleaker, more extreme example of Rose's own capacities for self-delusion.

But, then again, Verdi's right. Pete Rose never had to be taught "what it's all about." He was, for decades, an amazing, galvanizing force on the diamond, and that ability to push himself as hard as he could, at all times, seemed as much a part of his natural makeup as his craggy face.

Maybe some time down the road Rose will be remembered solely for what he accomplished on the field. Maybe someday he'll be allowed into the Hall of Fame. In the meantime, perhaps more so than with many of the pieces in this book, reading Ira Berkow's account of the man's greatest moment is eerily like opening a time capsule, except that we know what's inside this one, and still we can't quite believe it.

Pete Rose rounds first
after The Big Knock

# IRA BERKOW
*New York Times*

Ten miles from the sandlots where he began playing baseball as a boy, Pete Rose, now 44 years old and in his 23rd season in the major leagues, stepped to the plate tonight in the first inning at Riverfront Stadium. He came to bat on this warm, gentle evening with the chance to make baseball history.

The Reds' player-manager, the man who still plays with the joy of a boy, had a chance to break Ty Cobb's major-league career hit record, 4,191, which had stood since Cobb retired in 1928.

The sell-out crowd of 47,237 that packed the stadium hoping to see Rose do it now stood and cheered under a twilight blue sky beribboned with orange clouds.

Now he eased into his distinctive crouch from the left side of the plate, wrapping his white-gloved hands around the handle of his black bat. His red batting helmet gleamed in the lights. Everyone in the ball park was standing. The chant "Pete! Pete!" went higher and higher. Flashbulbs popped.

On the mound was the right-hander Eric Show of the San Diego Padres. Rose took the first pitch for a ball, fouled off the next pitch, took another ball. Show wound up and Rose swung and hit a line drive to left-center.

The ball dropped in and the park exploded. Fireworks being set off was one reason; the appreciative cries of the fans was another. Streamers and confetti floated onto the field.

Rose stood on first base and was quickly mobbed by everyone on the Reds' bench. The first base coach, Tommy Helms, one of Rose's oldest friends on the team, hugged him first. Tony Perez, Rose's longtime teammate, then lifted him.

Marge Schott, the owner of the Reds, came out and hugged Rose and kissed him on the cheek. A red Corvette was driven in from behind the outfield fence, a present from Mrs. Schott to her record-holder.

Meanwhile, the Padres, some of whom had come over to congratulate Rose, meandered here and there on the field, chatting with the umpires and among themselves, waiting for play to resume. Show took a seat on the rubber.

Rose had removed his batting helmet and waved with his gloves to the crowd. Then he stepped back on first, seemed to take a breath and turned to Helms, threw an arm around him and threw his head on his shoulder, crying.

The tough old ball player, his face as lined and rugged as a longshoreman's, was moved, perhaps even slightly embarrassed, by the tenderness shown him in the ball park.

Then from the dugout came a uniformed young man. This one was wearing the same number as Rose, 14, and had the same name on the back of his white jersey. Petey Rose, a 15-year-old redhead and sometime bat boy for as long as he can remember, fell into his pop's arms at first base, and the pair of Rose's embraced. There were tears in their eyes.

Most people in the park were familiar with the Rose story. He had grown up, the son of a bank cashier, in the area in Cincinnati along the Ohio River known as Anderson Ferry. He had gone to Western Hills High School here for five years—repeating the 10th grade. "It gave me a chance to learn more baseball," he said, with a laugh.

He was only about 5-foot-10 and 150 pounds when he graduated, in 1960—he is now a burly 5-foot-11 and 205—and the only scout who seemed to think he had talent enough to make the major leagues was his uncle, Buddy Bloebaum, who worked for the Reds.

Three years later he was starting at second base for the Reds, and got his first major league hit on April 13, 1963, a triple off Bob Friend of the Pittsburgh Pirates.

Rose was at first called, derisively, "Charlie Hustle." Soon, it became a badge of distinction. He made believers out of many who at first had deprecatory thoughts about this brash young rookie who ran to first on walks, who slid headfirst into bases, who sometimes taunted the opposition and barreled into them when they were in the way.

But never was there malicious intent, and he came to be loved and appreciated by teammates and opponents for his intense desire, as he said, "to play the game the way it's supposed to be played."

He began the season needing 95 hits to break Cobb's record, and as he drew closer and closer, the nation seemed to be watching and listening and wondering when "the big knock," as he called it, would come.

Tonight, he finished in a most typical and satisfying fashion. He got two hits—he tripled in the seventh inning—and walked once and flied to left in four times at bat. It wasn't just the personal considerations he holds dear. He cares about team accomplishments; he says his rings for World Series triumphs are his most cherished baseball possessions. And this night he scored the only two runs of the game, in the third and seventh innings, as the Reds won, 2–0.

After the game, in a celebration at home plate, Rose took a phone call from President Reagan that was relayed on the public address system.

The president congratulated him and said he had set "the most enduring record in sports history." He said Rose's record might be broken, "but your reputation and legacy will live for a long time."

"Thank you, Mr. President, for taking time from your busy schedule," said Rose. "And you missed a good ball game."

# MARTY BRENNEMAN and JOE NUXHALL

Brenneman: One out . . . and here comes the main attraction . . . And they're on their feet . . . Rose walking towards the plate . . . That number on his back emblazoned on the minds of sports fans probably forever and ever . . . The most famous number 14 in the history of this game . . . And trying to make history right here in the first inning tonight . . .

Show to the windup . . . and the pitch to Rose . . . and it's high, ball one . . .

And again the flashbulbs go off all over the ballpark . . . Last night the first time I have ever seen that in a baseball stadium . . .

One ball and no strikes . . . Rose swinging . . . and fouling it straight back . . . (*Enormous "Ohhh" from the crowd*) . . . And Show evens it up on him with a ball and a strike . . .

Pete batting .264, couple of home runs and 42 runs batted in . . . Both of his home runs against Cub pitching, and both at Wrigley Field . . . Right now just looking for a solid base hit . . . The 1-1 coming . . . And Rose takes it inside . . .

Hitless in four times up last night, and he did not hit the ball well but once, and that was when he lined to Martinez in the eighth inning with the tying run at second base . . .

He levels the bat a couple of times, Show kicks and he fires . . . Rose swings . . .

Nuxhall: There it is! There it is! Get out! Get out! . . . All right! . . .

B: Line drive, left center field, and there it is! . . . Hit number forty-one-ninety-two . . . A line drive single into left center field . . . A clean base hit, and it is pandemonium here at Riverfront Stadium . . . The fireworks exploding overhead . . . The Cincinnati dugout has emptied . . . The applause continues unabated . . . Rose completely encircled by his teammates at first base . . .

Bobby Brown of the San Diego Padres coming all the way from the third base dugout to personally congratulate Pete Rose . . . And a kind of outpouring of adulation that I don't think you'll ever see an athlete get any more of . . . Little Pete fighting his way through the crowd, and Pete being hoisted on the shoulders of a couple of his teammates . . . Tony Perez and Dave Concepcion, the last two of the old guard from the Big Red Machine days of the '70s . . .

Joe, quite an emotional scene here at the ballpark . . .

N: Quite a base hit . . . Ha ha . . . Yes it is, yessir . . .

# He Wanted to Bat

## KIRK GIBSON'S GREATEST WORLD SERIES HOME RUN
### October 15, 1988

**Sometimes it seems like** all the really, *really* great moments in baseball—the ones that are so preposterous, people shake their heads and laugh about them—happened way back in the past. Don Larsen's perfect game was 40 years ago. Bobby Thomson's home run was longer ago than that. Vander Meer's no-hitters? Six long decades ago. It's like a conspiracy, or something, so the old-timers can talk about how great the game used to be, and younger fans are forced to concede that, yeah, we've got some memories, but nothing like those stored up by the geezers.

And then along comes somebody like Kirk Gibson.

No, he did not win the 1988 World Series with one swing of his bat.

Not exactly, anyway.

What he did do, as everybody knows by now, is this: he hobbled out of the dugout in the bottom of the ninth inning at Dodger Stadium; stood in, with two outs, against Dennis Eckersley; took a couple of ugly, painful-looking swipes at pitches; and then slapped what seemed like a one-handed home run over the right-field fence, pumping his fist as he rounded first, screaming with delight, and generally freaking people out all across the country with the impossibility of what they'd just seen, or heard, or otherwise experienced on that October night.

He never batted again in the Series, but no one who saw that game can ever doubt that his one appearance at the plate somehow inspired the Dodgers—who were supposed to be trounced by the A's (there was a lot of talk of a sweep)—to a Series title in five games.

So, maybe every generation gets its chance, after all, to say, "Yeah, yeah, I'm sure being at (fill in your favorite moment here) was really somethin', but how about *this* . . . ?"

One last thing: In the radio transcript below, Jack Buck repeats the phrase

"I don't believe what I just saw!" several times after Gibson's blast. (He also asks, in one of the great sportscasting lines of all time, "Is this really happening, Bill?" in a voice that is as filled with incredulity—he sounds almost *fearful*, in fact—as one is ever likely to hear during a ball game.)

Buck's exclamation immediately brings to mind Russ Hodges's legendary call of Thomson's home run. Intentional? Probably not. It's more likely that Hodges's hair-raising shouts and whoops and yells are so deeply imbedded in the psyches of most ball fans that they're always lurking just slightly beneath the surface in any tense ball game situation, just waiting to be let out.

Or something like that.

# RON RAPOPORT
*Los Angeles Daily News*

*Dodgers outfielder Kirk Gibson, who is not in the lineup tonight, was examined before the game. Dr. Frank Jobe diagnosed a sprain of the medial collateral ligament and surrounding tissue in his right knee, an injury he sustained in Game 7 of the National League Championship Series. The knee was injected with xylocaine and cortisone. Gibson will be re-examined tomorrow and his condition is day-to-day.*

—Announcement in the fifth inning at Dodger Stadium Saturday night.

The camera panned the Dodger bench. Gibson isn't there, Vin Scully said. It looks like he's out for the night.

That's bullspit, said Kirk Gibson from his spot in the trainer's room, where he had spent the game. And he picked up a bat.

Thus began the most improbable chapter of the improbable finale that is now being written to the entire improbable 1988 Dodger season.

In a few moments after hearing Scully tell a national television audience he would not be factor, Gibson was telling Tom Lasorda something else. He was telling him he wanted to bat.

In years to come, the next few minutes of the Dodgers 5–4 victory over the Oakland A's in the first game of the 1988 World Series will be broken down moment by moment. They will be retold slowly and carefully, pitch by pitch and swing by swing.

But now things were moving much too quickly. There was too little time to analyze it. There was time only to see it, to comprehend it, to absorb it.

Gibson is standing in the batter's box facing Oakland's Dennis Eckersley, the best relief pitcher in baseball. Gibson is fouling off pitches. Gibson is working the count to 3 and 2.

And then, in one brief moment, in one stunning swing of the bat, Gibson is hitting a pitch into the right-field pavilion. He is trotting around the bases on a left leg that contains a sore hamstring and a right leg that has a sprained ligament numbed by cortisone only hours before.

The entire Dodger team is waiting for him at home plate, including Mike Davis, who has scored in front of him. Nearly 56,000 people are standing rooted in front of their seats as stunned and incredulous as he is. The Dodgers have just beaten the Athletics in the first game of the World Series.

*Eckersley's first pitch comes in hard. It is all Gibson can do to get his bat around on it. He fouls the ball behind him and slightly to the left. He looks overmatched. He looks hurt. He looks as if it has been unfair to send him up there in the first place.*

"I was in the training room getting treatment the whole game," said Gibson, whose left leg had troubled him throughout the Dodgers' seven-game National League playoff victory over the Mets, but who injured his right leg only in Game 7. "I asked the bat boy to bring me a batting tee and I started swinging the bat. I thought I could give it a try."

*Gibson fouls off Eckersley's second pitch, too. He doesn't get around on it any better than he had the first one. If you are a Dodger fan, you hope this will end soon. You hope Gibson doesn't aggravate the injury and ruin whatever chance he has of playing effectively in the Series.*

"I had the bat boy call Tommy in the dugout," Gibson said. "He came running up to the trainer's room. He said 'What!? What!? What do you want!?' I told him if he wanted to hit for Alfredo Griffin, I could hit for the pitcher. That was all he wanted to hear. He took off. It was like, 'Don't change your mind.'"

*Gibson finally gets around on a pitch. He hits a ground ball foul down the first-base line. It is painful to watch him run. The count remains 0–2.*

"I hadn't taken any live swings since the third inning of Game 7," Gibson said. "I tried to swing the bat in my living room today and I tried to do a little jogging in my living room, too. I couldn't. There was nothing I could do. And I had that wonderful injection come on the scene again. I'm not fond of that, especially at this time of year."

*Eckersley makes his first mistake, an outside pitch Gibson takes for ball one. He fouls the next pitch into the stands down the third-base line. Is he getting around on the ball better? The count is 1–2.*

"I came in yesterday and I couldn't work out," Gibson said. "I didn't think I could swing the bat very effectively. I thought I would be better off visualizing my swing because of the way my legs felt."

*What's the matter with Eckersley? He has just thrown two more balls. One is high*

Kirk Gibson hobbles
(loudly) into history

*and outside. The next is barely outside and as Davis steals second, Gibson appears to step out onto the plate. Umpire Doug Harvey can call him out for interference. He doesn't. The Dodgers have gotten a break.*

"I couldn't tell you how much pain there was because I wasn't thinking about it," Gibson said. "When I got out there, warming up, the fans were outstanding, the adrenaline started flowing. I told myself, 'You love these situations. Dig in.'"

*Eckersley does what any pitcher in his right mind would do. He tries to keep the ball away from Gibson. He throws a slider low and away. Gibson reaches out for it. The swing appears to be easy and deliberate, the swing of a man who can't take his full stride.*

"I wasn't thinking about hitting the ball out," Gibson said. "Davis was at second base and I just wanted to put the ball in play. A base hit would have got him in."

*The ball flies off his bat. There is no question where it will go. Gibson trots slowly around the bases. He has won. The Dodgers have won.*

"I think if somebody told me, 'If you hit a home run, could you make it around the bases?' I would have said, 'I think I could,'" Gibson said. "I've got to watch the way I walk, the way I run—if you call that running. If I step in certain ways, it grabs you pretty good."

He is at his locker now. Somebody has put a sign there that says "Roy Hobbs," after the hero of Bernard Malamud's novel *The Natural*.

"I'm the luckiest guy in the world right now," Gibson said. He went off to put ice on his legs.

# BILL WHITE and JACK BUCK
## on CBS Radio

White: . . . Jack, the guy you were talking about is coming out.

Buck: Hey, look at the way he's limping. That's impossible for him to come out and bat, isn't it?

W: We mentioned the ligament damage . . . now, it's not just the hamstring on the one leg . . . He has been diagnosed as having ligament damage, and of course that's Kirk Gibson who has a chance here to win the ball game. He represents the winning run at home.

B: He bats for Pena. Pena: two good innings, no runs, one hit, struck out three, walked none . . . and Kirk Gibson bats for Pena here in the ninth. He could win the game with one swing, against the best reliever in baseball this year.

He limps very noticeably as he walks to the plate. He's a left-handed batter, he's got a bad hamstring, and a bad knee. Davis is on at first. It's not beyond him to steal a base with Eckersley pitching.

W: Well, we talked about Eckersley . . . He keeps the left leg up a long time, and that gives the runner at first base a chance to get two or three steps.

B: Outfielders will be straightaway and deep, and this game will end on a dramatic note one way or the other with Gibson up there.

Tying run at first. Two out. Here's the pitch . . . swing, and a foul. Strike one.

W: And he's having problems. After he fouled that back, he put all his weight on that right knee and just hobbled out of there.

B: But he taps the dirt out of his spikes and goes back up to wait for another.

A two-out walk gives the Dodgers life here in the bottom of the ninth. The A's are leading 4–3. Davis at first, the tying run. Two out. Eckersley gets the sign from Hassey. Throws to first. The runner returns.

W: He can't forget Davis over there. Mike Davis has excellent speed.

B: Gibson steps out . . . Now the tough left-handed batter gets back in . . . And waits . . . Heeere's the pitch.

Swing and another foul, out of play, off to the left, and that's strike two. Gibson hit 25 home runs during the regular season.

W: Little tough here, Jack, with the weight shift. Of course, as you get the bat back, you have the weight on your back foot. In this case, the left foot of Gibson, but then he shifts through the front foot and all that weight goes up there as he swings through the ball, and that's where he's getting pain.

B: Two quick strikes on the Dodger star. Eckersley ready . . . throws to first again and Davis gets back. (*Boos from the crowd.*) He's there with the tying run. Two out, bottom of the ninth, A's leading 4–3 on the Canseco grand slam which occurred in the second inning. No balls, two strikes to Gibson. . . . He might have trouble stopping his swing on a bad delivery.

Eckersley gets the sign again . . . comes from the belt . . . throws to first again, and the runner returns. (*More boos.*) This Dodger crowd on their feet, ready to head for the exits, one way or the other.

The on-deck batter is Steve Sax. But there are two outs . . . Here it is . . . Swing, and a little tap foul down the right side, and Gibson can hardly run at all.

If he keeps the inning going, and doesn't win it with one swing, it'll bring up Sax, and he's a pretty good clutch-hitter.

Gibson struggles back to the plate . . . Picks up the bat. The count stays 0 and 2.

New supply of baseballs for the plate umpire, Doug Harvey. Four to three,

Oakland leading . . . bottom of the ninth. They've out-hit the Dodgers, 7–6 . . . there've been no errors. Mike Davis is at first, two out. Eckersley battling Kirk Gibson . . .

Outfielders deep, straightaway . . . Here it comes! . . . Outside, ball one . . . Throw to first . . . Davis had to struggle to get back, hand-first. And Hassey almost picked him off. That would have been a terrible way for this game to end.

W: Oh, my goodness.

B: One ball, two strikes the count. Gibson heaves a deep sigh. Digs back in . . . gets back in and waits. One ball, two strikes . . .

Here comes another! . . . The runner going . . . Swing and a foul, out of play, off to the left. Boy, what a tough cookie this Gibson is. Former football player, Michigan State, defensive back. Drafted by the Cardinal football team . . . elected to play baseball and the Dodgers are happy about that. And, of course, he was a big star in Detroit. We all know about him. He's playing hurt, hurt, hurt. He's up there with a one-ball, two-strike count, two out, tying run at first, bottom of the ninth . . .

The pitch! . . . High . . . two and two.

W: Well, we might see Davis take off again here . . . If he took off one-and-two, he might take off two-and-two.

B: How good a thrower is Hassey? The best?

W: Hassey? No . . . He can get the ball down there. He's not the best of catchers, but he does an excellent job.

B: Two-and-two the count to Gibson. Tying run at first . . . two out. Throw to first, the runner gets back. (*More boos.*) The A's are leading 4–3, the bottom of the ninth . . . Fifty-five thousand-plus for the first game of this '88 Series.

Gibson will get back in with a two-two count, and sooner or later Eckersley's gonna have to come to him again. He had a two-strike count, now it's two-and-two . . . Here it comes, the runner going . . . and it's outside. No throw, stolen base, tying run at second . . . Two out and 3–2 on Gibson.

You said it, Bill White, Eckersley doesn't hold 'em close.

W: Doesn't hold 'em close, Jack, and if Davis ran on one ball, two strikes, you figure he's gotta go on two-and-two . . . That pitch was away, and an easy stolen base for Davis.

B: And now an easier opportunity to tie this game, if Gibson can solve the . . . Dennis Eckersley, who saved 45 games for the A's this year, he's trying to save it for Dave Stewart. Mike Davis at second base with two out . . . Three and two to Gibson . . . A base hit would tie it, a home run would win it for the Dodgers . . .

If Gibson gets on, Sax comes up . . . From the stretch . . . Time called by Gibson . . .

W: And if he does get on, that would make Lasorda make another decision. He'd have to use a base runner, because he doesn't want that force at second base.

B: Yeah, he would run for Gibson and have Sax batting . . . But . . . we have a big 3–2 pitch coming here. . . . from Eckersley . . .

Gibson swings . . . and a fly ball to deep right field! . . .

This is gonna be a home run! . . . Unbelievable! . . . A home run for Gibson! . . . And the Dodgers have won the game! . . . Five to four! . . .

I don't believe what I just saw! . . . I don't believe what I just saw! . . . Is this really happening, Bill?

W: It is happening, and they've gotta help him home . . . The third base coach Joe Amalfitano had to give him a little push . . . and all the Dodgers are around home plate . . .

B: I don't believe what I just saw! . . . One of the most remarkable finishes to any World Series game . . . A one-handed home run by Kirk Gibson, and the Dodgers have won it . . . 5 to 4 . . . And I am stunned, Bill . . . I have seen a lot of dramatic finishes in a lot of sports, but this one might top every other one . . .

W: It was . . . (*Laughing*) It was a moment that we have never seen before . . . And the Athletics, they're obviously stunned, too, Jack Buck, they're gone, and all of them have got their heads down . . .

B: It was simply one of the most dramatic moments ever in the history of sports . . . Regular season . . . Post season . . . baseball . . . football . . . hockey . . . You name it . . . This is one of the most dramatic moments ever in sports . . .

Nolan Ryan notches his
seventh no-hitter

# In the Way of a Train

---◆◆◆---

## NOLAN RYAN'S SEVENTH NO-HITTER
### May 1, 1991

**The man just would** not stop.

When he threw his sixth no-hitter, against the A's in Oakland back in 1990, and became the oldest player ever to do so, that must have seemed like the end. He was 43 years old, then, and while he still had good stuff (obviously), the consensus seemed to be, "All right, Nolan. You've done it all. Nobody else is even close. You passed Koufax in no-hitters a long time ago. You've owned the career strikeout record for years. Maybe it's time to let the kids have the sandbox now, if ya know what we mean."

Thankfully—for Ryan, and for Ranger fans—he thought he'd stick around for another year. And so, on May Day, 1991, 44-year-old Nolan Ryan took the mound against the Blue Jays at Arlington Stadium, and pitched what was probably the best game of his career.

"The starting lineup the Blue Jays threw at Nolan Ryan last night," began a report on the game in the *Toronto Star*, "was an all-time, combined 7 for 56 with 19 strikeouts against the one and only.

"That same lineup, after the amazing fact, is 7 for 83."

For many of his teammates, of course, Ryan was a role model, father figure, and walking, talking mythological figure rolled into one. More than a few of them named children after the guy.

Maybe it's for that reason that the image I keep with me in my head when I think of Ryan's seventh, then, is the one described below by Gerry Fraley. He mentions the Rangers' shortstop and third baseman, both of them far younger than the man on the mound, running off the field together after Ryan struck out the side in the second inning.

It was clear to both of them, right then, that Ryan had the stuff to throw another no-hitter; and there's something immeasurably exciting about imagining the feelings of these two young men, knowing in their bones that they have a real good chance to be a part of history, running toward the dugout together, through the cheers, on a warm Texas night.

## GERRY FRALEY
*Dallas Morning News*

Nolan Ryan, feeling every bit the 44-year-old man, began Wednesday with an aching back.

He finished with another piece of history.

Ryan, going "into a zone where normal people don't go," according to Ranger pitching coach Tom House, pitched the record seventh no-hitter of his career, beating the Toronto Blue Jays, 3–0, before 33,439 fans at Arlington Stadium. No one else in major league history has thrown more than four no-hitters.

"This was the furthest thing from my mind," Ryan said. "When I woke up, I had more aches and pains. I physically had a bad day. Old age.

"I never say I have no-hit stuff. I know all it takes is one pitch. I took each inning as it came along. When I went into the ninth, I just felt like I was going to go right at them and be real aggressive and try not to make a mistake."

Ryan struck out 16 and missed a perfect game—retiring 27 consecutive batters from start to finish—by two walks on full-count pitches. He asked his defense to come up with one difficult play, and center fielder Gary Pettis ran down Manny Lee's shallow fly ball for the second out of the sixth inning.

Ryan was so dominant that the Blue Jays hit only four balls out of the infield. Ryan compared the quality of his pitches to his second no-hitter: a 17-strikeout performance against Detroit on July 15, 1973. The Blue Jays must live with the memory of this game until Tuesday, when they will face Ryan again at the Toronto Skydome.

"I had the best command of all three pitches. This is the best," Ryan said of his no-hit collection. "This is my most overpowering night."

Said Ranger shortstop Jeff Huson: "They were overmatched and it was no fault of theirs. They just got in the way of a train."

Ryan, with the crowd on its feet in a full-throated frenzy, finished by throwing his 122nd pitch—a hissing 93-m.p.h. fastball—past a swinging

Roberto Alomar for a strikeout. As they did last year when Ryan pitched a no-hitter against the defending World Series champion Oakland Athletics, the Rangers charged from the dugout and carried Ryan off the field.

In the clubhouse, the Rangers had their private celebration. Manager Bobby Valentine broke out a bottle of champagne that had been on the wall of his office since 1986. Valentine had vowed not to open the champagne until the Rangers reached a World Series. This was no time to wait on an even bigger miracle.

"I'm just relieved it's over with," said Ryan, who also has 12 one-hitters and has combined for two other one-hitters.

"I had hoped I'd get in this position to do it at home for these fans. I'm just thankful it worked out."

To grasp the magnitude of what Ryan accomplished, consider his final victim. When Ryan pitched his first two no-hitters with the Angels in 1973, his second baseman was Sandy Alomar. Roberto Alomar is Sandy Alomar's 23-year-old son, who as a child asked Ryan to help him become a pitcher.

"I won't be flipping baseballs when I'm 44," said Toronto starter Jimmy Key, who allowed Ruben Sierra's two-run home run in the three-run third inning. "The only thing I hope is I'm able to throw my kids batting practice."

There were doubts Ryan would see the middle innings. He woke up with a stiff back and took pain relievers all day before coming to the park. They did not help.

Ryan went through extra pre-game stretching and wore a heating pack on his back during the scouting meeting to go over the hitters. While warming up, Ryan turned to House, another 44-year-old, and complained about his accumulated years.

"I don't know how you feel at 44, but I feel old today," Ryan said to House. "My back hurts. My finger hurts. My ankle hurts. I've been taking Advil since noon and it isn't helping."

The aches were an omen. Ryan pitched his no-hitter last year shortly after coming off the disabled list because of a stress fracture in the back. As it did in that game, adrenaline took over.

"It kicked in in the first inning," Ryan said, "and it went better as the game went along."

Ryan carried an extra burden. This was his first start of the season on four days' rest. He threw a draining 131 pitches in a loss to Cleveland on Friday.

Ryan grew stronger under the workload, becoming more effective with the fastball, which hit a high of 96 m.p.h. on a pitch to Joe Carter in the fourth. Ryan had nine strikeouts with the fastball, six with the curveball and one with the change-up.

He struck out 5 of the final 10 batters.

Toronto presented a lineup full of Ryan fodder. Two of the starters—Glenallen Hill and Mark Whiten—had never faced Ryan. The other seven starters were a combined 9 for 66 lifetime against him.

Ryan had a few touchy moments in the first, going to two full counts and walking Kelly Gruber. Ryan escaped the first by getting Carter on a pop-up. In the second, Ryan gave signs of dominance.

He struck out the side, all on called third strikes.

The curveball froze John Olerud and Whiten. Hill could not react to a fastball low and away on the corner. Huson and third baseman Steve Buechele ran off the field together and shared the same thought.

"Right then, you could tell he could do it," Buechele said. "This wasn't like last year's game. There was a lot of pressure in that game. This was like being a spectator, he was so dominant."

## MARK HOLTZ
### on WBAP (Fort Worth)

Nolan Ryan with 15 strikeouts and two walks and a no-hitter through eight and two-thirds . . . 0 and 1 to Alomar . . . Here's the windup, and the Ryan pitch! . . .

Swung on and fouled back, it's 0 and 2! (*Crowd in a frenzy*)

Ryan may be one out away. He has retired all but two. He has retired 26 of 28 Blue Jays . . . The crowd goes crazy . . . No balls, two strikes . . . Alomar waiting . . . Nolan Ryan winds . . . Here's the pitch to the plate! . . . Low, for ball one . . .

One ball and two strikes . . . Ryan walks to the back side of the mound for a moment, lifts his cap twice, looks at the baseball . . . Roberto Alomar from the left side waits . . . Ryan steps on the rubber . . . Ball one and strike two, two out in the ninth . . . Ryan after his seventh no-hitter . . . Here's the windup . . . and the 1–2 pitch . . .

A swing and foul back, and the count stays at 1 and 2 . . . He hit a fastball back foul . . . This is a very pesky hitter.

So Ryan gets a new baseball . . . Alomar has struck out twice tonight against Ryan, both times swinging, in the fourth and in the seventh . . . Ryan is ready . . . One ball and two strikes . . . Here's the windup . . . The pitch to

Alomar . . . is . . . outside for a ball . . . He changed up on him, and the count goes 2–2.

And now Ryan wants a new baseball . . . This crowd is standing at Arlington . . .

Ryan wants a new baseball . . . Takes a look at those seams and how much that mud is rubbed in and now goes back to the mound . . . Two out . . . Top of the ninth . . . Two balls, two strikes on Sandy Alomar . . . If he gets him, it's seven no-hitters . . .

Here's the windup by Ryan . . . A swing and a pop up foul, that will be back and in the seats . . . So we'll do it again . . .

Give Alomar a lot of credit, he is battling away here at a couple of fastballs . . . Two balls, two strikes, two out, and a brilliant moment at Arlington Stadium . . . Nolan Ryan toes in on the rubber . . . Alomar stays right in the left-handed batter's box . . . Ryan the sign . . . here's the windup . . . And the 2–2 pitch . . .

He struck him out swinging! Incredible! No-hitter number seven! . . . Sandy Alomar has struck out, and Nolan Ryan has done it again! No-hitter number seven! . . . The Ranger bench has emptied . . . The crowd is standing . . . and Nolan Ryan, at age 44, does it one more time! . . . Roberto Alomar has struck out, as the Rangers have defeated the Toronto Blue Jays, and the unbelievable numbers for Nolan Ryan roll on . . .

What a moment at Arlington!

# One of Baseball's Loftiest Peaks

## CAL RIPKEN'S 2,131st CONSECUTIVE GAME

### September 6, 1995

**I suppose it's a** measure of how twisted my own — and probably everybody else's—view of sports heroes has become, that as Cal Ripken neared Gehrig's record, I had a queasy feeling in my stomach that something really, tremendously awful was going to happen to tarnish his unbelievable accomplishment.

There wasn't anything specific I was worried about. But when I think back on it now, I can sort of see the amorphous, ugly outlines of scandal. The man, it seemed, was just too damn *good*.

He was talented. He was dedicated. He had, it appeared, a healthy and happy home life, with a family that loved him, and whom he loved, deeply. He was, when I read about him or heard him interviewed, unfailingly gracious, articulate and, of all things, funny. I got the feeling that he even had a sense of humor about himself, could rib himself, which seems about as rare a quality in the world of big-time sports as modesty.

And Ripken had that, too. And, of course, he had the most intense blue eyes anyone had seen since *Cool Hand Luke*.

So, obviously, I thought there had to be something wrong, and as the night of September 6th approached, I dreaded the revelation of whatever it was that was wrong. I couldn't even imagine what his failing might be. Drugs? Gambling? A clandestine admiration for the books of William Bennett? What horrible secret was going to well up through the patently false veneer of Ripken's life?

And then, of course, the weirdest thing happened: absolutely nothing.

Ripken spent the entire day in a manner befitting a workmanlike superstar. Or, as Thomas Stinson put it in the *Atlanta Journal and Constitution*, Cal fulfilled his to-do list for the day: "Drop off daughter Rachel at her first day of school. Get ankle taped (a ritual). Chill out with the president. Hit a home run. Doff cap as required. Become immortal."

I am not saying that Cal Ripken, Jr., is perfect. I mean, the guy made an error some time back in 1989, or something, didn't he? My point is that, after decades of sports heroes who, in the end, turned out to be plain old human beings who happened to have better eyes or stronger wrists or fleeter feet or quicker hands than the rest of us (but all the same weaknesses, and then some), Cal Ripken turning out to be just a tremendously gifted, sweet, and deeply competitive man seemed . . . bizarre.

Bruce Jenkins, writing in the *San Francisco Chronicle* about all the talk of Cal Ripken "saving" baseball, said that "maybe baseball in its current state does not deserve Cal Ripken. He is better than that. He has joined us from some other time."

I understand the point. Baseball was in the middle of a strike-shortened season in 1995; the fans seemed unsure whether to let loose with a collective, prolonged wail or a final, titanic yawn; and one of the few unmitigated bright spots that season was Cal Ripken. Baseball was in pretty bad shape, and it was unclear (and remains unclear) where it was headed.

But baseball did deserve Cal Ripken that year. After all, it sometimes happens that—for brief moments, and despite every attempt to ruin it—the game actually seems to consist of nothing but the diamond, and the players, and the fans. There's something elemental about that relationship, and the game might just weather all the crap that, every so often, it seems destined to endure.

As fans, we deserved Cal Ripken in 1995. And maybe (and I don't mean this as an insult, Cal), just maybe, Cal Ripken deserved us.

# THOMAS BOSWELL
*Washington Post*

After 10 minutes, the cheers had not begun to subside. No matter how many curtain calls Cal Ripken took or how many fireworks exploded on the roof of Oriole Park at Camden Yards tonight, it was simply not enough. Not after the top of the fifth inning, when Ripken had just, officially, played in his 2,131st consecutive game, breaking Lou Gehrig's monumental record that had stood since 1939.

Seeing Ripken present his jersey and his cap to his wife and two small children brought enormous waves of warm applause, including cheers from the president and vice president of the United States. Also, the throng at Camden Yards was tickled to see the T-shirt that Ripken wore under his uniform, which carried the message: "2,130-plus. Hugs and Kisses for Daddy."

"See, Daddy's wearing my shirt," said 5-year-old Rachel, who was driven to her first day of school this morning by an extremely tired, but dutiful, dad.

So, realizing that more—much more—was required to make this moment of celebration worthy of Ripken's 13-plus-season feat, Rafael Palmeiro, Bobby Bonilla and the rest of the Baltimore Orioles pushed their shortstop out of the dugout and sent him on a lap around the perimeter of the ballpark. He'd never have done it on his own. Baseball can say a deep thanks that others forced the scene to happen. Because it was the tops.

Ripken shook the ballgirl's hand and then a security cop's big paw as he passed under the huge illuminated sign on the B & O Warehouse, which said everything that mattered: "2131." He leaped to slap the hands of bleacherites. He stopped at the bullpen to grab Elrod Hendrick's arm in both his hands to thank the coach he's known since he was a child. He noticed a fan drop his cap on the warning track and went back to pick it up to return it. The umpires threw their arms around him and every California Angel who didn't shake his hand actually grabbed Ripken in a bear hug. And he hugged the Orioles' clubhouse attendant, Butch, whom Cal has befriended with mock punches and pranks for years.

Golfer Hale Irwin ran around the 18th green in victory at the 1990 U.S. Open. It took seconds. He slapped the hands of strangers. Ripken's circuit of Camden Yards took 10 minutes because every time he'd started to jog, he'd see another old friend in some part of the stands and have to return for a greeting.

A sign in the stands said: "We consider ourselves the luckiest fans on the face of the earth. Thanks Cal."

For 22 minutes 15 seconds, such folks as President Clinton, Vice President Gore and even Joe DiMaggio seemed like extraneous afterthoughts.

Maybe baseball deserves Cal Ripken. Maybe it doesn't. The old game, taking a standing eight-count for the past year, was presented with an incomparably rejuvenating celebration of the sport tonight.

Ripken did it with his bat—hitting a home run for the third consecutive game. But he did it just as much with his heart. He melted this park with his beaming smile and his instant recognition of people, great and small, in every part of the park. No wonder that games in baseball, all across America, were stopped so that fans and players alike could give a standing ovation.

Ripken the ballplayer didn't do badly tonight either.

When Ripken celebrated his 2,129th straight game with a home run on Sunday, it was memorable. When he punctuated his 2,130th consecutive game with another home run on Tuesday, it was thrilling. However, when Ripken homered again tonight in the fourth inning—a signature, crackling line drive over the Crown sign in the left-field corner—it was an almost ridiculous command performance. You can't do that on cue in batting practice.

After reaching the summit of Mount Gehrig here on Tuesday, Ripken truly planted his solitary flag atop one of baseball's loftiest peaks tonight.

In sports, records are measured in many ways: by inches and split seconds, by numbers of home runs or touchdowns. However, the Gehrig record came to hold a special symbolic place in American games because it was calibrated in years. Until Ripken's arrival, no one had come within five years of Gehrig.

Like a climber who does nothing more spectacular than place each piton higher than the last, Ripken finally got to the top of a mountain which, for more than a half century, had been considered unscalable. Tonight, the sublime and the mundane were combined in a way almost everyone could comprehend: The sports world honored a man whose "impossible" feat was that he hadn't taken a sick day since May 30, 1982.

In the Oriole clubhouse before the game, Ripken told Clinton that all he did was show up for work everyday and do something he enjoyed. "This is the closest thing to an out-of-body experience I'll ever have," added Ripken to the president. "It's like somebody else is in your shoes."

Later, on national television, the president praised Ripken for combining "talent and joy with old-fashioned work." Then, in words that proved prescient within the hour, he added, "I think the games last night and tonight are going to do a lot to help America fall back in love with baseball."

To complete the linkage between Gehrig and Ripken, DiMaggio participated in postgame ceremonies. Thus, the Yankee Clipper, a teammate of the Iron Horse, bestowed authenticity on Ripken—the reserved craftsman who doesn't even have a nickname.

"Wherever my old teammate Lou Gehrig is today, I'm sure he's tipping his cap to you, Cal Ripken," said DiMaggio as postgame ceremonies stretched past midnight with the park still full to the top rows.

Ripken himself said at the conclusion of the ceremony: "I know that if Lou Gehrig is looking down on tonight's activities, he isn't concerned about someone playing one more consecutive game than he did. Instead, he's viewing tonight as just another example of what is good and right about the great American game."

This entire night resembled an all-star gala as much as a baseball game with 600 reporters on hand and special edition memorabilia spewing from concession stands. Even the balls used in the game were special commemorative souvenirs—thus radically enhancing their value and leading to extremely spirited competition for foul balls. In contrast to the commercial, carnival atmosphere, one bona fide charity angle—partly inspired by Ripken—elevated the affair; one-game only, $5,000-a-person box seats were erected, with $1 million of the proceeds going to Johns Hopkins University to study Lou Gehrig's Disease.

Around midnight after Game 2,130, Ripken allowed himself his first truly introspective reflections of this entire Streak season. "I'm looking forward to [setting the record]," he said. "And I'm looking forward to the end of it, too, to be honest . . . The last few days have been an eternity. Every time you look at the clock, it seems to move more slowly . . . It's time to celebrate it and enjoy it. But I hope the hoopla doesn't linger on . . .

"I've been very achy the last few weeks. Maybe it's the nerves. It's been a difficult time. It's been tough to eat. It's been tough to sleep . . . Usually, I sleep like a rock. But there's a switch in my body that won't turn off . . . It's been exhausting."

Game 2,131 was exhausting, but in the best sense. Like Game 6 of the 1975 World Series, this night of baseball-as-it-should-be someday may be seen as a turning point in baseball's troubled marriage with its public.

Whatever the future holds, this night clearly showed that the streaks of Gehrig and Ripken have taken parallel paths, leading to the same place. Both began as purely athletic achievements. Yet, eventually, both streaks became excuses for a nation to talk not about baseball but about the quality of the men. Gehrig said goodbye to his sport in one of the game's saddest, but most ennobling, moments. Tonight, with his warning track tour, Ripken greeted an entire ballpark, and embraced a whole nation of fans, in one of the game's most joyous evenings.

Cal Ripken fans applaud their man

# Acknowledgments

Grateful acknowledgment is made to the following writers and publications for permission to reprint the articles contained in this book:

"No. 1 Saga—Frustration, Unity, Love, Victory," by Ralph Martin: © 1969, *The Times Union*, Albany, NY.

"Rerun of 'ol 693," by Furman Bisher: © 1974, *The Atlanta Journal and Constitution*.

"The Best Game Ever!" by Ray Fitzgerald; "Fisk's HR in 12th Beats Reds, 7–6," by Peter Gammons: © 1975, *The Boston Globe*.

"Williams Gets 6 Hits in 8 Trips to Finish With Avg. of .406," by Burt Whitman: © 1941, *The Boston Herald*.

"Vander Meer in Second No-Hitter," by Lou Smith: © 1932, *The Cincinnati Enquirer*.

"Ryan Steals the Thunder," by Gerry Fraley: © 1991, *The Dallas Morning News*.

"Wild Finish Has Fans Delirious," by Bill Lee: © 1960, *The Hartford Courant*.

"Gibson's Best Shot," by Ron Rapoport: © 1988, *The Los Angeles Daily News*.

"Gibson Fans Record 17 in 4–0 Triumph," by John Hall; "Reggie Renames House Ruth Built," by Jim Murray: © 1968, 1977, *The Los Angeles Times*.

# Index